SILVER EMPRESS

Pathos, Book 2

2nd Edition

Tamara Henson

Tamara Henson Studios, LLC

Barbourville, KY, USA

Thank you for supporting the creative work
of Tamara Henson!

Published by Tamara Henson Studios, LLC
Barbourville, KY, USA
www.tamarahenson.com

ISBN-13: 978-1-968677-03-9

DEDICATION

To Ms. Lois Volpenhein. You are a treasure and an inspiration to innumerable souls. Your mark upon this world is immortal. Thank you for every moment you spent, every lesson you taught in art and life, and for every heart you touched, including mine.

I love you, Ms. V, forever and ever!

*　　*　　*

CONTENT NOTICE:

This work mentions and depicts parental death during traumatic childbirth and kidnapping. But there's fun Power Traits, gemflesh, and one random, awkward tantric psychic not-sex scene, so that should help soften the trauma a little?

CONTENTS

1: GODSKIN

The midwife Arcani, a close friend and neighbor to the expecting Rascha, arrived moments after the pregnant woman's first screams. Arcani carried her basket of child-pulling paraphernalia into the shadowy room, sensing the other woman's deep fear and panic. Rascha's pale face contorted as she suffered through another wave of agony, the bulge at her middle rippling with abnormal contractions. Arcani frowned. She pulled the woman's loose gown up to her ribcage.

"Lights!" she commanded, and the wall globes flickered to life.

Rascha's perfect opal skin shimmered white with glints of pink and green in the stark lighting, an Azelan racial trait specific to her noble bloodline. Across her distended stomach, dark grey splotches spread in an irregular pattern. *Azelans don't bruise grey.* Their crystal blood left glowing marks as bruises until the light in the blood dissipated. She leaned closer. Bright particles within the discoloration caught the light in a different way. They shone like silver. She pressed her lips in a tight line, clearly worried.

"She's been talking to me," Rascha said, her voice weak and drained. Arcani turned to the woman, forcing a smile. "She's learning very quickly! I think she's not the only one, but..." Rascha's voice trembled. "But the other doesn't talk to me."

"A twin child is a rare blessing, especially one with Power Traits." Leaning to sit next to her friend, she placed a cool hand on her forehead. "I'm here now. We will do all we can to see both blessings spanked and crying."

"You're a treasure, Arcani." Rascha's lips trembled. "A treasure, and a godmother, please." She followed her understated request with a pleading gaze into her friend's eyes. Rascha's slack face went tight again as another contraction wracked her slight frame.

"Well, sounds like the treasure is on its way." Arcani's wistful smile did little to comfort Rascha. The midwife worked hard to hide her jittery nerves, for once content that Rascha did not possess her bloodline's signature telepathy. *And I pray the pleading in her eyes isn't another premonition!* Arcani stood so she could face away from the younger woman and busied her wringing hands with her tools. *Her predictions have been far too accurate of late.*

Two young boys ran into the room bearing a large translucent box between them. They stared wide-eyed until the smaller child nudged his brother into offloading the box's contents. They pulled out crystal bowls, clear bottles with multi-colored liquids and see-through warming blankets, setting them within their midwife-mother's reach. Not a word spoken, and with a grim face, the midwife laid out her instruments on a low table and filled a bowl with blue antiseptic liquid. She dipped each cutting tool before returning it to its place. She dragged her hip-length red hair into a thick braid. Then she dipped her hands and arms, nearly to the elbow. Her ruby eyes settled on the writhing abdomen, then on her children. They gaped at the silvery stomach, understanding that something wasn't quite right and not knowing how to help.

"Jacan, will you take your brother back to Father?" Arcani thrust her chin in the direction of Forge Mountain. "I'm sure he needs both of you to help very much right now."

The smallest boy closed his open mouth and nodded, red spiky hair bobbing in front of his eyes. He turned to his taller brother, who had large hands and feet and a heavy jaw for so young a child, and tugged on his arm. The larger boy allowed Jacan to pull him toward the door, but he continued to stare.

"Please, Arcani. Don't send them away." Rascha gasped to regain her composure. Fear tinged her voice. "Unless..." She gave the boys a sympathetic glance. "Tell me?"

"Boys, wait outside." Arcani gestured to the boys who stood frozen in the doorway. "I'll call you back in a moment."

*   *   *

"Rashi okay?" the older boy asked in a heavy voice. But he obediently kept walking out the door.

"I don't know, Fagan. Now, quiet for Momma." Jacan tilted his head back to catch Fagan's wandering brown-and-gold-streaked eyes. "Let's play for a few minutes, over there."

Jacan followed Fagan to a dip in the front courtyard. Long ago, at least long ago in Jacan's memory, someone had dug a wide, deep circular pool and lined the edge with sparkling amethyst stones. A slight breeze rippled the surface of the liquid crystal, sending it sloshing against the amethyst stones. The bottom of the pool glowed with the gentle pulse of polished aquamarine. Fagan thrust his thick fingers into the liquid as Jacan stared at the tranquil ripples. Tiny fish flashed away from the boy's hand, catching the light in a rainbow of flashing gemstone colors. Fagan laughed loudly and dipped his other hand under the surface, trying unsuccessfully to catch the swimmers. Jacan smiled, but the expression held worry in so young a face. Rascha had been with him forever, and with his mother before that. And he knew that babies did not make metallic tummies. Gemflesh tummies, yes. Momma had told him once that all Azelans were gemflesh because they belonged to the Crystal Planet Azela. Not metal-flesh. Metal-flesh is for Gods, his mother told him. For the Golden Seer. *For Kameke*, she had said.

Jacan trailed his finger along the pool's surface, sure he had not seen anything as beautiful in all the years of his short life. The aquamarine substrate shined more brightly as he contacted the flowing crystal, filling him with a calm that drowned out the giggling of his brother, the lonely droning of a lesser avian in the distance, and his worry over his friend Rascha. He gazed into the sparkling liquid until the radiance within swirled in his eyes and the golden light climbed through the depths to brush his fingertips. He gasped and fell back, shaking the tingling sensation from his fingers.

"What did you see, Jacan?" Arcani stood just behind him, a picture of serenity.

"I didn't..." Jacan began, then cut his lie short. Fagan stared at him wide-eyed, mouth agape. Jacan rubbed his trembling hand on his leg. The sharp, electrical feeling did not go away.

"Rascha uses the meditation pool to focus her visions. The light never rises for anyone else unless there is something of importance to pass along." Arcani knelt before him and reached for his hand.

He relinquished the hand to his mother's inspection. She flexed his palm and prodded at each fingertip. He dropped his head, supremely embarrassed for the result of his curiosity.

"I saw amethyst eyes, Momma." His cheeks glowed in a warm blush. "And I fell into them! Forever!"

His mother looked from his hand to his face and back. He thought he saw her smile. He didn't understand what was funny. He had been scared! "Is that all?"

"And gray eyes, and shining all around." Then he puffed out his chest. "But I didn't fall that time! I wasn't scared at all!"

Arcani let go of his hand and ruffled his spiky red hair. "You should tell Rascha what you saw. She'd love to know!" She took each of her son's hands and walked slowly back toward the open door to Rascha's cottage.

"So, we get to stay?" Jacan asked, adding worry to his confusion.

"Yes, my children," Arcani said with a sigh. "But this is a unique experience for all of us. It may be even scarier than your vision, Jacan. And," she began, considering a lie and thinking better of it, "... and giving birth will make Rascha very weak. I'll need your help very much!"

"Yes, Momma!" the boys cried in unison.

Back inside, Jacan ran into Rascha's open arms, carefully wrapping his thin arms around her shaking body. She felt hollow in places, and he understood what his mother meant by weak. Fagan wrung his hands and stepped back and forth until Jacan moved out of his way. Fagan leaned his lanky form over the bed and landed a sloppy kiss on Rascha's forehead. He seemed too afraid of his strength to hold the willowy woman.

"I sent your mother as soon as I felt the power spike in my meditation pool." Rascha smiled. "It wasn't too scary, was it?"

"No. But I didn't mean to, I promise!" Jacan hung his head.

"You haven't done anything wrong, child." Her smile faded as she whispered. "I have been neglecting the pool lately, with good reason." She patted her large belly.

"I saw huge amethyst eyes, and I fell into them and never stopped falling!" Jacan waved his arms, speaking in a rush. He leaned in with a harsh whisper. "And I don't know why Momma thought it was funny."

"Fell into her eyes, huh?" Rascha grinned. "Well, you'll understand someday." Then to her belly she said, "You hear that, girls? He's talking about one of you!"

"And then there were gray eyes and lots of brightness..." Jacan blinked in silence. "Wait! Girls? There's more'n one baby?"

"Looks like." Then Rascha closed her eyes and gritted her teeth. Jacan caught her flailing hand and she squeezed hard.

Arcani examined her from head to toe after that contraction. "On the next one, we're going to have to push."

Rascha nodded and accepted the drink offered by Jacan. He knew that pushing was good and brought out the baby, but Rascha did not seem all that strong to him. Each time she pushed, she weakened. Jacan could feel it in her voice and the gentle grip she kept on his hand. On through the rest of that day and into the night, the pregnant woman labored, pushing with each contraction.

Fagan was a resilient treasure, fetching everything his momma needed from all over and never seeming to tire. Jacan did all the running and fetching within the house, always returning to his place at Rascha's side, hand in hand with the woman. He swept her long black hair from her eyes. He adjusted her folded pillow. He caught one too many worried looks from his mother to keep peace in his heart. But in his heart, he knew what Rascha knew. Two babies were on the way, and he was supposed to be happy! His heart thumped with fear and joy and worry.

His mother sent him outside for a break not long before dawn. All the moons shone pale in the night sky, in different degrees of fullness. He scratched his head, pushing back the red spikes obscuring his vision and stared straight up. He breathed deeply of the sweet smells of meadows filled with crystal flowers. He caught a hint of salt from the southern Distral Seas, blowing in from Forge Bay. He sent out a quiet plea, hoping it was heard in time.

"Kameke! Mama said that is your name. Great Golden Seer! I'm... confused," Jacan admitted. "How can bad happen at the same time as good? How can happy and sad happen at the same time? Why is Rascha so tired? If she's too weak, she can't take care of one baby, let alone two! I mean, Momma will help, but... She's happy that they're coming, but... but..." Jacan looked down at the ground and sighed. "Please, can you make everyone safe and happy?"

He listened hard for a long moment.

A strangled scream broke his focus. He sprinted back to the house and into the door, narrowly missing Fagan, who rushed out at a dead run.

"Hurry, Fagan! Remember! Delsin, The pre-Arkayn Healer!"

Jacan heard his bellowed acknowledgement. Arcani's hands and weight pressed fully on Rascha's bulging stomach. Rascha lay limp on the sheets, her lips quivering, and eyes clamped shut.

Jacan stared in horror as Rascha's belly bucked under his mother's weight. This time, Rascha whimpered, too drained to cry out. Jacan grabbed her hand and patted it gently, glancing from his mother to the laboring woman, not knowing what else he could do to help. But the look in Arcani's eyes told him too much.

"Jacan." Arcani stood, wiping the sweat from her brow with the back of her arm. "Get Mommy's cutters. Rascha, you'll have to hold on. If I have to cut you to get the babies, your skin will be breached. You're in more chance of slipping across the barrier if you lose consciousness."

The boy snatched the sanitized kit and laid it out on the bed beside Rascha. Then he took Rascha's hand again. Her fingers trembled. She squeezed back, drawing Jacan's eyes to her face. Her faint smile left his heart fluttering with uncertainty. Her internal light flickered and dimmed as her blood lost its strength. Still she smiled at him.

"You'll fall into her eyes forever," she whispered. "You'll watch over them for me?"

"Yes, I will!" cried Jacan. "I'll help *you* watch over them. I'll be right here with you."

Rascha's smile widened. She drew a deep, shaky breath and stared at the ceiling. Then she shook her head, blinking away the moisture that gathered in her eyes. She glanced at Arcani, whose hand had frozen over Rascha's stomach, scalpel at the ready, and her face a mask of realization.

"You *saw* this?" Arcani worked her jaw in frustration. "Why didn't you tell me?"

"You would have worried over something

you couldn't heal." Rascha drew a rasping breath. "It's who you are."

"But I could have done ..." Arcani's shoulders quaked in rage.

"You have been here for me," Rascha interrupted. "More than *he* was. You didn't disappear on me like their father. And now, you will be here for *them*." Her fragile, weak hand spread across her belly.

"My dear friend." Arcani laid down the scalpel and threw her arms around Rascha's shoulders. "I'll teach them everything. I'll make sure they know how much you love them."

"Rascha's going?" Jacan clung to her hand. "Don't! I want to keep you *here!*" He held her hand over his heart. "Right here."

Rascha smiled at him. "And so you will." Light gathered in her hand and swirled into Jacan's hands, spreading across his chest. "Right here." The light sank through his rich tan skin and flooded his heart with emotions he could not understand, with love for children Rascha would not live to raise, with her very essence. Jacan hugged her spirit to him as her hand fell open in his.

Then Delsin arrived, walking stiffly, dragged along by Fagan. Fagan saw the woman lying still. Her eyes held a final smile for both of them before they closed forever. Jacan clung to his crying brother for moments that dragged on for what seemed like hours before his own tears fell, piling on the floor as teardiamonds. Then his mother's voice, quivering and weak, called to him.

"Jacan, Mommy needs your help." She bit back the sorrow in her voice. "Get ready."

Jacan heard three firm slaps. A baby gurgled, then cried strongly into the stark brightness of the room. Jacan pried himself from

Fagan's strong grasp and hurried to his mother's side, anxious to see the new arrival. The little girl screamed and squirmed in the pre-Arkayn's hands, still dripping with softly glowing fluid. The umbilical cord lost its glow and fell away from the baby's belly. Arcani wrapped the child tightly and laid her in young Jacan's arms.

The baby calmed down, even when Fagan came over to watch her. Jacan stared at the infant. A tuft of black hair lay plastered against her head. Her pale opal skin—just like her mother's—sparkled as she waved her arms at his face. Her pale pink lips parted for soft cooing. Then she opened her luminous amethyst eyes on him, squinting into the bright light. He saw the eyes from his vision! He saw blurred pictures of palpable darkness and closeness to another presence. The inside of Rascha's womb. The infant's memories flooded out, overwhelming Jacan with the resonance of her Power Trait. And a wordless question reached his mind, a longing for someone from whom the child had never been parted: *Where is she?*

"Rascha?" Jacan swayed gently with the infant. "She's gone, my little princess."

The child blinked deliberately, sadness and understanding rising in her eyes. She shook her head. Jacan saw a blurred image of another child curled up next to her: *the other*. The gray-eyes from Rascha's meditation pool came back to him.

"I don't know yet," Jacan answered.

"One more to go." The pre-Arkayn's worried voice drew Jacan's attention. "But it's not moving."

Jacan hurried over to Rascha's bedside. The man lifted a limp infant from Rascha's open belly. Using the side of his hand, he scraped off glowing blood and amniotic fluid from the child.

Then he cried out in shock, releasing his hold on the still-slippery newborn. Arcani dove forward, snatching the infant from the air, cursing Delsin's carelessness. When he stared at her in horror, she looked down at the child in her arms.

Beneath the coating of glowing fluid, the baby's skin appeared incredibly dark. She held the child into the light. Her skin flowed beneath its form like quicksilver, swirling and gleaming. Arcani watched her surprised reflection in the child's mirror-skin. Then she had the presence of mind to flip the unconscious baby and give her three firm slaps to the backside.

In Jacan's arms, the other infant wailed in pain, calling out to protest the indignation of such treatment. Jacan startled, nearly dropping the child. But when Arcani turned over the baby again, her little mouth was turned down in a heart-wrenching pout. Her sad eyes whirled in orange, then settled into a smooth gray. Arcani turned to Jacan.

"She says what the other *can't*." A look of confusion spread across Jacan's face.

"So she does, and quite clearly," Arcani answered. She wrapped the infant in a blanket and stared at the body of her dead friend. "And this is your legacy, my dear Rascha. To give Azela these little miracles, and one of them a Metallic? I never thought to see such a thing in my life."

"The silver-skinned and the pale, born while I still walk," whispered the pre-Arkayn. He wiped his arthritic fingers over and over on his hand towel. "A child born with silver skin? It is not natural, I tell you! How very terrifying. The Arkayn Council must be consulted immediately."

Arcani caught the threat in his words. She forced her tone under control in response. "No need to fear infants. Right now, Delsin, these are just babies in *my* care," Arcani said, the mother-voice rising from within her. "We'll worry about the Council later. And my best friend needs a proper funeral. Would you please find her husband so we can arrange the honors?"

"O-Of course!" Delsin cried, limping for the door. "If he can be found." He retrieved a cane from just outside and leaned on it. "How silly I am, gaping like a novice when I'm already in this condition!" He indicated his cane with a disdainful scoff. "Forgive me, Arcani, for my disrespect and carelessness."

She nodded at him, expressing her sympathy with a cursory glance over his legs and hands. She sensed his hardening joints beyond the smooth surface of his skin. "You haven't a great deal of time until you go Arkayn."

He laughed in resignation. "I do savor the little mobility I have left, but serving on the Arkayn Council will be...good. But that final moment — I've heard it's unspeakably rough!"

"Hmph. I prefer a long servitude among the people rather than away from them," Arcani replied. "Good intentions through actions, then, please." She dismissed Delsin with a tilt of her chin. "Tonight, we celebrate both the sorrow of death and joy of birth." Arcani cast a final glance at her friend's cooling body. She then clamped her mouth shut and forced down her dark feelings, lest the perceptive infants suffer with her. "We'll gather the supplies later. Come along, boys. And guard your hearts to keep the babies calm."

Arcani watched Jacan press his lips into a tight line. She had always privately criticized the Arkayn Council for their isolation and distance from the concerns of the common good. But she believed strongly in Kameke, the Golden Seer.

She stared down into the entrancing eyes of the baby Jacan carried. Then looked down at the metal-skinned girl in her arms. *Metal-flesh is for gods*, she had always been told. *And gods are meant to rule.* The Arkayn Council would probably claim her for that role soon enough. At the same time, they would expect to make a figurehead out of her rather than a rightful heir to power. Deep inside her heart, she buried that knowledge from the boys. But Jacan would be bound to ask at some point. So she distracted him.

"Jacan, you know that Rascha named you?"

The boy nodded.

"That means I get to name her firstborn, too." Her longsuffering smile barely reached her tired eyes.

She stopped walking along the cobbled path to their home near Forge Mountain and turned to the bundle Jacan carried. "Do you like the name Briescha, little one?"

The amethyst eyes sparkled. The baby smiled. "Good." Arcani smiled back. "Your mother would have liked it, too, dear baby Briescha. Now for this little sweetheart."

"Silver?" Jacan asked. "Briescha shows me a picture of shiny silver as a name."

"Just Silver?" Arcani groaned, teasing little Briescha for her choice of name. "I don't know. Do you like Silver for now, tiny baby?"

Silver smiled up with wide eyes. Briescha cooed.

"Alright, then. Briescha, Silver, let's get you home." Arcani sighed in exhaustion. "You have a lot of living to do, and a lot of love in store."

Jacan stared into baby Briescha's amethyst eyes and fell into them. He did not stop falling. He didn't mind it so much, after all.

TAMARA HENSON

stop falling. He didn't mind it so much, after all.

2: MEADOWDANCE

"He's not dead, Silver," Briescha whispered. She tiptoed through the sparkling blue meadow grass to where Silver knelt by Jacan's prone sleeping form. He had not crawled far from Forge Mountain before catching his nap in the open.

Silver's doubtful eyes answered Briescha with a swirl of orange. *I shook him and shook him,* Silver's voice rang in Briescha's mind, brandishing her fistful of ruby flowers like a warning flag.

"Jacan just sleeps too soundly!" Briescha dismissed the young man with a wave of her hand. "Daddy Ganan says he just works him harder than the others, cuz he's gonna take over someday."

Awful clumsy, though. Silver leaned in to inspect a fresh scratch that ran the width of his back. Briescha nodded, agreeing that Jacan was all knees and elbows lately, and way too tall now to move right. Silver poked him with her finger, her expression wistful. *Sure he's not dead?*

Briescha clamped her hand over her mouth to stifle her giggles. "Well, at least the pink scars are pretty against his topaz skin."

Then Silver remembered the ruby flowers she carried. Briescha saw the mischief brim in her sister's eyes before she heard Silver's mind-voice. *Red goes with orangey-yellow, too? And his red hair?* Briescha grinned back at her and knelt by her side. Together, the girls wound all the sparkling flowers into Jacan's spiky hair. He did not budge, nor even stir in the slightest.

All out! Silver abandoned Briescha to pick more flowers. Briescha rearranged the flowers in Jacan's hair. Then she tucked the older boy's hair behind his ear and wiped a smudge of cave dust from his cheek. She let her hand linger there, felt the warmth of Paz bounce back onto her hand and saw how her pale opal hand contrasted with his rich golden skin.

She lazed in the warm sun, drawing in its energy, wiggling her small fingers to make them sparkle against Jacan's cheek. Lately, he did not let her cuddle him as much. He said he was busy a lot, and tired a lot, and could not play as much with the twins anymore. She was not allowed to sit in his lap or even hug him anymore, and definitely could not kiss his cheek. She missed him a lot.

Only six years of living, and Briescha knew something was wrong. Daddy Ganan said that's how boys are when they grow up. But he was only thirteen! Mama Arcani said Jacan did not want to stay so close because the girls were moving to their new home in Xepaqua—half a world away—and after their first solo Council, they'd be ordained as future rulers. He knew it was not "proper" to treat royalty like family. So Jacan was either growing up or acting properly or both. And Briescha didn't like it one bit! But young Briescha didn't buy either of those excuses! One day, she would get to the bottom of why her big brother didn't love her anymore.

He still loves us, silly head! Silver scolded. *Can't you tell?* Briescha jolted alert when she realized Silver heard her musings, her pale blood rising to her cheeks in a shameful blush. She jerked her head toward Silver, barely a gleaming dot on the edge of the meadow. But Briescha sensed the rare sad, scolding expression Silver used when Briescha was too hard on herself. *Sorry*, Briescha thought back. *You're right.*

With that, Silver turned and continued her hunt for flowers. Briescha returned her attention to Jacan. He slept on, impervious to the noonday sun and the silent conversation shared between the sisters. Briescha smiled at his peaceful expression and his silly hair wreathed in flowers. She felt drawn to him, to the boy who played the perfect big brother all her life. She rested her ear against his ribs and listened to his steady heartbeat. She draped a thin arm over his lanky chest and hugged him. Then Briescha pushed her black hair behind her shoulder and leaned in to kiss his cheek. *One last time*, she thought, *and I'll let you grow up.*

Briescha's lips brushed his cheek for a second, long enough to catch a flash of Jacan's dream—of amethyst eyes surrounded by onyx hair. Briescha froze by his side. The eyes— Briescha's eyes—appeared wiser, more mature, and deep as forever. Then Jacan turned in his sleep toward Briescha, a dreaming smile on his lips as he mumbled *my princess*. His lips raked against hers and she sprang to her feet, her face burning, her mind racing and her hands clamped over her tingling lips. *Why does he see my eyes?*

Never mind that, Silver answered in her matter-of-fact tone. *I found another dead one over here.* Briescha backed away from Jacan, then raced silently across the meadow to Silver, as much to answer her sister's summons as to distance herself from Jacan. By the time Briescha arrived, she had managed to drag her hands off her mouth long enough to look at Silver's latest "dead one".

The boy was not much older than them, but he looked sickly and weak in comparison. His sallow skin peeked through a tattered uniform, the identifying emblems long since gone. Mud, twigs and weeds dried in blue-streaked gray hair that framed a too-thin face.

"Wow, Silver! This one really is kinda dead. Wonder how long he's laid here?" Briescha shook him. "Hey, wake up! Come on!"

Silver pulled at his torn shirt and patted his pants pockets, looking for his card identification. Briescha kept talking to him, trying to bring him around. She saw her frantic expression in Silver's mirrored skin and forced herself to calm down. The back of her hand rubbed against his arm and came back slimy. Silver reached past Briescha. She grabbed his pale left arm and turned it to reveal a long, infected burn that ran from his wrist to his elbow. The intricate brand indicated he had been claimed by Ouranos for training.

Silver's open, sweet expression soured. Something like the rumbling of an earthquake sounded far off and Silver winced. *Ouranos*, Silver hissed in Briescha's head.

Briescha felt Silver's anger as her own. "Yeah, but what's he doing all the way out here?"

Silver shook her head and released his arm. She gasped when her fingers left deep gray depressions. *He needs something to drink!* Silver ran toward Forge Mountain.

Bring Daddy Ganan, too, Briescha reminded her. A regular Azelan replenished liquid once, maybe twice a year, and more often when injured. *But he won't take a drop if he stays unconscious.* Briescha placed her hands on the boy's bare chest and leaned forward in concentration, like she had seen Arcani do.

The faint beating of his heart amplified in her head. She listened beyond that to his stomach, which churned audibly, unlike the near-silent workings of a healthy Azelan. Then she streamed her consciousness upward into his mind. She knew she shouldn't mess around in there, but she looked for what Arcani called the switch. She repeated Arcani's explanation in her head. Bright means conscious, dark means unconscious. When you filter your light into the switch, the person wakes up.

She found the dim beacon in his mind and wondered at how dark it had become. She started filtering her light into it. Then strong hands clamped onto her physical wrists, jerking her out of her concentration. She clenched her eyes in pain as her mind rejoined her body. Then she stared into the boy's blue-streaked gray eyes.

He heaved in deep breaths, and then finally sighed. "Looks like you saved me. I owe you one."

"Y-You…Your eyes are weird," Briescha stammered. "B-But in a pretty way."

He coughed out a laugh and said, "Likewise. And nice to meet you, too, Miss."

Briescha blushed, having never been called "Miss" before, especially by someone so young. She grabbed his hand and pulled him to a sitting position. "What're you doing coming from the deep woods?"

"Sightseeing. My name is Kyros." He gave a weak smile. "Thanks for asking."

"I'm so sorry." Briescha cried out in frustration. "I'm usually not so rude. Briescha is my name." She bowed with the easy grace of practice.

Kyros scrambled back and stared at her, slack jawed. "Briescha? *Princess* Briescha?" He shook his head. "Of all the bad luck. I'm here to protect you and *you* end up saving *me*."

"I'm not that princess-like at all." She replied with such authoritative disdain that Kyros laughed. Angered, Briescha yelled, "And what do you mean *protect* me?"

Almost there! rang Silver's voice in Briescha's head.

Then Kyros tried to stand. His legs gave out and he pitched forward against her side. She struggled to keep the boy upright, but he was much taller and heavier than he looked. She sank to the ground with his head on her shoulder. "She says she's almost here."

"Who?" he slurred, clearly disgusted with himself.

"My sister, the one who found you."

"The Godskinned?"

Briescha cringed at the awe in his voice. "She's touchy about that. Kyros, she's just my sister. Just Silver."

At that time, Silver ran up with a crystal pitcher full of blue-tinted liquid and a heavy pack on her back. Arcani's medical supplies. As an apology, she cringed and said, *Daddy Ganan was in the deep forge.* Silver deposited the heavy pack on the ground. She smiled that he was awake and alive, then she leaned in toward Kyros' awestruck face. She saw the meaning behind his look and sighed. She pinched his hollow cheeks until his mouth opened and dumped some water down his throat. Though he sputtered a moment, he regained his senses enough to guzzle the precious drink.

Arcani came rushing over the low hill to

where the boy sat leaning against Briescha while Silver nearly drowned him with the rare Azelan water. Arcani would overreact. Briescha shared a knowing smile with Silver, even before Arcani cried out in shock at the boy's condition.

As Arcani fluttered over him, a half-dozen forge workers appeared behind her by Ganan's orders. By habit, she immediately ordered them to task, getting Kyros hauled directly to the forge cottage's clinic wing. And at every chance, Kyros continued to turn and gape at Silver's gleaming mirrored skin.

*　　*　　*

"What in the world!" Arcani listened to the boy's belly.

Kyros' middle protested loudly again, rumbling and quaking. The boy gripped his waist and looked at her in apology. Pain registered on her listening device.

"I heard that before." Briescha felt awkward and useless. "Only it was quieter then."

"Before? Quieter..." Arcani pursed her lips. Then understanding alighted in her eyes, followed by quick anger. "I told you to stay out of people's heads until you gained more control. You could've killed him!"

Briescha gasped, horrified. "I only tried to... He was...I'm so sorry!"

"But." Arcani drew a deep breath. "You didn't. Just learn more before you try healing again, Briescha. Promise me?"

Briescha nodded. Tears brimmed in her eyes. She never wanted to almost hurt anyone again!

"I think I'm just hungry," Kyros mumbled sheepishly. "It's my weak blood."

"You're a Flawed, er, a Delvan?" Arcani

sighed in relief. "*That* I can handle. And that explains your color, your eyes, everything!"

Kyros ducked his head in shame.

"No, I didn't mean anything bad by that." Arcani scolded rather than apologized. She placed a hand on his shoulder. "It means I know how to help you now."

"Mama Arcani?" Briescha looked from Kyros to Silver and back. "Silver asks what is a 'Flawed'."

"So, normal Azelans only eat after they're born or when they sustain some type of injury, right?" She waited for Silver to nod her understanding. "Flaweds, or more properly, *Delvans* have special stomachs that need food more often than that, almost daily." Arcani gestured to her belly. "Delvans have other minor differences, but that seems to be the only one hurting our new friend at the moment."

Briescha caught Arcani's eye and headed to the clinic's pantry. She dug through the preserved, condensed foods they kept on hand for healing and found a few of the tastier looking options. When she brought them back out, she found Silver staring a hole through Kyros. She prodded at his sunken cheeks and felt down the length of his uninjured arm. She again stared into his eyes. All the while, Kyros stayed silent and still. Arcani watched with her arms crossed in front of her chest, a calculating look in her sharp eyes.

"What're you doing to him, Silver?" Briescha smiled at Kyros, apologizing with her gaze.

Well, Silver began, *since he's called "Flawed", I was looking for flaws. He looks perfectly normal to me. So why is he called flawed?* She turned her confused look on Briescha, then on Arcani.

"I don't know." Briescha relayed the

question to Arcani.

"I guess it's because they're different than the majority of Azelans, and are often referred to as a subspecies of Sentient. Though I don't know if anyone has proven that correct." Arcani shrugged. "It's an ugly term, and I'm sorry I used it," she said to Kyros.

Kyros lowered his eyes, mumbling his forgiveness.

It's okay, Silver whispered in Briescha's mind. *I'm different, too!*

Kyros smiled back, understanding Silver's sparkling eyes without Briescha's translation. The boy's eyes crinkled at the corners. A broad smile lit up his face. Briescha's heart fluttered right along with Silver's.

Then the girls fawned over him with such chattering that he barely had time to notice they were shoving food and drink down his throat at an alarming rate. Then Arcani ordered him to rest, saying he needed time to digest that much food. She promised Kyros and the girls they could visit in the evening, when Ganan returned to fully discuss the boy's ordeal.

*   *   *

Kyros awoke to the three staring faces of Silver, Briescha and Arcani. When Arcani had made him eat and drink again, she settled into an interrogation.

"You're my, uh..." Kyros scratched his head. "You two are my first assignment, but I got lost on the way. I'll be your private guard from now until you're safe within the city, maybe even afterward."

"Private guard?" Briescha frowned. "We need a guard?"

Arcani was livid. "Look at your injuries, at

your health. You have enough trouble taking care of yourself, kid! How am I supposed to relinquish the girls, *my* girls, to someone like you?"

"Now I'm sure, my dear..." Ganan arrived at last, tall and strong and concerned. "...the boy won't be completely on his own. He'll have a mentor of some sort?"

"Yes, sir, Forgemaster, sir!" Kyros cried, responding formally to something in the older man's military bearing. "He's a mid-rank with Hyperion in the city! Until Xepaqua, I'm just a trainee, though, living in the local barracks. He'll be coming by to tutor me, or I'll be traveling there. His name's Deraddian."

"Deraddian, huh?" Ganan drew his brows together in thought. "We'll see about this Deraddian fellow. Until then, you're welcome to come and visit, Kyros. And practice your drills. And keep your *respectful* distance." The chilling look Ganan cast on poor Kyros wilted the boy where he sat. Kyros mumbled his gratitude and managed a sloppy salute from the bed. With that, Ganan waved off his salute and strode out the open door.

Moments later, Jacan stumbled in, tired and cranky, with Fagan spilling in the door behind him, poking at something in Jacan's hair. Jacan scratched his head and frowned, pulling out a handful of lovely ruby flowers. And then another, and another. He sighed. "Who's hurt, Mama?"

Arcani laughed. "You slept through the commotion. Meet Kyros, the Ouranos trainee responsible for our girls' safety from now on."

"Ouranos, huh?" Jacan pursed his lips, a habit he picked up from his mother. "Doesn't it seem odd that they waited this many years to assign a guard after those zealot soldiers tried to assassinate them? That was right after we presented them to the Council as infants!" The bitterness spilled out with his words. "Silver still can't stand Ouranos to this day and doesn't even remember why!" He leaned around the corner. The girls listened intently to a story told by a strange boy with pale eyes.

Arcani leaned toward Jacan, a clear cup in her hand. She steered Fagan aside to carry a plate of food. "Your father is checking out the boy's credentials. Don't worry. We won't leave them alone with him until Ganan is okay with it." She placed the clear cup in Jacan's hand.

"Darn right, we won't," Jacan grumbled. He shoved the bouquet of red flowers he carried into his belt and made his way to the narrow bed. His mother chuckled behind him, mentioning how he sounded like his father more and more these days. Fagan peered silently around the door facing, waiting for Jacan to meet the boy first.

Jacan offered the cup to the new kid and managed a polite-enough introduction. Kyros met his eyes with a hint of challenge Jacan had not expected. Jacan's temper flared at the possessive feeling he picked up from the younger boy. All the distance he tried to put between the girls and him collapsed under the new feeling of jealousy. Suddenly, Jacan felt very protective of the girls. Kyros was their official guard, but he was weak.

Jacan skipped the small talk. "I expect that your intentions are pristine regarding Briescha and Silver?"

"Pristine? Really? Well, uh, of course!" Kyros stared a hole through Jacan's forehead.

Jacan leaned in close. "Credentials or not, that doesn't mean I'm okay with you disrupting my girls' lives. They. Are. Happy. Here." He punctuated each word by poking a forefinger into Kyros' shoulder.

"Jacan." Briescha sighed, surprised by his outburst.

"Maybe so." Kyros smiled up at Jacan, a small twitch in the corner of his mouth. "But they won't be here for much longer. It is more important that they stay safe. Happiness will follow."

"Spoken just like a coldhearted soldier." Jacan bristled again, remembering the horrible terror of the Ouranos extremists attacking Ganan, Arcani and the children in Xepaqua just days after the twins were born. They had not counted on Ganan's training and Arcani's unorthodox defense techniques. But they all survived! Then, under Ganan's persistent line of questioning, they admitted their plot to kill the girls. "All it takes is one misstep to lose my trust, if you can gain it at all."

"Jacan…It's okay. We're all right." Briescha tried again to divert his attention, to ease the tension.

"You haven't realized it, have you?" Kyros clenched his jaw in anger. "If I had any intention of hurting them, I would have done it already. But I didn't."

Jacan's eyes darkened. "I can't imagine an Ouranos I would trust with their safety."

"Then you'll just need me to help you imagine one." Kyros sneered. "And when I am successful with this mission, they will bump me up to the Hyperion level. And I'll be with them *there*, too."

"You arrogant prick!" Jacan took a step closer to Kyros.

Briescha appeared between them. "That's enough, both of you! You can continue this silly contest of yours later, but just stop right now!" Silver grabbed Jacan's arm and clung to him, hugging him into submission.

"I'm sorry, my Princess. I'm sorry, Silver." Jacan bowed from the waist, his face glowing with embarrassment.

"I know you're worried, but Daddy Ganan will find out if he's okay to stick around." Briescha grinned back at Kyros. "And if you're lying, he'll just gut you like a swaysnake."

Kyros, already pale, managed to blanche even further. Jacan shook his head, clearly not comforted. He ducked his head and mumbled his dismissal. He turned on his heels and swept out of the room in one grand motion.

Briescha smiled after Jacan's gruff departure and patted Kyros' thickly bandaged arm. "Sleep well for now. You're in the best hands." Briescha turned to the door. "Fagan? I saw you out there! Come on in. Kyros won't bite!"

The giant of a boy ducked his head to clear the door and placed a full plate on the bedside table. His bony shoulders were twice the breadth of Kyros' and strung taut with banded muscle. Lanky, with hands and feet that were too large for their limbs, Fagan stood inspecting Kyros from a great height. "You're different," Fagan said.

"So are you," Kyros replied, staring up at Fagan with utter shock. "I've never met anyone like you!"

Taking it as a compliment, Fagan pulled up a stool and folded his knees up to his chin to sit. He chatted for some time with Kyros about anything and everything that came to mind. Kyros kindly and patiently answered him and even got in some questions of his own. The exchange was a far cry from Kyros' conversation with Jacan. Briescha listened and watched, talked and laughed with the boys and Silver until everyone's eyelids drooped with exhaustion. Fagan yawned audibly and wiped his eyes.

Then Arcani came in, sighing and fussing about Jacan's behavior, shooing Fagan off to finish the chores that time forgot. She ushered the girls to their bedroom, calling for the wall lights to dim as she left. "What's your nighttime light preference? Red? Yellow? Green?"

"No red, please." Kyros looked everywhere but at Arcani. "My eyes don't see that spectrum very well."

"Really?" Arcani called for green instead. She walked over to him and pulled the covers up to his chin. "That's an interesting trait. Would you mind telling me more about it tomorrow?"

He smiled weakly at her, only vaguely annoyed at being tucked in like a child. "That's the first time someone said that. So yeah. And... thank you, ma'am. Thank you so much!"

"Well, you're welcome. But you should really thank the girls." Arcani leaned in with a confidential tone. "Silver found you. And if Briescha hadn't had the silly sense to try something I told her not to try, you probably wouldn't have made it."

With a wink and a flip of her thick braid, Arcani left Kyros with his thoughts.

3: FORGESONG

"Girls, it's time for Council!" Arcani cried over the hum of the rock cutters. "Gracious! Why do you always disappear like this?" She grumbled and shrugged her thick red braid behind her shoulders.

The midwife picked a nimble path over the huge gemstones piled around Forge Mountain. The workers paid her no mind, accustomed to the woman's constant search. She slipped past the spindly earth movers and other huge equipment, all the while calling for Briescha and Silver. As she passed a high work platform, someone caught her wrist and spun her about. She gasped in surprise until the man's deep voice rumbled in her ear.

"Hello, my beautiful Arcani." Ganan wrapped his arms around her in a tender embrace.

Arcani's stomach fluttered despite her artificial frustration. She smiled at the man and laughed as she wrenched loose from his grasp. "You get no free hugs, Master of the Forge, until my work is finished for the day."

The man pushed back a lock of streaked orange hair and flashed a smile that melted

Arcani where she stood. His kind blue eyes regarded her for a moment. Then he propped his chin on his scarred hand in mock concentration. He smiled again. "Our daughters are scaling the rainbows of Hindaro and flying with the sacred Mietina on Vesuvior!"

"You're a silly dreamer, Ganan!" Arcani scolded. But she smiled lovingly at him.

He took her hand and kissed her open palm. "Or you'll find them with the boys, as always, in the tinkering cave, making 'pretties' from the discarded jewels."

"Ah," Arcani said with a smile. "I'm forgetful in my old age."

"You're ageless in my eyes, my dear," he whispered.

She rolled her eyes and turned toward the caves.

*   *   *

Jacan particularly loved the ringing sound the diamond hammer made as it connected with the hot gemstone. The stones sang to him, each with a different note. And he was happiest when listening to their music as he molded them into various shapes. Well, one thing made him happier. He held his most current work in the light. He turned it in his rough, bare fingers, watching the glow fade from the heat of forge fire. The deep violet hue glinted back at him, reminding him of Briescha's searching, determined eyes, eyes that reached back from the future to ensnare him.

Jacan placed the amethyst gem on the table with a sigh. Immediately, Briescha and Silver crowded around.

"This one was cracked?" Briescha leaned in closely. "But I can only barely see the seam."

Jacan shrugged. "I'm getting better at

sealing them. Dad always says, 'With the right heat, even flawed gems can be made perfect.' The same goes for people." Jacan stole a look past the girls at the ever-present Kyros, challenging him with that taunt.

"Depends on what you consider a flaw, Jacan," Kyros replied in a low voice, full of warning. He unfolded his arms and stood glaring at the Forge apprentice. Jacan stared back. Another full year at the Forge Mountain barracks had broadened Kyros' shoulders and filled out his slim chest. His hair grew longer, and his face kept its chiseled cheeks and hungry eyes. Yet Jacan still outsized him twice over.

"Not this again." Briescha sighed. She slipped between them and pushed at Jacan's chest. "Stop it. I'll not have you two hurting Silver's feelings again. Plus, there's Fagan to consider. You know he's grown attached to Kyros."

Jacan grinned down at her, then at her thin hands on his bronzed chest. "Of course, my Princess." He let Briescha shove him back to his worktable. Briescha, ever the caretaker of her sister, failed to notice his idiotic grin and the subtle possession he placed on her title.

Kyros noticed. He excused himself with some measure of disgust in his voice and said he would be waiting outside. Silver gave him a confused look and followed him, her skin reflecting forge fire back at Jacan and Briescha.

Briescha stared after Kyros. She shrugged off the feeling, then realized her hands still rested on Jacan's chest. She mumbled an apology and snatched her hands away.

"What's gotten into him lately?" Briescha twisted her waist-length onyx hair into a quick braid. "He's just been acting so moody lately."

Jacan plastered on a calm expression and answered her. "Probably upset that there isn't much he can protect you from here at Forge Mountain."

Then they heard Arcani's voice ring through the cavern.

Briescha cringed. "I forgot about Council on purpose. It is half a world away from this place, from my real family. And this will be the last time we go before the move is permanent."

Jacan heard the sadness in her voice. She did not look at him, so he knew she was trying not to cry. After a lifetime with Briescha, he heard the words between her words.

"Briescha, I..." Jacan began.

She turned to him and forced a smile on her pale pink lips.

"I will be the best Master of the Forge Azela has ever seen." Jacan tried to smile for her. "Because Azela is getting the best leaders they've ever had." Not what he wanted to say, but what he needed to say, for Briescha. He let his eyes say *I'll miss you, I love you, I'll think about you every day*. But she was not good at reading his eyes. She did not reach out with her telepathy, so his thoughts were safe for the moment. She only looked out for Silver, never Briescha.

4: STONEHEART

Arcani and the girls boarded the blue longboat, running their fingers over the smooth, swirling gemstone. Kyros boarded with exquisite dignity, then immediately flattened his body against the cabin. Briescha smiled at him and shook her head. Kyros hated crossing the sea, hence his solo overland excursion to Forge Mountain last year. Briescha stared down, thrilled to see the bottomless liquid crystal ocean descending beneath her feet. The wind caught in the translucent sails and they went zipping along the water, flying across the crests of waves.

The sailors gave them a wide berth at first, staying noticeably quiet. But when they saw how much the girls enjoyed their work, how Briescha asked questions about sailing on behalf of Silver, they warmed to the girls, smiling and gladly explaining every detail they questioned.

Later, Arcani pulled them away to a walled upper deck that was open to the sea and blocked the shipside workings. They needed to review Council procedures. Briescha sighed her farewell to the water beneath her and the friendly sailors and tried to focus on Arcani's lesson.

"Now practice like I showed you!" Arcani adjusted her posture to her own instructions. "Shoulders back, head up. I said head up, Silver, dear. Don't slouch so!"

But there's pain, Silver whispered in Briescha's head. Silver wrapped her arms around her middle, pinning her cloak to her sides.

Briescha held Silver's trembling shoulders, feeling the pain with her. "She hurts, Arcani."

Arcani's sharp eyes cut into Silver. The medic in her crushed the worry she had about the silly Council meeting. "What kind of hurt? Explain it to me."

Silver spread her fingers over her ribs and rubbed them back and forth. Arcani pressed her hands over Silver's abdomen.

Briescha's head swam with worry. She answered, "She says it's a rumbly hurt, like her heart is pounding too hard."

"When did it start?" Arcani closed her eyes and listened to Silver's belly, trying to find the source of the pain. Briescha stared between Silver and Arcani, feeling helpless and fighting her rising panic. Silver had never been sick before.

Ouranos, Silver clenched her teeth. *When we found Kyros.*

"Over a year ago?" Briescha wrung her hands. "You've been in pain that long, and hid it from me?"

It wasn't that bad, just an ache. Silver wilted under her sister's scolding. *I didn't want to worry you! But it's worse now.*

"Worry me, please!" Briescha felt tears well up in her eyes. "Otherwise, what use am I to you?"

You're my sister. Silver pushed away the

hurt in her eyes and leveled Briescha with a glare of her own. The pain subsided. *I love you, and you're of plenty use! Stop thinking you must do everything, or you'll be sick, too!*

"Girls!" Arcani grabbed Briescha's arm and shook her. "That's enough! This is bigger than secrets. Do you remember the exact day the pain started?"

"The day we found Kyros." Briescha frowned, her mind swimming with why that mattered.

"Do you remember the news we received late that day?" Arcani had a hand on each girl's arm. Her eyes were full of calculating concern. "That same day, a massive earthquake leveled Birim, a little farming village to the east. Around noon. When you found Kyros. And we all heard the distant rumbling."

Silver looked horrified, both in remembering the story and in realizing its implications.

"You can't mean Silver caused the earthquake?" Briescha trembled with fear. The sound had hit just after Silver's scathing reaction to Ouranos. How could she forget so easily?

"I'm not saying she caused the earthquake." She shook her head, staring at Silver. "Your pain isn't coming from within you. You can feel that, can't you?" Arcani nodded along with Silver. "I've examined you and studied you since you were born, and never heard it before today. You've had other sharp pains before?" Silver furrowed her brow in thought, then shrugged. "And I'd bet they all coincide with some geological event on Azela."

Then Arcani glanced at Briescha. "Nothing inside is hurting her. There's a pulse, like a beacon, and it's so strong. It speaks without words. It's...It's asking Silver to fix it, to control it. Like the very core of Azela is crying out for help! The only reason you've never heard it is because it's not Silver's voice."

Silver took Briescha's hand and placed it on her breastbone. *She's right, Briescha. Listen.* Briescha listened with her weak telepathy and then pressed on with the health analysis technique Arcani taught her. Deep in Silver's chest lay a pulse enshrouding her heart, sparking, roiling and compressing. The voice— for what else could Briescha call it—cried out with each expansion and whimpered with each contraction, as if begging for help. The mental noise terrified Briescha. The presence was inside Silver, inside *her* Silver, and she could not push it out. It was too strong, too much a part of Silver. A part Briescha could neither purge nor understand.

Then she looked closer. A tiny thread sparkled in the light that represented Silver's heart. Briescha followed the thread upward, losing track of it several times, pressing her consciousness through Silver's neck and into her head. There, the tiny thread sank into Silver's brain, into the special lobe Azelans use for extra-sensory abilities like telepathy and telekinesis.

"That's it!" Briescha cried. She withdrew from Silver's mind too quickly, at once writhing in pain on the floor as she held her head. But still, she laughed. "That's it!" She groaned, and then laughed again.

"What is it?" Arcani asked, her eyes wide.

Silver heard Briescha's conclusion before she could voice it and hauled Briescha from the floor. They danced back and forth in glee. *That's what it is! It must be!*

"There's a thread, a telekinetic or telepathic link from the dark stuff to Silver's brain." Briescha explained. "So she can learn to control it! You just pushed it down a few minutes ago to show me you were going to be okay, didn't you?"

Silver's cheeks glowed with embarrassment. But she nodded.

"What if you can learn to control it, to stop the earthquakes and other things?" Briescha cried, amazed by the potential for such an ability. "You could save so many people. You could wave your hand and crush a mountain, or raise your hand and build one!" Briescha danced about with such joy, waving her hands to crush mountains.

Then she noticed that Silver looked concerned. She stared from Briescha to her own outstretched hands — hands which trembled in fear. Briescha threw her arms around Silver, murmuring words of comfort, telling her she didn't mean to scare her. She was just so happy to finally realize Silver's true power that she overreacted.

"The Arkayn Council will be skeptical about this discovery," Arcani whispered. She wrung her hands, pursed her lips and paced the deck, as she always did when deep in thought or worried. "When they claimed her at birth, I thought she would rule by virtue of being a Metallic, a so-named Godskin. But her power is potentially more literal than we could have guessed. Earthquakes, big waves, great storms, the tumultuous core of this planet producing too much despite continual mining... Azela has been a dangerous home for all my life, and even for every Arkayn in that hall in Xepaqua. And I've had a gut feeling that this started changing on your birthday, girls."

Still clinging to each other, the girls faced Arcani. She slumped into a chair, rubbing her face with her hands. Then she looked at them with tears glistening in her eyes.

"I'll bet Rascha knew how special you two are." Arcani shook her head and smiled. "She knew from the moment you were conceived. And she was afraid to tell me, even in the end. She knew I believed, and that I'd raise you like my own, that I'd figure it out one day."

She reached out to the girls, who rushed into her arms, kneeling by her sides. "My baby girls. Your power has awakened, Silver. We now have to make the Council understand what that means, and try to demonstrate it somehow. We only have a few days, but whatever we can show them will help us make a smooth transition." She sighed into Silver's swirling hair.

"And that telepathic thread? I really didn't see it." Arcani chuckled. "Looks like you've improved more than I realized, my little girl." She leaned in and kissed Briescha's forehead.

"Now let's get ready to show the Council how powerful my baby girls are!"

*   *   *

A handsome, tall man awaited them at the docks, his crimson robe floating on the sea breeze along with his flowing emerald hair. A host of curious children and more composed adults lined the pathway leading to Xepaqua's main thoroughfare, anxious to steal a peek at the new arrivals.

"Long time, Caslorius," Arcani said, biting back the venom in her words. "The girls nearly forgot they had a father."

"A pleasure as always, Midwife Arcani." He dipped his head in a bow and took her hand in his firm grasp, his sharp amethyst eyes never leaving Arcani's. "Business has kept me away, I assure you."

"And I assure you, Minister, the girls are well-loved and well-taught, even in your regrettable your absence," Arcani offered with a graceful flourish. She nudged Briescha's shoulder. "Greet your father, girls."

"Father." Briescha glared at the man with open anger.

The girls curtsied formally, fanning out the hems of their longgowns on the dock. Caslorius stepped forward, his face an emotionless mask, and awkwardly embraced his daughters in a greeting expected by the crowd, pausing a long moment before pressing his face against Silver's gleaming cheek. Silver hugged him back, but Briescha stiffened in his embrace, clearly suspicious of his very public display. *Why bother now, after so many years?*

"To what do we owe the honor of your personal greeting, Father?" Briescha asked in a biting tone, looking up at him. She walked down the path with her hand tucked in the bend of his elbow and Silver on his other arm.

"It is only proper that a father should attend his daughters after so long an absence from them." Caslorius warned her with his tone.

"Under duress?" Briescha made sure that neither their travel companions nor the crowd heard her bitter voice. "Proper, perhaps. But unwilling. Because we didn't see you at all during our last three Council sessions."

"My work has kept me from my daughters." Caslorius spoke calmly, though his jaw twitched in anger at Briescha's allegations. "You must understand, young lady, that this world does not revolve around your personal issues."

He stole a glance at Silver, who dragged her feet, wilting in the oppressive atmosphere between Caslorius and Briescha. "Not yet, anyway." Silver cringed away from her father.

"Maybe not yet, but when Silver ascends, you'll see how the world really feels!" Briescha's voice welled with bitterness born from hurt. "Not even your Ministry of Core Geology will matter, then!"

"That's Ministry of Core-based Theology, Briescha." He stopped walking and opened his mouth, thought better of it, and kept walking. They continued a moment in silence. Then he sighed, the worries of the universe on his shoulders. "You don't even know what I do for you girls."

"Not like you tell us anything!" Briescha cried. Several people in the crowd gasped. "All I know is Rascha founded the ministry when she was young. For all I know, you are just spitting on our birth-mother's hard work!"

He spun Briescha around, holding up her arm by the wrist. Still controlling the volume of his voice, he hissed indignantly, "I protected you, just as I struggle to preserve the spirit of your mother's ministry. You have been safe, loved, and well-taught, except in self-control." Caslorius dropped her arm in disgust. "You should show some respect, ungrateful child, for every moment I'm not with you, I'm fighting for you!"

Briescha bowed her head in shame and anger. *That's enough!* Briescha heard Silver's mind-voice falter, and then sputter into silence. Briescha's heart started pounding in the silence, though everyone around them buzzed at the spectacle. Suddenly, the air around her thinned. The sky spun overhead. Her knees turned to jelly. Briescha collapsed against her father.

"What's wrong?" Caslorius asked, his voice ripe with unaccustomed worry. He shook her shoulders to get her attention. But his voice still sounded far away. "What happened?"

"Briescha?" Arcani appeared before her bleary vision. "Hey! I'm right here. Just breathe for a moment! What's going on?" She held her hand over the girl's heart, searching for some sudden illness to explain her collapse. She glared frequently toward Caslorius, who wrung his hands in helplessness.

Briescha mumbled, "Silver! Where is she? She's not here anymore." Then in rising panic, Briescha cried out again and again, "She's not here! Not here! Not here!"

Arcani's jaw dropped. A difference in Briescha's telekinetic lobe caught her attention. "Silver just...shut down their mental link! Briescha's suffering from shock. She'll be okay, but... Kyros!"

"Yes." He attended but seemed just as helpless as Caslorius. He could not protect them from something he didn't understand! Silver must have disappeared in the throng of people. It would be easy. Or was it kidnapping? Kyros froze with indecision.

"Find Silver!" Arcani glanced all around. "She'll be scared and alone. Chances are, she didn't know what she was doing! She's probably hurting just as much as Briescha. And now that the link is broken," Arcani added, with a note of fear, "she'll be practically invisible to even the telepaths."

Kyros nodded, masking his uncertainty. "Caslorius," the young man said under his breath. The man shook his head and attended Kyros' requests. "I will need as many Hyperion contingents as they can spare, and a search team. She will be afraid and she'll run, but I'm more worried about what the other Xepaquans may do if they find her first."

Wide-eyed, Caslorius set his jaw in determination. His daughter could be in even more danger than he realized. He led Kyros away to organize the search.

*   *   *

Silver ran away, for the first time. Frustrated and sad and scared, she slipped past cityfolk who stared at the angry outburst by Caslorius and Briescha. They whispered about earthquakes and distrust and hotheadedness running in the family. They muttered about Godskins and nobility, dripping curses from venomous tongues. She clamped her hands over her ears and ran. She willed silence to engulf her, so that she couldn't hear their hateful words. She wished so hard for quiet, longed for it, that she cried out in her silent voice.

That's enough!

And then the world was quiet. The fighting and roiling emotions stopped flooding her senses. For a moment, she was deaf to anything but the beating of her own heart. That, too, dulled to a distant thunder.

Silver reeled in the absolute silence, clutching her cloak around her shoulders. Confusion kept her feet flying from the anger, from the vile feeling of something not quite right. When she slowed down and tried to get her bearings, Silver recognized an alley on the outskirts of town. The light of day rarely reached this spot, try as it might to stretch beyond the thick amethyst walls. But the inky shadows were at once comforting, then terrifying. Even brave Briescha had shivered when she saw this place. Silver had run the length of the city undetected. No one would know where she was except Briescha, when she showed her sister the dark place.

Defiance reared inside her heart, then faltered as Silver turned again to the dirty backstreet. She released the tension in her shoulders and dropped her head. She pictured the place strongly and projected the picture to her sister. Briescha would come for her. *Why did I run?* Silver trembled. *I did little but scare myself, and this solves nothing.*

Then Silver realized her dilemma. The air she drew smothered her. Darkness entered her sight for a long moment. She slumped to the ground, a quivering pile of fear. Her words, for the first time since before birth, didn't reach Briescha. *I'm sorry. I'm sorry. I'm sorry. Please.*

But who was she asking? To whom was she apologizing? No one could hear. No one ever heard, except Briescha. She couldn't call out with her voiceless mouth. She couldn't call out with her mind. The strongest telepaths had no access to her thoughts. She was alone, in utter silence. And inside, alone with her mind, she screamed over and over, curled into a ball at the center of the grimy alleyway.

I must get back to them. Silver still clutched her head. *I'll be Empress soon! This is no way for royalty to behave!* With much effort, and a long time later, she arose on shaky legs. The light faded evermore from the sky, and the dark backstreet loomed more terrifying than ever. The shock of separating a lifelong bond left her exhausted. Her first steps forward robbed her of breath. She leaned against the wall, feeling the nicked and pocked surface under her fingers.

A crystal window rattled. A door creaked open. Silver's heart pounded. The last of Paz's light crept across the pavement before her, then flickered behind the amethyst spires. She knew they were beautiful from a distance, glowing in the reflected light. No one sought the dark paths by daylight. The dark paths only open at night to those who prefer moonlight, to the lawless and forgotten. To the outcast Delvans and night workmen. To the dissidents and assassins.

The stories she had heard amplified her hearing. The shadows shifted and rolled in her peripheral vision. Or was someone there? She couldn't ask. She could only run from them, and run she did. She concentrated all her fear into running toward the light. She focused on the dissidents who hated her, who made the others hate her through fear, and the assassins who threatened her very life. What would they do if they caught her? She saw Briescha's face in her mind's eye and wanted her nearby more than anything. But she still didn't answer. *I'm helpless.*

She was sure the shadows followed her, chasing her down another street, veering her off her direct path toward the sunset. Silver began to panic, worrying at her weakness and shaking from fear. *Am I imagining things?* When her path gave way to another cluster of shadows, she knew she was trapped. All too late, she spun to see her pursuers. She squinted in the night and shook her head when she saw the edge of a hem here, a fray there. The dark shadows ebbed and flowed. But now she knew the shadows were flowing fabric that warped the light.

"Took you long enough, Empress." A sparkling yellow face emerged from the darkness. A pale hand pulled at her face covering. "You know they're combing the city for you." The woman scoffed. "It's a shame they won't find you unless they pay a hefty price."

Silver sobered when she realized her opposition, her pursuers, were just Azelan thugs. If they were assassins, they would have killed her by now. And Briescha was looking for her, which meant that Kyros was coming for her. Maybe even Caslorius. She pushed down her fear with a façade of dignity and waited, even as her emotions settled into a steadily rising anger.

The woman whispered, "Wonder how much they'd pay for a Godskin?"

Silver shook her head, hoping they would believe that no one would pay a ransom for her. She turned and looked all around, up the walls, seeking out handholds for a quick ascent. She had been deft at climbing back at Forge Mountain. She backed against the wall as she sought her escape, hoping to gain enough ground to jump to a ledge overhead on the other side of the alley.

"We need to get her out of the street before we're discovered," the topaz-woman said, waving her hand.

The shadows crowded closer. Silver frowned. She couldn't escape without hurting one of the poor fools. She considered struggling against the shadows, but strongly felt their desperation. This group did not take her for politics. They took her for pay, and whatever motivations brought them to that desperation. And yet if Silver could slip past them, if she could be sure they wouldn't harm her, she could leave them in the night where they chose to live.

One of the shadows stepped forward to bind her hands. She watched his blue hands emerge from the shielding fabric and saw the thin scars striping his weathered, trembling fingers. He worked hard at his trade, whatever it was. The scars reminded her of Jacan, except this man was afraid of her, of touching her silver flesh. The man wrapped a silken rope around her wrists and fumbled with the knot.

She stared deep into the inky blackness of his shrouded face, willing him to release her, to aid in her escape. He seemed to stare back for some time before he sighed and stepped back. Silver struggled with her logic that kidnapping was not as life-threatening as murder, that they had never offered to kill her outright, and that they only struggled for survival, however desperate. Her cold, fearful eyes smoldered, brightening from mercury gray to a warm orange. She could forgive their desperation but could not reconcile the man's unprovoked fear of her!

Silver clenched her jaw and shook her head at the man. He stumbled backward, into another shadow. Silver forced her wrists apart, twisting them in their silken binding. The topaz woman cursed and barked a raspy order. The shadows regrouped. *They are going to take me away now!*

Twitching in fear mingled with anger, Silver watched them close in on her. She felt the heat rise to her face as her eyes blazed orange and yellow. *I wish I could give them a reason to be afraid!* Her heart pounding, she ran for the weak spot in their formation. The gap closed and they descended on her, grabbing her ankles and pushing her to the ground. Silver shouldered one shadow aside and kicked another across the alley, but wasn't strong enough to escape their bruising hands.

She screamed inside, in terror and rage, willing them to understand her and wallowing in the loss of Briescha's mind-voice, in the hollow fear of loneliness. Then the pain from her chest exploded, the blackness enshrouded her heart, and she collapsed unconscious in her captors' hurtful embrace.

*   *   *

"Silver, wake up!" A voice, as through water, reached her ears.

A cold hand pressed against her forehead. The pressure made her flinch. Her head ached beyond any pain she'd felt, and her breath came in ragged gasps. Her chest pain had subsided to a dull throb and an occasional sharp jolt...normal. *What happened?* No one replied. Panic arose in her until she felt faint from the fluttering of her heart.

"Calm down, child, or you'll hurt yourself!" Arcani rapped her flailing knuckles with the back of her thermometer. She pressed a cold cloth back over Silver's eyes before she could open them. "Your eyes are a little swollen, so keep still!"

Silver caught her breath. Turning to jelly on the ground, she trembled all over. She clenched her fists and caught gravel in her palms. Confusion clouded her relief. She had been in the city just a moment ago, trying to run from her would-be kidnappers. They'd bound her wrists again — they were still raw and sore — and tried to catch her. Then the pain.

"Silver?" whispered an apprehensive voice to her right.

Briescha's voice! Silver cried in her heart. *I'm okay! See? I just hurt a little, but I'm here!*

Nothing.

"Just give us a minute, Briescha." Arcani's familiar scolding voice couldn't begin to comfort Silver in her silence. "We need a few moments before she can be moved. Briescha? Are you listening?"

"My Silver!" Briescha cried and threw her arms around Silver.

Searing white light filled Silver's mind, blinding and painful and pure. New agony amplified her many aches and pains, the likes of which she had never known. When the pain died down, she lay quaking from the experience, curled in Briescha's protective arms.

I didn't mean to do it! Silver clung to her sister in terror. *I never wanted to hurt you! I'm so sorry! So sorry!*

The long silence that followed was more

terrifying than her ordeal. Then a wave of love poured into her from Briescha, refilling the void of their severed link. *Me, too,* answered Briescha across their re-forged connection. *Me, too.*

The moment shattered when Arcani slapped both girls in the back of their heads. "I told you to wait! That I needed more time before you tried to reconnect! You could have fried her brain, Briescha! Did you think of that? No! Now *move!*"

Scary though she found that prospect, Silver felt far more terrified of Arcani's wrath. She caught the wet cloth that fell from her eyes, sat up with great effort, and stared from Briescha to Arcani. And when Arcani shoved Briescha aside, sending her toppling over into a pile of rubble, Silver cringed. Then Arcani hugged Silver, squeezing the life out of her.

"You gave us a real scare, Silver!" Arcani cried, then whispered, "Don't you ever disappear on me again!"

Silver squeezed her, too, her mind filled with a mixture of relief, terror and the fuzzy feeling of displacement. Briescha scrambled back over to hug them both. Silver's mental link sparked with ferocious love and worry and every other emotion Briescha had felt. Silver welcomed that embrace as well.

For the first time since she awakened, beyond the consoling family, she stole a glance at her surroundings. The dark alley was brighter than before, as Paz crept over the horizon. The building that formed half of the alley no longer blocked the light. Confusion took hold. Someone piled rubble all around. Cracks etched across the smooth gemstone plates of the sidewalk, and crumbling amethyst walls framed the sunrise.

Thinking perhaps they moved her, Silver asked, *Where are we?*

Briescha sat back on her heels and gazed into Silver's eyes. "Remember that scary dark part of Xepaqua I hate?" Briescha glanced around at all the rubble. "You ran straight here, of all places. And Caslorius said some thugs attacked you."

Silver stared at the shattered amethyst laying all around. She clenched the broken rocks in her hand. *What happened?*

"Caslorius, uh, Father found you unconscious right here." Briescha sifted a pile of pebbles through her fingers. "He saw some guys running away, but they knew the backstreets and the dark paths too well and Hyperion couldn't catch them."

No, Briescha. I need you to tell me. Silver trembled. *What happened to the building, to the ground?*

Briescha pressed her face into Silver's neck. "An earthquake."

Silver stared at the destruction, knowing she had somehow caused it. And now she had confirmation in Briescha's face. And there were verified witnesses to her power. *Stop blaming yourself*, Briescha said in her head. *You can't control it yet!* But Silver knew that she was at fault. She shivered. And as weak as she was, Silver posed more of a danger to the Azelans than ever. All of Azela finally had a reason to fear her.

*   *   *

Briescha refused to unlink her arm from Silver's, terrified that her sister would just disappear again, despite Silver's adamant promise to stick by her side. And Silver, to her credit, had bounced back from her ordeal, except for the one dark spot.

Two days had passed since the incident,

delaying their meeting with the Arkayn Council. Hyperion scoured the city for Silver's assailants to no avail. Rebuilding commenced on the destroyed buildings in that dark corner of the city, no tenants had been hurt, and they were getting new city-funded housing. Yet she still had not forgiven herself for the earthquake incident that she may or may not have caused. There was no convincing her that her power didn't work in that direction, too.

Arcani squeezed Silver's limbs, listened to her chest, grabbed her chin and stared into her gray eyes. "Well," she said, pulling at the girl's eyelids, "the black and purple has faded a bit, but it still looks like you lost the fight. Do your eyes still hurt?"

Yes. But...They didn't hit me in the face, Silver repeated. Briescha relayed the message. *My eyes hurt like they're burnt, not like they're bruised.*

"Burnt?" Arcani pursed her lips. "That would explain the blackness. We've never had to treat someone with metal skin before, and you've never been burnt. Didn't think it could happen, honestly."

"She said her eyes were glowing when it happened," Briescha said, pulling the thought from Silver. "Like when she's mad, only brighter. White light."

"The Arkayns will sort it out, I am certain." Arcani released Silver's chin. "And I'm sure this will be added to the other report about your connection to the planet."

She turned away, mumbling her thoughts as the girls crowded behind her. Arcani led the way to Council, with Kyros and an entire Hyperion contingent all around. After the scare from the other day, Hyperion finally decided that Silver's safety was of utmost importance. Other than the danger of Silver losing control, they apparently couldn't imagine what would happen if she died. Silver hated their reasoning. *I'm just me*, she told Briescha, who held her tighter.

Hyperion searched the Council Hall and premises, and then led the girls past the gate, into the Inner Sanctum and deposited them before the Arkayn Council. Briescha wondered why such measures had been deemed necessary. Kyros was enough, and they trusted him. The girls only had to stay around him. No more running away, or childish fights, or ego trips. No more drama. Just allowing themselves to be protected.

The mosaic gemstone map glowed beneath their feet, as always. A hundred multi-colored spotlights shone on just as many statues, the immobile planetbound shells of living Azelan elders known as Arkayn. Their lights flickered in unison with a collective greeting. "The Arkayn Council welcomes our future Empress, Salakind Velonsacor Eranklaya, the Princess Briescha of the Salakind, daughters of Rascha the Seer. Welcome to Arcani, godmother and midwife, and Kyros, the Warbound of Hyperion."

The group bowed low at the center of the map. Arcani stepped forward. "We arrive on orders of succession, to this, our last Council before the girls have reached the age of maturity and join the Arkayn Council of Xepaqua. They have worked diligently in their studies, but much preparation remains. We bring many pressing matters before the Council this day."

The Council agreed, having caught wind of the recent events. They settled down to listen as Briescha wove her account of the past year's studies and various joys and hardships. They often complimented her lilting voice and intricate wordplay, as anyone's skill in storytelling was of particular interest to the Arkayn, who could not venture beyond the Hall walls. Certain that they could all but feel the meadow grass between their toes, Briescha stepped back for Arcani's account. She reported on Silver's growth and physical condition, the nature of her physiology as compared to others, and, in response to their prodding, the goings-on at the Forge.

Old business aside, Arcani and Briescha worked with Silver to reconstruct the full story of her physical link to planetary disturbances, beginning with finding Kyros and ending with the earthquake that destroyed part of the city just two days prior. They included her temporary severance from Briescha and the possible impact it could have on her psyche. They discussed the thread that connected the shadow in Silver's chest to her mind and the shroud of power that encapsulated her heart. Feeling very exposed, Silver stepped forward at their request so they could inspect her with their amplified power.

"Impressive that she's repressed this power for such a long time," one Arkayn said through his wavering light.

"Still can't access her thoughts. Never encountered such a barrier before!" said another in wonder.

"I see the thread! Briescha was right. It resides in the Power Trait cortex. Seems fragile but," the Arkayn female paused, "but the stress test proves that there is little danger of severing this connection as she severed Briescha."

"Appears that the thread is spreading and strengthening," the first Arkayn said. "See the flickers as it turns? Those look like new tendrils. The connection is stronger than it was a moment ago."

"I can't really see past the darkness, but it does have resonating emotion," said the second Arkayn. "Not the will or mind of a Sentient, though. Something more basic and animalistic, but far stronger than any animal."

"The core is rumored to be alive in many ways, therefore a symbiotic relationship with one as powerful as Silver seems not only possible, but probable," they said as a collective entity. "Her power surges as the planet stretches and recedes when the planet rests. And if any part of her emotion recoils down the connecting thread, it stands to reason that the planet would also react on her behalf."

Silver bowed her head, knowing at last how she may have unknowingly caused the earthquakes.

"Power surges within Silver in line with the core?" Briescha cleared her throat. "Has that ever happened before, to anyone else?"

The Council murmured and whispered for some time, searching the records for any mention of such a Power Trait. They returned no evidence of any Azelan having such a power before. "Many Azelans have developed Power Traits to some extent, as you know, but never have we witnessed one with such potential for widespread destruction."

Silver shivered under a wave of terror that ripped through her body. Then she straightened her shoulders. Briescha spoke up. "Silver says she'll just have to learn to control it, to give the core an opportunity to relinquish its suffering to her, and in the process, help synchronize the planet's productive and destructive forces."

"Future Empress," spoke another Arkayn, "your single power will be like unto Arkayn. Though you are yet young and mobile. Can you be sure to gain control of such wild forces?"

If I cannot do such a small thing for my Azela, then I do not deserve to rule as Empress, Silver replied. Briescha relayed the message, and an approving rush of energy flooded the room.

"That said, are you ready to suffer, to

know true suffering?"

For my birthright and my loved ones, yes.

"We do not sense that she can gain full control in her current shielded state," murmured the other Arkayns. "If that is true, then we shall help her fully awaken today, to know the full extent to which we must prepare. For this, we must dissolve the many barriers she has erected. Are you prepared for this process?"

Briescha still held her hand, feeling wave after wave of worry from her sister. Silver gulped down her fear, telling Briescha she was sure that she could tolerate anything, would in fact have to rise above any task set before her, to embrace her future. She nodded to the Council.

"Stand aside, others."

Briescha clamped down harder on Silver's hand, wide-eyed with fear.

Silly head, I'll be fine! Silver pried her hand from Briescha's in a show of bravado and stood at the center of the Azelan map.

Briescha stepped back into Arcani's encouraging embrace, feeling no comfort from her sister's reassuring expression. Silver stood there, strong and proud and unwavering. She waited for the Arkayn Council to fully awaken a power they did not understand. Briescha watched her sister smile, felt her sigh as her own. Then she opened herself to the Council.

"The future Empress possesses multiple subconsciously existent self-placed barricades," whispered the Council as one. "We must dissolve them to effect a full awakening. The natural barrier protecting her mind should shield her from the worst of the process."

The Council's inner lights flickered in unison, then flared, illuminating the room in white. They focused their power on the layers around the presence shrouding her heart. Silver dropped to her knees in pain, her arms wrapped around her middle. Briescha gasped as the pain flooded her own body. Flame seared her chest across Silver's mental link. She collapsed in Arcani's arms. Briescha felt the first of many layers dissolve. A surge of power flooded her mental link. Darkness came in waves and blotted her mental image of Silver.

"No!" Briescha, stumbled forward, crying, "You're hurting her, you monsters!"

The onslaught of destructive power stopped. Silver heaved in air, falling forward on her hands. Briescha knelt beside her sister, cradling her head in her arms.

"Your fire burns, sister of Silver, where Silver's cannot," an Arkayn said from the front of the Hall. "Yet her strength is far beyond yours. We give her a means to control the power, rather than muffling it."

"Fear not, for we are only amplifying the inevitable," said the Arkayn immediately to Briescha's left. "This newfound core power will cement her claim to the empirical throne, where only her Godskin could not. Azela will truly take a knee before her now."

"Take a knee? Then the Seer Kameke, the Golden One," Arcani said, speaking carefully about a touchy subject. "You believe in her?"

The Council murmured and agreed. "Yes, at least, in her teachings and insight. We see more truth in Kameke's teachings daily. Caslorius has spent a great deal of time in research, and we do not fail to acknowledge the fruit of his studies, and that of Rascha. And yours, as well, Arcani."

"Then you believe that the Great Peace Unequalled is grounded in planetary harmony?"

"Yes," they said. "But not because of any prophetic works. We focus on the science of discovery. But much has been revealed by the future Empress' birth. We did not believe that Metallic Sentients ever existed until we met her. But now we must surmise that Kameke, too, existed possibly as a Metallic, and provided insightful teachings. Put simply, we must learn more, through our observations. But should she fail, the planet will likely fall to chaos again."

"That won't happen!" cried Briescha, clinging to Silver. "Silver is stronger than me, but we are stronger together!"

"And so together you shall be," the Council assented. "Please allow us to finish what we have started today."

With that, knowing the Arkayn could not lie, Briescha stood down, remembering the murmurings and assassination attempts and pain of her entire life. Silver pushed gently at Briescha's shoulder. *Back up, silly head! I've got this.* Briescha did as she was told.

Now tell them to block our connection for the rest of the process, Silver ordered.

"No! Let me share the pain with you." Briescha reached out to her sister. "I can help."

Silver held out her hand to stop Briescha, knowing that the process was necessary, and gave that sweet smile that was just for Briescha. Briescha dropped her head and relayed Silver's order. Terrified once more, Briescha felt one of the Arkayn Council shut down her link to Silver. She couldn't hear her sister. She couldn't feel her pain. But she knew Silver better than anyone. She sat on the floor in silence, watching her beloved suffer through the worst pain of her life.

Barrier after barrier fell from the darkness around Silver's heart. As Silver bore the pain, the darkness arose in her mirrored skin, across the surface of her chest, flowing like black smoke in icy tendrils, etching an intricate design from shoulder to shoulder across her collarbones and dropping between her breasts. Briescha watched, astonished, as the smoke dissipated and left a rainbow of gemstones in its wake. Silver crumpled to the floor, exhausted, while the inner lights of the Arkayn Council dimmed.

Briescha's link with Silver came back in a rush. Silver's pain dulled for the time being. She beamed with some private understanding. Briescha and the others ran to her side, turning her this way and that, checking for visible injuries. Briescha slid her fingers across the edge of the mark on Silver's chest. Contoured and seamless with her silver skin, the design was composed of innumerable colors and types of gems, all gemflesh to the touch but faceted beneath like cut stones. Briescha gasped and jerked her hand away from the mark.

You felt the voice, then, didn't you? Silver grinned up at Briescha. *It's like the core just sighed in relief, like it is content for once.*

Briescha nodded and reached out her hand again to marvel at the smooth stones shining inside Silver's skin. "It feels like a birthmark, doesn't it?"

"We believe it is a Key," said the Council. "She suppressed it all her life, so we agree it is a birthmark. Over time, we believe she will fully synchronize her will with that of the planet. Already, we can feel the core relinquishing its control to Silver."

"But we have no idea how she will gain control, or how it will affect her physiology?" Arcani paced before the Council.

Silver stood between Arcani and Briescha on trembling legs. *Nope. Not yet,* Silver said to no one in particular. Briescha heard a quiet rumbling beyond Silver's mind, something she could only hear because she touched Silver's arm. Silver went silent, as though speaking to another entity. The next moment, Silver bit down on her lips in pain. Then she surrendered to the feeling, throwing a sweet apology to Briescha before she fell unconscious at last.

The presence of the Arkayn Council flowed across Silver immediately, inspecting her status and recording her vitals. "We will observe her for several more days to make sure she is stable," said one Arkayn Council member. "And to make preparations to further assist with this process when she joins us permanently."

Another Arkayn said, "We sense that her power will increase in waves, each one stronger than the last. If she is found to have periodic surges, then those will increase in frequency and intensity over time. And with that scenario in mind, measures will be taken for her comfort. For now, she must gain control of the basic levels of her power."

The Arkayn Council adjourned the meeting. Kyros called upon several Hyperion officers to help carry Silver to their secure lodging. As Briescha followed them out the door, the Council called to her once more.

"Let it be recorded that when next she arrives before us in the next year of confirmation at Council, Salakind Velonsacor Eranklaya will be proclaimed worthy of the Throne, betrothed to planet Azela, and sole inheritor of title of Empress before all Azelans."

"And Princess Briescha, at which time your sister gains full control of her powers, we will hold a grand coronation. She will be crowned Empress in sight of all, and reign with you at her side."

Briescha's heart fluttered, feeling her sister would no longer be denied before her subjects. Now, however, the problem rested with Silver's physical trials. With a deep bow of gratitude, she excused herself. Her light heart tinged with worry, Briescha hurried after her sister.

5: BLOODEMBER

Briescha stood on an amethyst boulder that jutted from the cliff, looking out across a sea of rippling blue meadow grass. The light of Paz danced on the waves. This day was like any other—warmth and brightness and beauty all around. The humming of heavy machinery buzzed from Forge Mountain as workers went about their daily duties. Other workers dozed in the tall grass, taking advantage of the good weather. Briescha knelt on the wide stone and peered over the edge, as she had when she was a child. Her heart ached to feel the grass between her toes once more. But a Princess on her way to Xepaqua didn't have time to play in the meadow. She stood with shoulders slumped, her fluttering azure longdress drifting on the breeze, wrapping her arms tightly around her middle to ease the nervousness that gripped her. Briescha's heart felt immensely heavy, all the joy fleeing her as she considered what she would lose this day. The breeze lifted Briescha's long black hair from her shoulders, whispering a mournful goodbye.

Something bounced off the stone at her feet, startling her. She stared at the small diamond as it spun in a circle where it landed. Briescha touched her face, unaware the tear had fallen. She knelt to pick it up and inspected the smooth surface. A teardiamond. *Only Sentients cry.* Briescha examined the small stone, turning it over and over in the light. *And I'll be a leader of the Sentients soon, held to a higher standard than those I lead.* She clasped her hand over the stone and squeezed her eyes shut. *For Silver's sake, this must be the last tear I shed.* She heard muffled footsteps behind her and turned to the one who drew near.

Jacan approached, one large hand half-outstretched and a defeated look of sorrow on his face. He worked hard to hide his expression, folded his arm across his waist and bowed deeply before Briescha.

"Hello, my Princess." Jacan's throat sounded tight, his voice full of gravel. He rose to his full height wearing a calm expression.

Briescha shoved hard at his shoulder, punctuating her words with a stab of her finger. "Stop that! The last thing I need is you treating me like some greater-than-thou outcast, too. It's Briescha to you. It'll always be Briescha to you! Got it?"

Jacan stared into her angry eyes — anger that masked her very real grief — and down at her thin finger gouging a dent in his shoulder. Something glinted in her palm. He held out his hand for the gem she carried. Ducking her head in childish embarrassment, she relinquished the evidence of her sorrow. Jacan turned the stone over and over in his fingers, feeling the sadness seep from the stone and creep up his arms, swirling into the vortex surrounding his heart — the light that was Rascha's essence.

"Got it." His reply was thick with his shared sadness.

She held out her hand to him.

"There's no way you're getting this back." Jacan slipped the stone into a hidden belt pouch and grinned at her. "It's one of a kind, after all!" He winked.

Briescha pouted. "You really are a jerk, you know!" Then she socked him fiercely in the shoulder.

"Haha!" Jacan covered her fist with his hand, clasping it to his shoulder. "That's not very princess-like, my Princess."

She yanked her hand away with a grand flourish. "What did I tell you? To you, I'm Briescha!" She turned away from him, back toward the dancing blue meadow.

"You did tell me that." Jacan ducked his head. "But I came over when I noticed you were staring down at the meadow. And from your favorite perch on this big amethyst." He tapped his foot on the purple rock. He looked across the meadow with her. He leaned in close and whispered in her ear, "Why don't you go down once more before you leave?"

She snorted in derision, crossing her arms. "Because Arcani sends us off within the hour."

"Has that ever stopped you before?" His ruby eyes were full of mischief.

Briescha grinned over her shoulder at him, then bolted for the narrow path that led to the oft-traveled handholds and footholds down the side of the boulder. He followed on her heels, skidded past her down the slope and rolled to a stop as she reached the bottom, dropping the hem of her longgown. He lifted her from the last ledge and set her on the ground, barefoot in the meadow. Briescha felt the cool blades of grass slip between her toes and the soft pillow of the spongy ground beneath her. The wonder of childhood came back in a rush. She closed her eyes to embrace her fond memories of growing up at Forge Mountain.

Then Jacan had her hand and was pulling her on a jaunt through the meadow. Briescha hiked up the hem of her longgown again, trying to keep up. She tossed her head back in laughter. Then movement in the distance caught her attention and silenced her.

"Jacan! Look!"

He skidded to a stop and followed her pointing finger. "I thought they were all but extinct in the wild!"

A band of Mietina lingered at the edge of the forest, grazing in the shadows. The small group of animals were equine in shape, with smooth coats in colors of gemstones. Fine hair called feathering flowed from above their cloven hooves. And upon each broad forehead sparkled a unique patch of scales that refracted the light like cut gems — a scale pattern that also flowed down the center of their back. Briescha crept toward them to get a closer look, hoping they would not notice her.

"Did you know the winged Mietina are still around, breeding in the caves of Vesuvior?" Briescha glanced back at Jacan. He stared into her eyes instead of at the glorious creatures that fascinated her. Briescha's cheeks burned with a blush. "Daddy Ganan told me so." She focused on the Mietina again. "These are only common Mietina, but they're easier for the poachers to catch. Caslorius says there are less than a hundred reported in the wild. The rest are in a special program at Divinia."

"The huge sanctuary in the south?"

"Yes. It's a pretty amazing ecosystem." Briescha shook her head. "I had to study it since it's under government regulation, and I'll be visiting often."

"Does Divinia house any of the winged, horned Mietina?" Jacan teased, trying to clear the sad clouds in her eyes.

"No, you brat!" Briescha couldn't hide the note of exasperation in her voice. "Dezul is a legend. There are no more."

"You can feed other folks that line all you want, about not believing." Jacan peered at her past his spiky red hair. "I know you better than that."

"Do you, now?" Briescha leaned into his smug face.

"I do, my Princess." His warm whisper flowed over her cheek.

Briescha gasped and turned away. "I told you to call me Briescha!"

The loud noise startled the band of Mietina, and they galloped off into the forest. They, in turn, frightened a flock of avians, who filled the air with a thousand vibrant colors and a gust of wind. Briescha stared in wonder at the beauty, drinking in the scent of warm earth and the feel of air on her skin.

"But you're my Princess," Jacan whispered. He stood just behind her shoulder.

"I guess I am." She smiled at him. "But you're still my Jacan, whether you want to be or not!"

Jacan stared openmouthed at her. She turned and sprinted back across the meadow, realizing how far they had traveled in what seemed a short time. She ran faster, hoping to justify the pounding of her heart.

Climbing up the cliff to the amethyst boulder once more, Jacan followed easily behind Briescha. He gave her foot one final shove and she tumbled onto the amethyst boulder, laughing. The impatient tapping of Kyros' boot greeted them. Briescha scrambled to her feet.

"Sorry to keep you waiting, Kyros." Briescha giggled, a grin still plastered on her face. "I couldn't resist one last run in the place where so many good things happened to me."

Her voice softened on that last bit, and Kyros flushed, remembering the girls had found him nearly dead in the meadow many years ago. He stood at attention. "N-No. It's the prerogative of the princess to take her time."

"It's more like I'm stealing time, now." Briescha turned back to the meadow, to Jacan as he stood up behind her. "I suppose we should be going."

Kyros nodded, giving a curt bow. "They're waiting for us."

Briescha looked back toward Forge Mountain. Silver exited the gem discard cave with a small box carrying all her remaining treasures. Her head drooped forward. Their mental link was silent but carried a sullen tone. Briescha could offer no words that would comfort her.

Jacan arrived at her side, shaking the dust from his pants. He offered the crook of his elbow to her, once again formal and distant. He'd hidden the worry on his face, but his jaw still twitched. She heard his teeth grind together more than once as he stared down at Kyros. Briescha hooked Jacan's elbow with one hand and clung to him for support. Jacan, with a reluctant sigh, guided her back toward Forge Mountain. She fought the foggy part of her brain that wanted to shirk responsibility and stay here, in her home. She fought both her sadness and the sorrow welling in Silver. At last, she quit dragging her feet and walked proudly over to her waiting family.

Arcani and Ganan stood nearby and waved to Briescha from the entrance to the Forge. Silver sulked, running her fingers over the carved treasure box and pulling her cloak tightly around her neck, drawing the hood over her bright hair and gleaming face. Fagan fidgeted nearby, shifting his weight from foot to foot nervously, carrying a huge pack on his broad shoulders. He'd be joining them and entering guard service as a low-level recruit in Kyros' squadron. Briescha relinquished Jacan's comforting support to the hugs and kisses from her foster parents.

"You know, it'll be a long time before we can see each other again." Jacan clapped a hand on Fagan's shoulder. Fagan nodded and ducked his head, an odd gesture from a giant of a man who stood a head taller than Jacan with shoulders nearly twice as wide. "You look out for yourself and our girls, okay?"

Fagan bit his wide bottom lip. His brows knit together, and he nodded again. Then he threw his arms wide and caught Jacan up in a rib-crushing hug that Jacan returned the best he could.

"I'll miss you, too!" Jacan laughed, pounding Fagan on the shoulder as he caught his breath again. "But with that strength, you'll make any bad guys think twice before doing anything stupid!"

Briescha tore her wandering eyes from Jacan's roughhousing with Fagan. Jacan caught her staring. She clenched her jaw to stop the quivering of her bottom lip. She squared her shoulders and lifted her chin, determined not to cry.

Ganan watched them with misty eyes. He spoke in a soft, reminiscing voice. "Seems like only yesterday, we welcomed you into our home. And seems like moments ago, you both were running across the field to the discard cave with Jacan, your heads barely clearing the meadow grass."

He held out his palm above Silver's drooping head and settled his hand on her flowing metallic hair and hood. Her shoulders heaved and she collapsed against his side, wracked with silent, tearless sobs. Briescha froze. Silver's emotions slapped her full force. She bore the brunt of Silver's breakdown and then managed to soothe Silver into calmness. Briescha stood still and met Ganan's fatherly gaze, her own eyes showing her love mingled with determination. She knew if he hugged her, she'd break down and never be able to leave them. Seeing her strong front, Ganan shared his best smile. His blue eyes caught the light.

"But here you are now." Ganan lifted Silver from his chest, where she had collapsed. "Strong women, ready to lead Azela into a new age of peace. And a strong son to help protect you." Ganan smiled for Fagan. He then held Silver by both shoulders at arms' length and beamed at her until she timidly smiled back — an unsure, wavering smile on her lips as she regained some of her composure. "And I'll be sure to see you off at the docks myself."

Silver's face lit up at the offer. *He's coming, Briescha!* Silver slipped free of his grasp and spun, grabbing Briescha's hands and dragging her along in a dance of pure delight. *He's leaving work and coming with us!* Briescha felt Silver's joy and her own, dropping her formal façade and grinning at her foster father as he whirled into view. As kind as he had always been to the twins, as much of a true father as he had always been, he had never left the Forge for them. His work was simply too important to warrant such sentimentality.

"But Ganan," Arcani said with a silly grin, "what about your very important work?"

"My very important work will have to wait," Ganan answered, "for something even more important!" To the small crowd of forge workers, he cried, "Long break today, everyone!

To the docks!"

The workers made as much pomp and circumstance of their rare midday break as their send-off duties for the twins and Fagan. Silver let go of Briescha and ran over to Ganan, who draped a cradling arm around her shoulders and wrapped his other arm around Arcani's waist. Giving his wife a quick kiss, he led the cheering troupe toward the long cliff pathway that led down to the deep bay used as the harbor for Forge Mountain.

Fagan and Kyros marched ahead with great purpose, looking back occasionally to where Briescha still stood, smiling. Briescha felt some of the sadness lift from her heart and smiled after them, soaking in the moment while it lasted. She started, realizing they'd left her alone with her wandering memories. The forge was quite lonely and dark without the ringing voices of the workers, without the laughter of her friends.

Then she heard footsteps beside her and looked up into Jacan's eyes.

"If you think it feels empty now," he began, "it'll be worse when you leave. But I know you must go. I don't want you to feel bad for doing something you have to do. But...I..."

Briescha took a step closer, tilted her head back and looked up into his guarded eyes. "I'll miss you, Jacan. I'm gone for now, not forever, you know!"

Jacan tried to smile past the pain he felt in his chest. "Not forever?"

"Not forever." Briescha smiled up at him. "I'm still just Briescha, remember? This is just my job, now, like Forgemaster will be your job." She paused, deep in thought. "Hey!" She grabbed his arm and shook it. "When you finish your apprenticeship under Ganan, aren't you required to make the trek to Xepaqua to confirm your Inheritance before the Council?"

Jacan nodded, briefly confused. Then his eyes widened as he realized her intentions. "I'll be in Xepaqua in just a few years," he said slowly, deliberately considering each word.

"We'll all be really busy until then, getting our lives in order." Briescha's heart fluttered, glad to have something beyond duty ahead of her. "So, we'll definitely meet up when you come to confirm your Inheritance!"

His expression grew pensive. "That's a long time from now. What if you change your mind?"

"I won't, silly!" Briescha shoved at his shoulder. She turned around to find that the group was a distant thunder on the cliff path. "It's decided, then." Then she started toward the path.

"Just a minute," Jacan said softly. "I wanted to give you something, but you can't open it until you're at least on the boat."

He pulled a small crystal box out of his belt pouch. A blush of red shone through the clouded box. "We'll call this a down payment on the worth of that one of a kind, priceless tear I stole!" He gave her a lopsided, goofy grin.

"But it's not stealing if you pay for it." Briescha pursed her lips like Arcani, like Jacan. She stared at the box in his hand for a long moment. Then he arched his eyebrow, gave her a broad smile and shoved the box into her hands.

"Well, I guess, if you insist." Briescha settled the sealed box down into her small bag of travel items. "I'm on my way, then."

"Wait." Jacan caught her hand in his and pulled her around to him. "I... I don't want to go just yet."

Briescha felt his arms wrap tightly around her waist. An odd feeling. He hadn't hugged her since she was much younger. She folded her arms and rested against his broad chest, like she was a little girl again. Only this time, he felt different to her. His heart pounded beneath her hands — hands spread across smooth skin that covered thick bands of muscle. Her head lay on much broader shoulders than she remembered.

Her heartbeat doubled. She had never realized how much like a man he'd become. *He's not like a man,* she told herself, sounding to her own mind like Silver scolding. *He is a man, now, silly!* And leaning against him with his arms around her was so relaxing, even though she heard the pounding of her heart in her ears. She nestled her head into the hollow above his collarbone and sighed.

Jacan gasped, releasing her gently. "I'm sorry, my Princess! I'm such an idiot!"

"No," she said simply. Briescha rested her hand on her heart, willing it to calm down. "I just felt so at peace right there." She stared at the place where her head fit perfectly, smiling. "Such an odd feeling."

She shook her head and blinked several times to rid herself of the foggy feeling that led her back to his shoulder. Glancing up at Jacan — whose face glowed with a profuse blush, obviously embarrassed or something more — Briescha forced her idiotic grin into a smirk. "And I thought I told you to stop the Princess stuff?"

"That you did, my Princess," Jacan said with a smirk of his own.

He ducked her backhand and followed her as she stormed off down the path. But his heart still pounded, and he wasn't even sure if she understood why. It wasn't an intelligence issue. She was the smartest woman he knew. Briescha just focused so closely on Silver's needs that she had never acknowledged her own. And he did not have any right to sway her from her path. He clenched his fists as he followed her. He could not even tell her how he felt about her, not as long as Silver filled her sight.

Or maybe she knew exactly how he felt but refused to acknowledge him because of her duty to Silver? Or perhaps she was not remotely interested after all? Jacan plodded on behind Briescha, his heart and mind in turmoil, until he fell so far back that she stopped to wait on him.

She looped her arm through the crook of his elbow by the time they caught up with the group, making small talk and fully pretending nothing of interest had transpired between them. Jacan's heart sank, and he drew up his own indifferent façade as they arrived at the docks.

Forge Mountain's docks lay inland, in a great artificially created bay formed by Forge Canal's inlet of water into a bowl-shaped valley. High, sloping sides protected the bay—and the huge gemstone freighters—from the worst weather. Many workers and settlers had built homes, shops and access routes directly into the mountainside.

Briescha loved the look of the bay in the morning, when the light of Paz first shone on the still water, burning off the thin, odd mist that rises from liquid crystal. Briescha paused at the crest of the cliff path and stared down, knowing that morning was long past, but hoping to see the normally tranquil bay. Instead, the ground, docks and mountain-inset villas were crowded with surprising throngs of people.

The forge workers descended the wide path and blended in with the sea of other locals, shouting greetings to those they knew. Briescha stood with her mouth agape. *Why are there so many people at the docks?*

To say goodbye, silly-head! Silver sang out

in her head, startling Briescha after such a long period of silence. *More people like us than you think!*

Jacan closed his hand possessively over Briescha's hand where it rested on his arm. Then he walked with full regality through the crowd and to the docks. The crowd parted, bowing briefly before their resident Princess, until sometime later, they stood again with Ganan, Arcani, Fagan, Silver and Kyros at the edge of their pier. The same blue messenger ship awaited them, looking bright and shining new, even after so many years since their last visit to Xepaqua.

Jacan gave his best courtly bow and lifted Briescha's hand to his lips in farewell. The fire from his kiss leapt from her heart to her face. She blushed, knowing that in childhood she had kissed him often with no such consequences. Why is this kiss any different? Silver chuckled in her head. *Look up,* she said. And the answer to Briescha's question lay in Jacan's smoldering eyes. She pulled her hand from his with great difficulty, opening her mouth and finding no words that she was permitted to speak to the man. But he smiled at her, finally realizing he had finally gotten through to her and content with that knowledge. Then he withdrew to the edge of the dock and busied himself with checking Fagan's pack straps and closures.

Briescha turned to the shining eyes of Arcani, her foster mother. The midwife had mourned their leaving in so many ways the last few weeks, but now, as the actual event loomed, she looked on with bottomless pride for her daughters. Did she notice what just happened with Jacan? Briescha's mind was suddenly a jumble. *Of course she did,* Silver answered with a mental giggle. *Silly.*

Briescha blushed again. She then

wondered if Arcani would cry when they left, and the thought threatened to drag her heart down. But Silver appeared at her side and took her hand. *It's time to go*, she told Briescha, pointing to the shipmates as they unfurled the thin sails. Both girls kissed their parents, curtsied to their well-wishers and shyly accepted a small fortune in flowers and trinkets from would-be suitors they knew they would never be permitted to entertain. Briescha's heart fluttered and she searched about for Jacan. He leaned against a lamppost, content to watch her every move as she left. He saluted her formally, winked at her in his mischievous way, and when she raised her head again, he was gone. She stood on the ship deck, feeling bereft and lonely. Silver grabbed her hand again, squeezing with all her might and waving with her free hand to the crowd.

Fagan squish-hugged his father and clumsily kissed his mother before walking carefully up the gangplank to the main ship. He waved as enthusiastically as Silver, though his jumping and great weight caused the ship to sway a bit. Briescha allowed herself one last sad thought before plastering a smile on her face and waving alongside her sister, burying her emotions and past behind a mask of determination.

* * *

Kyros bowed to Ganan and Arcani, then walked behind them and knelt to hoist up his travel bag. He sensed someone in front of him, moving through the press of bodies.

When Kyros straightened up, Jacan stood within a hairsbreadth of the young man's face. Jacan caught Kyros' eyes and glared. "You'll take good care of them. Of her." It was not a request. It was a warning.

Kyros narrowed his pale eyes, seething with jealousy. "That's my job, Jacan. I will be in service to the Empress and her sister for the rest of my life, while you continue playing with pebbles in this quaint little town. I'll have plenty of chances to demonstrate my loyalty in your absence."

Jacan grabbed his arm as he brushed past. "I took you for no more than a swaysnake, pale and parasitic. Prove me wrong, and I may forgive you for your words, and for taking her away from me."

Kyros jerked free of Jacan's grasp. "I have nothing to prove to you, and you have nothing but empty threats to levy against me. They are with me now, under my care. In the hands of a Flawed. And you're too Forgebound to do anything about it!"

"I'd take your place in a heartbeat, Delvan," Jacan growled, "if it meant being with her."

"Really?" Kyros leaned forward. "If you only knew what that meant. No. In a heartbeat, huh? Well, mine's still beating, and you're still here." Kyros hauled the pack to his back and headed toward the gangplank.

Jacan worked his jaw in anger, remembering his promise to Briescha. He clenched his fists impotently, knowing that any violence he showed toward a member of the Hyperion faction could ruin his chances of Confirmation, or at least delay his meeting with Briescha. He resolved to let nothing come between him and that future meeting. He had to let Kyros win this round.

"Hey, Kyros!" Ganan called out, waving his hand to get the boy's attention. "One final word of advice. Steer clear of that Deraddian fellow.

Word is, he's bad for the whole regiment."

Kyros paused on the gangplank, signaling his thanks. Silver bounced up and down on the deck with Fagan, waving both hands frantically in farewell, her well of dark emotion finally dissipating in the reality of departure. Jacan let his glare bore into Kyros' head until he was aboard. Then all he saw was Briescha's beautiful face, her false smile and courageous mask of happiness in the face of leaving behind all she loved. His heart pounded again.

"Goodbye, my Princess," Jacan whispered. "My Briescha."

6: WINDBLOWN

The great bowl of Forge Bay narrowed and closed into the forced-water strait of Forge Canal, sending the small ship gliding through the passage along manmade currents. The crowd lining the docks blurred into a wavering line. Then even that was gone from her sight as the ship entered the open sea.

Briescha felt a flutter in her stomach as the port to Forge Mountain slipped away toward the horizon. She stood still on the deck as a stiff wind pulled her hair back. The ship's captain barked orders to drop sails and pull oars. Fagan ran about, scrutinizing the crew's every move in his attempt to learn on his first boat ride as an adult.

After inquiring about Briescha's wellbeing, Kyros retired to his cabin, nauseous from movement aboard the ship. In Briescha's mind, the voices faded. Soon, the soothing, lonely sound of ocean wind rippling across sails filled her ears, casting her into a haze of melancholy. As Paz sank into the sea before them, even the overexcited Fagan settled quietly at the bow, lulled by the gentle rocking of the ship.

Silver arrived at her side, fresh from staring at the lingering flashes of glowfish surrounding the ship. Silver took Briescha's hand. *Don't you think it's time to turn around, my sister.* Briescha started, pulling her eyes for the first time from the long-gone arch of Forge Mountain. Silver's courageous expression beamed in the darkness, reflecting the orange light of Paz in her mirrored skin.

"Am I being silly?" Briescha's lip quivered. "They're not dead, they're not gone. I'm just away from them."

Silver shrugged, giving a shy smile. *I don't know if I can cry*, Silver said, *but if I could've, I would've today.* She touched Briescha's cheek, at the corner of her eye. *I know what it feels like, though.*

"I thought you weren't listening earlier." Briescha squeezed the hand that held hers.

Silver shook her head. *Even if I'm not listening, I can hear. Always.*

"Always," Briescha sighed, rising from her melancholy. "I'll never lose everything as long as I still have you, right?"

Silver leaned in close, resting her forehead against Briescha's forehead. *Right.*

"Then I guess I'll turn around now." She winked, and then faced the prow of the ship. "And start facing the future, huh?"

Scary, huh?

"What? Getting ready to help rule a whole society with my sister?" Briescha slugged her sister in the shoulder. "Watching her be crowned Empress in the sight of all Azela?"

Yeah, that. Silver sighed. She shivered in the chill air. *I don't know. I'm scared. Really, not pretend, scared.*

"Is it the politics?"

No. Silver placed her hand over her heart, over the dark gemstone key that pulsed beneath her fingers. *It's here, my heart, and the planet. The more in-tune I grow, the more the power surges cripple me.*

Br"escha nodded, knowing this was one way in which she could not protect her sister. The surges had become more frequent with time, and more debilitating. "Then I'll take the burden of the politics whenever I can, until you're fully synchronized with the planet, assuming the Council will allow me. They acted concerned, a little wary, when you lost consciousness before."

Silver's shoulders slumped.

"Stop that!" Brescha scolded, shaking the hand she held. "Not like you did it on purpose! But I'll make them understand that it won't always be that way, that I'll stand in for you as your voice. That's how Arcani says this would work, right?"

Right.

"Then it's a plan," Brescha said, her focus restored. She grabbed Silver by the hand. "By the time Paz rises at our backs, we'll be in Xepaqua, ready to face the world. And we've gotta rest, right?"

Right.

"Onward, to sleep!" Brescha cried, startling the handful of crewmembers on deck.

To sleep! And Silver knew they were both far too wired for sleep from then on.

*   *   *

Brescha giggled and whispered late into the night, until Silver succumbed to sleep. The pale Azelan stared at her sister's peaceful face and listened to the gentle rise and fall of her breath for a long time. Then she finally sank into a restless sleep of anticipation and worry, rising finally at the sound of a gentle rapping at her private compartment door. She pulled her thin robe tightly around her waist and went to the door.

Kyros stood at attention outside her room. He apologized for the intrusion and stumbled when she grabbed his arm and pulled him into the room.

"Paz rises in less than an hour," he announced. Then Silver stirred in her sleep. He lowered his voice. "I'm sorry, again. They've spotted our landfall. We'll be at Port Vestra by sunrise."

"Then we should get ready." Briescha smiled. "Thank you."

She stared at her small bed, where Silver had curled up next to her. She turned toward the bedside table and bumped into her travel bag, knocking it over. Briescha gasped. Kyros dove forward, snatching the bag from the air before it hit the floor. Only a few items clattered from the opening, leaving the larger crystal bottles inside undamaged. Kyros stared up at Briescha with such an intense expression that she felt the blood rising to her face.

She stammered a thank you and knelt to gather up the few objects that fell from the bag. One such item was the gemstone box given her by Jacan. Kyros eyed the box, working his jaw. Briescha guessed that he knew from whom it came.

She smiled at Kyros. "A going-away gift." She blushed when she realized her robe had fallen open between her breasts. She clasped the fabric tightly around her neck.

"I'd like to think," Kyros said, following the line of her throat with his eyes and glowing in embarrassment as well, "that the gift I received is better, dear Briescha."

His blazing pale eyes caught hers. Her heart fluttered again, and she stood. He took the box from her hand. She saw his white-knuckled grip on the amethyst. At the moment when Briescha was sure he would hurl it out of the small porthole window, Kyros placed it into the bag and cinched the top closed, settled the bag gently on the table and excused himself with a curt bow.

Briescha stood, her mouth agape, mulling over Kyros' words. She had one hand on her closed travel bag and the other on her robe.

Did you get him a present? Silver mumbled in her mind. *Cuz I didn't.*

"I think he's talking about us coming to the city with him," Briescha whispered.

That's not much of a present, since we're just coming to work. Silver sat up and stretched mightily. *We won't even get to see him outside of work.*

"Not quite," Briescha whispered again. "He'll be with us almost all the time. He's our personal guard, even more so in Xepaqua than at Forge Mountain."

Oh. Briescha heard the smile in Silver's mind-voice. *So he'll spend more time with us than Jacan did back home?* Silver skipped over, her flowing hair catching the dim light of the room in ever-changing distortions.

"Kyros was jealous of Jacan?"

Silly-head, Silver answered. She pulled the amethyst box from Briescha's bag and placed it in her hand. *Open it.*

Briescha gazed down at the translucent box. She traced the intricate carvings with a trembling finger and slid her hand across the smooth facet across the lid. Her heart pounded again.

"But he didn't get you a parting gift."

Silver beamed at her. *Yes he did!*

"Really?" Briescha swallowed hard, her throat suddenly parched.

But it's a secret, Silver said, *and you don't*

get to know.

"How is that fair?" Briescha felt very silly to place some type of romantic importance on the gift in her hand. Of course he would give a gift to both girls! He'd been around all their lives, and they were leaving home.

You really are a silly-head, you know. Silver's tone was soft, full of some emotion Briescha couldn't identify. *Open it.*

"Brighter!" Briescha commanded of the wall lights.

She flipped open the hinged lid with Silver's face hovering at her side. Her jaw dropped again. A huge ruby flower filled the box, faceted to catch every glint and tone of red, from the deepest maroon to the palest pink. She lifted the flower from the box with trembling fingers.

So pretty! Silver cried in Briescha's head. *Are those words on the petals?*

Briescha leaned in closer and nodded, squinting at the tiny etched inscription. The words began in the center of the flower and spiraled outward, artfully curling across each petal and forming the detailed veins across the surface.

Briescha gasped. "Oh, Silver! Listen to what he's written: A childhood, fleeting and full. Kisses pure as Paz on my face, and bright as ruby flowers in my hair. As all mountains crumble with passage of time, only one flower blooms eternal. When at the heart of all wonder, a child's heart blossoms into beauty and duty and love, so shall this flower bloom forever."

Jacan's such a sappy guy. Silver's knowing tone clanged around in Briescha's mind even as her heart fluttered. *And he's nearly perfected the technique, the joining together of stones.* She ran her finger around the smooth edge of a seamless petal. *These are the red flowers I put in his hair when we were kids!*

Briescha nodded, her stomach twisting inside her, full of clashing emotions and unease and wavering. She held the flower close to her heart, feeling the stir of something deep in her chest. Silver hugged Briescha's shoulders, emanating the warmth of understanding that Briescha so often left by the wayside in favor of duty.

Silver shook her a little. *Silly-head.* She took the flower from Briescha and swept a lock of her sister's hair to her left side, pinning the large flower securely above her ear. She grabbed Briescha's chin, twisting her face this way and that, beaming her smile so brightly that Briescha snapped out of her reverie. *I wish you would let yourself take care of your own heart, too.*

"You know, you're pretty smart." Briescha shrugged off her feelings and pulled up her façade again. "I sometimes forget you're the younger sister."

Silver socked her in the shoulder. *Like a few minutes matter! Stop playing grown up to me. Remember, I can always hear, even when I try not to listen.*

"I'll remember that, you little brat," Briescha said, love filling her voice.

Both girls startled when the docking bells rang within earshot.

Here we go. Silver tensed up. *Are we ready?*

"Yes," Briescha said. "Here we go!"

*   *   *

Both girls gathered their belongings and trod up the steps leading from their room. As dawn broke and Paz began to climb higher above the ocean, they stepped into the warm rays of morning. The light fell first on the impressive carvings of the moors, as Xepaqua's docks had been forged from gems and carved in the most ornate curves she'd ever seen — curves that closely resembled the very ocean on which she'd arrived. Jacan had told her the design and project were Ganan's first commissions by the capitol when he took over from the previous master, and it had been quite the undertaking, spanning many years. Afterwards, Ganan wasn't much interested in ocean travel, saying he'd had his fill carving it in along the coast of Xepaqua.

Briescha tilted her head back, staring up at the multi-hued spires of Xepaqua rising beyond the shoreline, like a great crystal forest. Her heart pounded when she saw the press of people nearly spilling from the docks into the sea, felt the city loom above her, sensed the hands reaching all around her. Her throat tightened and her chest ached from the closeness of them all. Country living suited her best. She clung to the memory of the grass between her toes, of the scent of flowers on the evening breeze. But she felt the air disappear around her and she wanted to bolt for home, swim across the whole ocean and strait if she had to. As the panic rose, so too did her worry. She locked her legs so she wouldn't run. Then Silver grabbed her hand again.

It's okay, Silver whispered in her mind. *No turning back, remember?*

Her eyes held more fear than Briescha felt, but she faced forward, forcing the smile on her lips and the pride in her posture, just as Briescha had done for so many years. Briescha's anxiety lessened. The air seemed to flow back around her, across her face, into her lungs. She regained her composure and squeezed Silver's hand. *No turning back,* she reminded herself.

On deck, they were met with a fanfare rivaling that at Forge Bay. But the turnout was much larger, with many attendees standing quietly among the more boisterous young people, simply observing the arrival of their future Empress with the arrogance of detached indifference.

Kyros scrambled in front of them and scanned the crowd with a menacing glare. Briescha felt quite comfortable with Kyros to her left and Fagan on her right, beyond Silver. She couldn't quite understand why Kyros assumed assassinations would happen in broad daylight in the core city of Azela. If they wanted to oust Silver, they'd do it when she's more vulnerable. Or, more likely, they'd do it through justifiable means, not through hack-job mercenaries. From what she understood about Xepaquan politics, a lofty and powerful public image paired with sound logic were often everything, followed by a persuasive tongue.

She put her hand on Kyros' shoulder. He craned his neck to look at her. The tension never left his face, not from his hard eyes or the twitching of his chiseled jaw. Briescha smiled, and then stepped lightly around him toward the lowered gangplank. Silver joined her at the rail of the ship. Together, they bowed to their new neighbors and future subjects. Most of the welcoming party applauded politely. The warmest welcomes came from the young men who had pushed to the edge of the dock, plus a few young children splashing in the shelf of water lining the dock carvings.

Silver grumbled in her head. Briescha followed her sister's line of sight and stared straight into the amethyst eyes of their father, Caslorius. His emerald hair floated on the ocean breeze along with his flowing crimson robe, but his eyes bored into her. Just as she remembered him. *It's okay*, Briescha told her sister. *We'll get to know him better this time around. Maybe he's not so bad? He did find you the last time.*

Silver laughed in her mind. *Your confidence isn't convincing about this issue, silly.*

I'm nothing if not hopeful, Briescha replied.

"Silver, Briescha." Kyros greeted them with a curt bow as he rushed in front of them. "This way. Your possessions will be hauled up while you meet the dignitaries." He gestured to a group of young recruits waiting in the crowd. "Bring everything to the tower." They scrambled to gather the packs and packages. "Will you go with them, Fagan? Make sure everything gets to the building in one piece?"

"Yes, sir!" He nodded and saluted sloppily, hoisting his own heavy pack and three others while the recruits rushed to gather everything else.

"Sorry, Kyros," Briescha whispered in his ear. He led each woman by the elbow down the gangplank. "I didn't feel we were in danger at all!"

He nodded. "I must assume there is danger anywhere, always. What would this world do without you?" He stammered and corrected himself. "Both of you."

He turned away on that last part to hide his embarrassment.

"Well, I know you'll keep us safe." Briescha leaned in to whisper. "Always."

He marched ahead of them; his head lifted proudly. The crowd parted at a respectful distance. The girls tried to greet them all with a smile. But even though they were rushed and pulled along by Kyros' hurried pace, the girls still ended up with their arms full of gifts and flowers from those who greeted them most ecstatically.

At the top of the rise, Kyros paused, looking about.

"Caslorius is gone." Briescha bit her lip in

irritation.

"I was bringing you to him as quickly as I could!" Kyros clenched his jaw again.

"He doesn't stick around for long." Briescha shared a glance with Silver. "But don't worry about him. We'll run into him, eventually."

Silver tensed at Briescha's side. "What's wrong?"

Hyperion, Silver growled internally.

A double line troop marched down the incline to meet them, wearing the formal gray uniforms reserved for ceremony. Briescha pleaded with Silver to calm down, that Kyros was Hyperion, and he was a good guy. Then a short, stocky man with slick black hair halted the group. His deafening order still rang in the air when Kyros stepped in front of Briescha and Silver. He held his back straight and broad shoulders level. Briescha expected him to salute, or stand at attention. But he only stood calmly, breathing and waiting for the other man to speak.

"Recruit," the officer spat. "Deraddian, Rank C Lieutenant presiding over Squad Four of the Hyperion Faction of Ouranos Organization has received orders to escort Salakind Velonsacor Eranklaya and her sister to the dignitary court at the Council Hall. You're hereby relieved."

Deraddian? That's the guy Daddy Ganan said couldn't be trusted. Silver glared.

Briescha knew that Daddy Ganan could be trusted to provide accurate info. She kept one eye on the short, angry man, and another on Kyros, wondering if he'd remember Ganan's words.

"Hyperion is late." Kyros stared, unflinching, at the man.

Deraddian bristled and stepped up to Kyros, standing a hairsbreadth from his chin.

"Who are you to question Hyperion's actions?"

"My humblest apologies, sir, for not displaying my proper rank and uniform in this transitional time." Kyros lifted his branded arm and two-year-old rank promotion. "I am Kyros, Rank A Lieutenant presiding over Squad One of the Hyperion Faction of Ouranos Organization, in the capacity of a special S Rank mission. My orders, as issued by the Hyperion faction, are to remain in service and in attendance to these two ladies until relieved of duty or reassigned by an officer-leader of S rank or higher, fellow Lieutenant Deraddian. I must respectfully decline your order."

"And you understand, Kyros, that since you are out of uniform, it is my right to inspect your identification card and orders?"

"I suppose I have changed in the years since my assignment, Deraddian." Kyros declined to announce the man's rank, handing over his identification card to the older man's snatching fingers. "I suppose you would not remember me by my appearance or even name alone, particularly since I have been reassigned beneath a superior more befitting my rank." He smiled, watching Deraddian's eyes cloud as he read the card. "However, my memory of your reputation then, and word of your reputation do no justice to the man who stands before me now."

In reply, Deraddian's expression soured. He shoved the card back in Kyros' hands.

"You'll lead the way now," Kyros ordered, his voice low with warning.

"U-Understood," stammered Deraddian. "We...We shall follow our orders for the escort of Salakind Velonsacor Eranklaya and her sister at the inclusion of their personal bodyguard." His voice betrayed him. He was insulted and ashamed, and snide. But his salute was proper and somewhat enthusiastic.

"The future Empress is her title, and her sister's name is Briescha, Lieutenant."

"Of course," Deraddian answered. "Future Empress Salakind Velonsacor Eranklaya and Lady Briescha Salakind." Derision dripped from his lips.

"Good," Kyros replied.

Kyros kept his tone even, but the tension in his shoulders did not ease. Briescha realized she was frightened by this dark, controlling side of Kyros. She knew he was quiet and always deep in thought. She knew he overreacted on occasion, showing great emotion. However, she had never felt such a chill in his presence. She wasn't entirely sure it was just an act in front of fellow Hyperion soldiers. But *her* Kyros was anything but cold. At that thought, she blushed.

This tiny Deraddian guy is an egotistical swaysnake, Silver informed her, with a little mental laugh. Briescha answered, *Yep.*

The recruits back on the ship were low in rank. Kyros also outranked the first officer he met. And since they lived so long in Kyros' presence—in normal Kyros' presence—neither girl really knew his rank change from two years ago was so significant. She also found it odd that he met so much resistance against a lower-ranking officer. The older man had to follow Hyperion's code of conduct, regardless of his personal feelings. Yet he openly insulted Kyros' claim before checking facts. Deraddian would be one to watch, as Daddy Ganan already warned.

"Briescha?" Kyros broke through her thoughts with his calm even tone.

A smile tugged at the corner of his mouth when he caught her worried eyes. Baffled by the Deraddian's incident of rudeness, she felt only more perplexed. Silver called her a silly-head again, at that point, and took the arm Kyros offered. Briescha looped her hands through the crook of Kyros' other elbow. They walked along the gemstone path toward the city proper, toward the great Arkayn Council Hall of Xepaqua, an entire Hyperion contingent flanking them and marching noisily.

Briescha drifted in her thoughts. The year of Silver's confirmation had arrived, at long last. Silver would be officially tested and named as Empress-elect in just a few days, with all the formal responsibilities that follow.

Briescha shoved down her confusion and brought up her façade again. She remembered her plans, her goals, and her purpose. Silver smiled excitedly on Kyros' other side, pointing to show Kyros her favorite buildings. Briescha stared at all the twining spires of fragile-looking structures, all sparkling in the light, and wondered about the genius who designed them.

She stared with a longing sigh at the rolling blue-green hills far in the distance and resigned her focus to the towering city of Xepaqua.

7: LIFEBANE

Deraddian screamed for a halt before a new tall structure next to the in-progress palace construction site. By habit, Briescha searched the cylindrical pedestal for a door seam. She wondered why they had not continued on to the Council Hall. Then she glanced at the soldiers around her. Each was carrying a package, each opened and carefully checked for explosives or other dangerous implements, from the multitude of greeters who swarmed the group along the way.

"I guess he wants us to drop off the gifts before we continue," Kyros whispered.

Briescha did not stifle the laughter that rippled across the overburdened contingent. They squirmed beneath her good humor. Silver's eyes lit up.

"Yes, my dear Silver," Briescha answered her unspoken question. "Looks like this is our new home!"

"Yes," Deraddian answered in his gruff tone. "It's built to the Arkayns' specifications to help with the synchronization process."

Kyros stared up at the top of the building.

He guided Briescha and Silver over. "What specifications?"

"Sir! The Arkayn Council developed some type of gravity-control technology," he answered, following Kyros' lead. "To control the internal fluctuations, ah, caused by the process. It's just been activated this morning."

Briescha shivered, remembering how Silver's body almost ripped apart from the inside out before she collapsed with each episode over the last few years. Silver spent a long time under heavy scrutiny by the Council to determine what would help her. Telekinesis was deemed too weak. Finally, they had reached this decision. Multi-point forced gravity would not ease her pain, but it would keep her weakened body together for the duration of her episodes.

"How do we get inside?" Briescha reached out and traced the near-invisible door seam with her finger. A beep sounded and she snatched her hand away. The door parted in the center and receded into the wall with a light whoosh. Silver slipped away from Kyros and darted through the opening with Briescha on her heels. Kyros headed after them, clearly worried.

"Don't worry, Sir," Deraddian slurred. "That's the safest building in the whole city. Won't open to anyone but her bloodline or Arkayn blood. The tech reads her DNA." His tone made Kyros stop and glare at him. The short man rubbed his chin thoughtfully, staring at the open door. "Opens to Kyros, too, we're told, if protocol demands."

Briescha screamed halfway up the first set of stairs. Kyros bolted into the building and skidded into a giant of a man carrying a huge pack. Briescha broke down into a laughing fit with Silver buckled over at her side. "One of the Council gave them access to drop off their packages, then moved on to another task before releasing them."

"Kyros! We were stuck here!" Fagan cried out, but in good humor. "We got in, then we heard beeping. Then the door wouldn't open!"

"Good gracious, Fagan! You scared me to death!" Kyros cried, beating the large man on the back in relief. "I don't know what I would've done if..."

Then Kyros stared into Briescha's laughing eyes. She smiled for him, then ran up the stairs. Fagan showed them excitedly around their new home. The ladies directed one soldier to place their load here and another there, listened to the relief of the trapped low ranks and the haughtiness of the mid-ranks led by Deraddian. Then the other men left, allowing them to freshen up. The door slid closed behind them, leaving only Briescha, Silver and Kyros in the dim entryway.

"We do feel safe here." Briescha sighed, glancing from Silver to Kyros. "A little entombed, but safe."

Kyros gave a curt bow. "And I feel you are safer with me. In the future, I will limit myself to outside for my rounds, when things have settled down. But now, please allow me to stay with you."

"Silver says you're very cute when you're so serious," Briescha relayed. Kyros blushed. "And she's right," Briescha whispered. "And she also misses the 'real' Kyros. We hope we get to see him again, very soon."

Kyros shook his head with a smile. "Go get ready. This is hard enough to maintain without you looking at me with so much concern. 'Mean' Kyros will keep you safe for now, okay?"

"For now." Briescha ran hand-in-hand with Silver up the winding steps.

At the top of the first flight, the girls continued to the next level, then the third to a sealed room marked Induction. Silver slid her hand across the sensor bar and the door slid open. She tapped her hand on the wall inside the door — for she couldn't call out for the lights the regular way — and the lights came on at once, illuminating a huge circular room with a domed ceiling. The air around them smelled funny, like electricity and chemicals. Sensors on the wall pointed toward the center of the room, where a large concave circle sank into the floor.

"I guess you'll stand there and activate it."

Silver walked forward and Briescha grabbed her wrist. "Better not try it just yet. Let's go to the living space."

The door closed behind them and they descended the steps to a huge sleeping room with panoramic views of Xepaqua. Facing the center of the city, bloodline-sensing doors opened up onto a spacious balcony that circled half the cylinder. One huge circular bed filled half the floor, veiled by draping, translucent fabric hanging from the ceiling. Silver's room, they decided. The first floor had various smaller rooms, one of which would serve nicely as Briescha's bedroom. The girls ended up in that small room, dropping the remainder of their new possessions onto the bed.

Briescha collapsed on her bed, exhausted from lack of sleep and her long journey, as well as their amazing ordeal. Silver flopped down beside her, laying her head on Briescha's shoulder.

"We made it!" Briescha said with a sigh. She listened to the comforting pattern of her sister's breathing for some time, feeling the rise and fall of her chest, and began to drift off to sleep.

A soft knock on the door shattered their brief peace. Kyros called quietly, "I'm terribly sorry. They've sent word that they're ready for you now."

"Thanks, Kyros! Just a minute."

I knew it was too good to be true! Silver ducked under the sheet.

"Hey! Now Silver, remember what you said?" Briescha yanked the cover from Silver with a laugh. "We're here to work, right?"

Silver grumbled in Briescha's head. She sat up, shaking her head back and forth. *Now I'm the one looking to the past!*

Briescha hugged her. "I don't think that's bad. Being afraid to move forward is worse!"

Well, Silver began, *at least we have great experiences to remember. We know what we're trying to protect!*

"Yes, we do!" Briescha cried.

Together, Briescha and Silver descended the spiral staircase that led to the lower door. Each girl looped an arm through the crook of Kyros' elbow. Then the girls stepped out into the bright afternoon light of Paz. Briescha felt sluggish and tired. Her heart pounded.

Silly-head, it's just noonday break time, Silver goaded. *I guess they don't do that here.*

Briescha agreed. She willed her body to be more energetic. She mustered the strength to step lively toward the council hall.

Deraddian's men stood at attention before the great Arkayn Council Hall. An oddity amid the amethyst spires, the Council Hall cut a wide swath, sprawling under a sapphire dome in the center of a walled courtyard. Briescha let Kyros guide her through the tall gates. She peered around members of the Hyperion contingent, trying to sneak a look at the artfully manicured gardens encircling the building. She felt a pang of longing. Her toes itched for cool meadow grass and the evening mountain breeze.

On either side of the wide paved path, the legendary statues rose above her, guarding the entrance against intruders. When Briescha first came to the Hall as a child, she didn't get a close enough look at them because Arcani said staring was rude. The years after, she had been in such a hurry always. Briescha had been rushed so often before that she simply froze in her stride and stared at the beasts. Kyros faltered beside her, taking his next step and then looking back at her in confusion. He followed her gaze to the huge serpentine Draklian whose clawed hands formed the doorway to the Council Hall.

"You never got to see them up close, did you?" Kyros looked between Briescha and Silver. Briescha's jaw dropped and she blushed, feeling guilty for her selfishness. "Then let's take a moment now." He steered the future leaders of Azela between the guards who stood still, trying to keep their composure.

"Begging your pardon, Sir," Deraddian interrupted. "But the Arkayn are waiting."

"The Arkayn," Kyros answered blithely, "have waited for centuries. A few more moments are nothing to them."

"Very well, Sir," Deraddian replied, clearly annoyed.

Briescha, meanwhile, stood enthralled with Silver at the base of the huge Draklian. His carving was exacting, minute and so detailed that Briescha could have sworn they were gemflesh instead of mere sculpture. Each purple and green scale of his back, each curve of his muscled body looked natural and real, though Briescha hadn't seen a thing like him except in story books. Each of his four wings arched higher than the top of the sapphire dome, each bony digit spreading in the noonday light to support the translucent orange and yellow membrane between the bones. His diamond eyes sparkled gloriously. Briescha felt like he was staring into her soul.

"Why are his eyes so piercing?" she mumbled.

She looked around, but Kyros was staring at another huge statue across the way, running his hand across the creature's smooth feathers. Deraddian ambled over and answered her.

"In the legend, the Draklian's center of power is his all-seeing eyes." Deraddian gestured to his own eyes. "He can see the past, the future, your thoughts, your dreams. The Draklian sees the beginning and end of all things in the universe."

Briescha shivered. "What a terrible power!"

"Why do you say that?"

"To know everything and to be incapable of changing anything means he is weak." Briescha laid her hand on what she could reach of the creature's scaled flank, sensing again that he was more like gemflesh than carving. But unlike the immobile Arkayn, no light arose at her touch or voice in the Draklian. "I feel sorry for him. He's bound by his wisdom instead of empowered by it."

"Maybe, but it would be a power worth having, nonetheless." The short man gave his chin a thoughtful stroke. "Think of what can be done with such power! Think of how one could rule!"

She met his eyes for a long moment, steeling herself against his overflowing hubris. "I have, Officer Deraddian, and have decided that a true ruler would die before sacrificing hope to such helplessness."

"You are as headstrong as I have heard." He chuckled, the sound a dark rasp in his throat.

"Perhaps." Briescha fixed him with her penetrating gaze. "And you, as overbearing as rumors suggest."

"Ah, my reputation carries well, then." He

slicked his hair back with a stubby hand. His laughter was disingenuous.

"I wouldn't say it carries well, Officer."

He scoffed as she turned away and walked toward the large ruby Avian of Flame. Briescha greeted Silver and Kyros. She sighed deeply.

"Don't be overwhelmed by him," Kyros muttered. "He's just a bit gritty. I'll have him straightened up before long."

"He's quite ambitious," Briescha said, with a note of warning.

"Many Hyperion soldiers are." Kyros rubbed the Ouranos brand on his arm. "And they'll do anything to climb the ranks, including under-the-table mercenary jobs."

Silver's temper flared. Her eyes glowed orange like lava. One time of being hunted for assassination was enough for both girls, and they were thankful for Daddy Ganan, Jacan and Fagan for saving them. Briescha leaned against Silver's shoulder and willed her to calm down. *We're safe now*, Silver finally repeated her sister's chant. *So it'll be okay.*

Kyros studied Silver's reactions and calmed down when her eye color subsided to a cool mercury. He explained how the ruby Avian of Flame represented the Forge, but Ganan had told them that in infancy. Her huge wings and tail flowed in fiery curves almost too delicate for Azelan hands to carve.

Briescha smiled, finally getting the chance to run her fingers across the beautiful creature's legs and bottom wing feathers. "She dies and lives, representing the eternal cycle of change, purging and recreating just like Daddy Ganan and Jacan." A pang of hurt settled in the pit of her stomach. She missed the Forge. "Her power is in her feathers—her wings and tail can change the direction of the winds, of the tide, and even time if she so wishes it."

Dezul loomed above her next, larger than the biggest Mietina stallion she'd ever seen and reared on his massive back legs, feathered wings aloft as if he would take flight at any moment. His twining lapis lazuli horn glowed darkly in the light from Paz, casting a dark blue shadow across Briescha's outstretched opal hands, his sinuous neck frozen in a deep, proud arch. Her fingertips reached past his flank, still half her height away from his broad blue back. She remembered all the times she and Silver had dreamed of scouring Mount Vesuvior in search of a winged unicorn Mietina like Dezul. But Dezul seemed real enough, at least, to keep her childhood dream alive. Somewhere, she had to believe, they exist.

Then she caught a far-off glimmer of Silver's mental voice. Her sister wasn't speaking to her. Silver's smoldering eyes had fixated on Dezul's muzzle high overhead. She had both hands pressed against his knee. Her mind was whispering to him in words even Briescha could not understand, with a deep gaze of stern concentration knitting her brow. Then she sighed deeply and dropped her hands, defeated. Seeing Briescha's confusion, she ran over and grabbed her sister's hand, her eyes swirling in excitement.

I could've sworn that there was a glimmer in there. Silver grinned. *I just know if I could concentrate hard enough, and push hard enough, he would answer.*

"But what are those words you were saying?" Briescha furrowed her brow.

Silver glanced away, her eyes glassy, thinking. *I can't remember, but it just felt like he would understand them.*

Puzzling over Silver's answer, Briescha absently took Kyros' offered arm again.

"What is it?" Kyros looked back and forth between the women.

Briescha gave a mischievous smile. "She was trying to wake Dezul."

With Kyros blinking at her, and Silver pinching her for the disbelieving tone, they made their way finally through the sliding doors that opened on the column-lined hallway leading to the Inner Sanctum. At some point in the transition, they shed their Hyperion escort. Kyros must have dismissed the men at the wide entrance while Briescha was in deep conversation with her sister.

So what happens if they all fight each other? Silver waved her hands like a fighter.

"Silver!" Briescha echoed, then gasped in the dead silence around them.

"What is it?" Kyros urged once more in a low voice, still walking casually between the girls. Briescha told him Silver's musing.

He smiled at them. "The Avian would call the forge-fire from Azela's core to burn the ground. She would make the very wind catch fire. The Draklian would evade her attacks and stomp on the earth, causing the planet to shake apart. Dezul would watch them destroy one another, then take his rightful place atop a mound of charred space rubble, ruling the vast nothingness of the shell of Azela."

Briescha and Silver stopped and stared wide eyed and open mouthed at Kyros' serious face, both taken aback by the total destruction and power wrought by these creatures. *Perhaps awakening them would be a bad idea.*

"Is that the legend?" Briescha's expression was one of abject horror.

Kyros' face split in a grin full of mischief. "Nope. I just made it all up."

Both girls took the opportunity to pinch the closest, softest part of Kyros' arm before dragging him off in a huff to the Inner Sanctum as he alternated between chuckling and crying "Ouch!"

The atmosphere within the Inner Sanctum immediately calmed the group as they entered with courtesy as they were taught. Above, as always in the high dome of the hall, the whole wide sky shone in shades of sapphire. Below, the gemstone mosaic map spread across the floor. And along each tier, in nearly every spotlight, stood a gracefully posed Arkayn statue, each frozen in an elegant stance, lending beauty to his or her respectable servitude of singular power and guidance. The scene both moved and terrified Briescha every time she laid eyes upon it. To be immobilized was to be helpless, and helplessness was her greatest fear.

The Arkayn Council had composed a touching elegy to welcome both girls as the Godbound of Azela. Silver beamed as the lilting voices from all the circular chamber's residents mounted into a haunting melody that filled her heart with joy. As the song drifted away, all three Sentients bowed before the immobile ones, profoundly moved by the touching tribute to Silver's transition.

"We are honored to receive your song, your blessing and your acknowledgement, Arkayn Council." Briescha arose again to her full height. She glanced at Silver. "My sister wonders at your intricate composition, and the immaculate execution of the arrangement."

"Our future Empress enjoys and studies music in detail," the Council noted.

"Singing elevates a common tool to an instrument." Briescha maintained her cheerful tone. "In lacking that common tool, a voice, she has found true appreciation in what many could take for granted."

The Arkayn Council expressed profound

understanding with many comments on Silver's steadfast and practical nature, showering their approval on one who would also take joy in supporting the arts.

The meeting turned to several structural matters after that. The Arkayn Council outlined the basic duties expected of Azela's new leaders, roles they would build upon over the next years until Silver gained exclusive ruling authority. Briescha attended with rapt interest, keen on reciting her many roles with complete accuracy. Interpreter. Philanthropist. Coordinator. A whole lot of overseeing, managing, attending, traveling and such. Just basic support details. Silver had all the hard work of ruling and aligning with the core.

Silver stood beside her, a tight bundle of nerves, but straight and strong. The little girl from their youth, swaddled in a brown cloak to hide her skin, clinging terrified to Briescha's side, was gone. Briescha watched her sister, sensing her quiet resolve and the static of worry.

"The most important element to assure your shared success in leading Azela is controlling how you are viewed — by the public, by officials in power, by the youth." The Council emphasized their intent with a wave of power that rocked the girls back on their heels. Kyros stumbled backward. "We, for instance, were once merely Azelans possessing Power Traits. At the point when we became immobile, our Arkayn power purified and refocused. The people viewed us as more than what we once were. Regardless of our personal inclinations, we are now Arkayn above all else."

"You would have us be all to all?" Briescha let the question hang on the air a moment. "Even though we are not gods?"

"You must be all to all," said one Arkayn, "because you are not gods."

"The people expect infallibility in their leaders, no matter that they are mortals," said another Arkayn. "You must be more in your darkest hours than they are in their brightest. You must be a pinnacle they cannot reach."

But they will be afraid of us, Briescha! Silver's eyes pleaded with Briescha.

"We do not wish to lead through fear," Briescha announced.

The Council joined their voices in approval. "Arcani has taught you well. Prepare, then, our leaders, for you must find a way to lead through love," the Council said.

Following the full psychic inspection of Silver's metaphysical connection, the Council determined that Silver's synchronicity was escalating toward resolution within four or five years, at which time she could ascend to the Imperial Throne. They explained how the Tower's gravity chamber functioned, how Silver could use it during her episodes, and provided a long list of things not to do regarding the room, foremost of which involved never opening the door prior to decompression. Also, during training and various temporary separations that would occur between the sisters, their mental link may or may not temporarily terminate when the chamber was in use.

Briescha's heartbeat quickened, but Silver calmed her down with silent encouragement.

"We know that this causes you great distress, Princess Briescha," the Council began, "but as the termination will be temporary and for the preservation of your mental health, we must insist."

"The Council is just and kind in this ruling," Briescha stated. "I accept and will abide by it."

The long meeting concluded with the presentation of a very full schedule, keeping

Kyros ever in attendance. Briescha, Silver and Kyros bowed deeply when they were finally released. The psychic energy of the room pressed all around constantly, affecting even the most willful people with anxiety and weak knees after a long time. Heaving in the thick courtyard air, Silver sat on the Draklian's huge foot and stared ahead.

"Don't be overwhelmed, Silver." Briescha sat next to Silver and tucked a loose lock of hair behind her ear. "We'll manage just fine, once we have a system in place."

Silver scoffed and crossed her arms. *You're just as scared as me!*

"Haha. So I am! But they must cram a lot of training into just four or so years, I suppose. We will plan it out on a chart and just learn everything by then."

Silver stared at her, blinking. *Is that all? Just put it all on a chart?*

Maybe, Briescha answered. She liked having a way to be more involved, records or no.

"Ladies, it's time to head home," Kyros said, his voice low. His eyes darted to and fro.

Briescha stared around the darkening courtyard. Evening was upon them, with a new schedule to commence tomorrow. Even so late, the flowers sparkled with a special, natural look that made Briescha long for the Forge Mountain meadow once more.

Kyros chided two sleepy guards who leaned against the doorway. "Is this all Hyperion can afford to protect Azela's future Empress?" He raged against their slack-jawed appearance. "I'll have words with Hyperion tomorrow on their ineptitude, and you two will be front and center!" He stabbed a finger against their chests to punctuate his last three words. "Funny how Hyperion disappears when no one is admiring their patriotism," Kyros grumbled. "I will work on that attitude. Especially with Deraddian."

Briescha and Silver clung to their escort's arm as darkness fell around them. *It's okay, Silver. Kyros is here.* Street lights flickered on overhead, the surreal light blending with the glow of stepping stones underfoot. The trailing guards stumbled along and apologized once too often. Kyros ordered one on point, the other behind, and demanded their silence.

Many spires and towers around them glowed with internal light as citizens went about their nighttime duties. Several lights winked out as Briescha and Silver watched. They made a guessing game of the lights for some time — one light belonged to a seamstress finishing up her last longgown of the night, one belonged to a child whose father read her to sleep with great stories of adventure. And so the walk back to the tower progressed.

The point-guard — now fully awake — called out a warning. Too late. A shadow barreled past him. The guard cried out and fell to the ground. The shadow streaked toward Silver. Briescha saw the outline of the head and shoulders, then some type of flowing fabric that bent the light. Silver cursed in Briescha's head. *It's them again.*

Kyros moved between them and pulled his sword up to block a wild swing by the shadow. Something heavy bounced off the diamond blade. He knocked the assailant off balance and flung aside the shroud, pinning her shoulders with his weight. A muffled crack was met with a piercing scream. A woman with a sparkling yellow face and wild blue hair cursed and glared at him, then scratched at his hands to free herself. Then her hands fell limp. She breathed heavily, but offered no more resistance.

"Her back is broken." Kyros fought the

remorse in his voice. "She's dying."

Silver stepped forward. *It's her. The one from the last kidnapping, when I ran away.*

"Silver knows her," Briescha said to Kyros. "From when our link was broken."

The yellow-faced woman screamed incoherently as Silver approached. Her lifeless hands trembled of their own accord. Then Briescha heard a word she knew well.

The woman cried out, "Monster! I saw what you did! Monster!"

No, Silver answered, nodding to Briescha for relay. *You saw nothing. You were blinded by greed and desperation. And now you hunt me?* Silver knelt at the woman's side, reaching out to the woman's face. She turned away. *Tell me why I am a monster to be hunted.* She leaned into the woman's seething stare. *Please, before you die, tell me!*

"You are a monster because they want to put you in a cage," she answered. "But their payment wasn't worth that day. That awful day! Those glowing eyes! That horrible power!"

"Who wants to kidnap Silver? Tell me." Kyros held his blade to her throat.

The woman cackled, unhinged from that first attack on Silver, from the fear and shock of Silver's uncontrolled power. She laughed and laughed, until the light dissipated in her blood and death took her at last. Silver looked distraught, kneeling as she was with her hand outstretched to the dead woman.

"So she wasn't just trying to collect a ransom back then." Briescha clenched her jaw.

"Identify yourselves!" cried the guard in the rear. He fumbled with his gun.

Kyros spun to face the new arrivals. He sheathed his sword and pulled his pistol from a rib holster. More shadow-cloaked figures emerged, ambling toward the four remaining targets. Kyros leveled his gun at their leader's head and steadied his breathing.

The locator on the dead guard beeped to life. A siren wailed in the distance — finally — to signal Hyperion forces to their fallen comrade. The rear guard jumped at the sound, and one of the shadows descended on him, ending his life promptly. Exposed and terrified, Briescha knelt beside Silver and clung to her, trying to shield her with her body.

"They'll be here soon, Silver." Briescha forced her eyes on the movement of the enemy.

She stared up at their friend. Kyros kept his aim.

"Great Hyperion, always ascending and falling away," said a measured, smooth voice.

"Let me see your face," Kyros ordered, "and your hands. Otherwise, you will die."

"It's foolish of you to think I would die without reaching my objective," he said from beneath the distorting cloth. Kyros blinked and squinted. His shrouded hand gestured to Kyros. "First, I must kill you, then the girl, then take the Empress."

Kyros pulled the trigger. The man fell back against his followers, a waft of smoke drifting from his forehead. He dropped one after another, squinting into the darkness. Briescha tried to follow his aim, but she could only see a telltale shift of the shadows. Kyros killed them as if they attacked in daylight.

A shadow attacked from the side, swinging a shrouded weapon at Kyros' ribs. Briescha cried out as Kyros landed beside her. She saw the pain on his chiseled face. He pressed a hand against his ribs. With great effort, he stood, his pistol in his hand. He shot the man who knocked him down and searched for the others. They retreated, carrying the body of their leader with them. Their other dead remained. Kyros limped over to the girls.

"They ran away." Kyros gasped. "Whoever they are. Are you girls okay?"

That one isn't dead. Silver stared beyond Briescha's vise-like grip at a twitching shadow whose shroud flipped up to reveal his legs.

Briescha reluctantly released her sister to inspect Kyros' wounds. "Let it go for now. I'll live. See if that one can be saved. We need him."

She pulled the distortion fabric over the man's head. His pallid skin and pale hair lost light with each second. "He's Delvan?"

Kyros looked over her shoulder. "Looks like." Then he continued standing watch, guarding against a new attack.

She placed her hands on his chest and reached for his heart. The beat slowed and slowed. She ignored it and pushed past his chest into his head. She sought the switch, to put more light into it. The switch was near-invisible and the light she pushed in disappeared into a void, as if the switch was bottomless. Suddenly, she felt weak. Her hands trembled and went numb. But a name reached her ears. She clung to the sound of it with feeble psychic hands. She felt her body lying on the ground. Her head ached in waves that lessened with the numbness that spread inward from her hands and feet. Her heart beat slower with each ragged breath. And then, as all her parts stopped working, agony swelled from her core with a monumental shuddering that would end in silence.

Silver shook her over and over, bouncing her head off the ground and screaming in her mind-voice to snap out of it. Briescha screamed over and over, rolled to and fro in pain beyond any she had ever felt. Quaking in abject terror, she finally lay still, heaving in breath like it was life. Each breath made her shudder. When she looked up, Silver's infuriated orange gaze filled her vision.

You dummy! Silver fumed. She shook her sister again. *You idiot! You almost died!*

"Ow! Stop! What happened?" Briescha heard her own voice through a tunnel, tinny and distant. She trembled uncontrollably. Someone draped a blanket over her.

"You joined with him." Kyros paced before them, quietly furious. "You tried to save him, but he was too far gone. It's my fault for asking you. If we had lost you, I can't..."

"Hush." Briescha's lip quivered. "I knew something wasn't right, but I didn't stop. You're right, Silver. I'm an idiot! Please, forgive me?"

No, Silver crossed her arms and turning away. *Not even close. Dummy.*

"You must never place yourself in harm's way again." Kyros' low voice held a warning and something Briescha couldn't quite identify. "Promise me."

"You know I can't." Briescha felt a sharp pain in her ribs. Silver kicked her a second time for good measure.

Dummy. Silver poked her with her toe again and stormed off.

Kyros gaped after her. Briescha noticed for the first time that they were surrounded by an entire contingent of Hyperion. A sizable number flanked Silver as she left. Briescha sighed.

"They sure were late." Briescha stared all around her.

"That, I can promise, will never happen again." Kyros raged against their incompetence. "Reform, no matter how drastic, is in order within Hyperion. I'll make sure it happens for you both." He stretched his hand to Briescha. She noticed she was lying on a manicured lawn of the mid-city park. Taking his hand, she labored to stand. Her head pounded.

"Are you okay?" His eyes were all old-Kyros, all concern and sincerity.

"I'll be fine." She rubbed her forehead. "Even after all of Arcani's training, I didn't even know that could happen. I think Silver hurt me more in the end!" She chuckled and grabbed her ribs.

"Silver saved you." Kyros stared into Briescha's eyes. "She realized something was wrong and dragged you away just in time. She was the only one who could tell what was happening."

She stood for a long while considering the possibilities. "Let's go home, now." Briescha sighed and listened for Silver. "She isn't speaking to me now. She was very worried, so she has the right to be mad."

Walking with Kyros, swaddled by an entire half-contingent of fully alert Hyperion soldiers, Briescha felt safe again. Her head cleared finally, and she remembered what she had learned from the dying man. "I have a name. That's all I got. It wasn't some faction of Hyperion that I know. It wasn't Ouranos, I think. They may be working with the other factions. It was someone or some group named Visett."

Kyros dispatched his summary with that name, promising a full report and full disclosure in the morning. He ordered research by Hyperion for any name relating to the word. "I haven't heard of it before, but I'll figure it out."

They walked in silence and thought for a long time. "You did well." Briescha squeezed his arm.

"I killed people." Kyros looked down at his hands, disgusted. "The dead were mostly Delvan from the lower classes. Like me."

"You did what you needed to do." Briescha grabbed the hands he hated. "I...I don't like killing anyone, but I understand when it needs to happen. I don't want anyone to die ever. But...if you can't understand sacrifice, you can't lead, right?"

Kyros nodded. They continued in silence for some time. She finally released his hands.

"I wondered then," Briescha whispered. "How did you see the shadows so clearly?"

"What do you mean?"

"Your aim was perfect, even though they blended into the shadows so well."

"They blended in?" Kyros shook his head. "Their cloaks had sort of a fuzzy glow around the curves. Like white light."

"No, they didn't," Briescha said. "But..."

"But what?"

Briescha leaned in close. "The fabric was wired. It bent the light. I would bet that the research team finds that a higher red-spectrum concentration is emitted around curves to break up the outline. And..."

"And I can't see it." Kyros laughed heartily and leaned in to whisper, "I never thought this weak blood of mine would serve a purpose."

"I knew." Briescha hid her shaken nerves with a wide smile. "And there's nothing weak about you." She felt Kyros breathe against her cheek and knew her point had hit its mark. "Ah, we're home."

She stared warily as both halves of the Hyperion contingent rejoined and dispersed around the circular base to their Tower home. She sighed, and knew without asking that they would be staying the night. She turned her eyes on Kyros. He released her arm and bowed.

I think it's time to add self-defense to our lessons, Silver told Briescha. *And weaponry.*

Oh, we're on speaking terms? Briescha asked playfully.

Hush, just bring him in, Silver ordered.

Tonight will be our first lesson.

Her tone held such regality that Briescha burst out laughing. When she caught her breath, beating her hand against Kyros' shoulder, she managed to pass on Silver's command. He watched her eyes light up. He blinked several times to refocus. Then he nodded his agreement.

"I'll begin self-defense training tonight at the future Empress' request," he informed a lower-ranked commanding officer. "I need a volunteer who can take a beating."

The Hyperion officer smiled and called forward a recruit named Dirco with broad shoulders and a strong jaw, jade skin and amethyst hair. Kyros approved of the boy and followed Briescha into their fortress. He ordered Dirco to relinquish his weapon before he passed through the door. Confused, he complied. Kyros smiled and led the way. The door locked behind him.

Briescha and Kyros walked the recruit down the stairs sometime later. Dirco was bruised but alive. He laughed periodically. When the commanding officer demanded to know the joke, the recruit shrugged.

"She's stronger than me," Dirco said with a snicker. "But she apologized more often than she hurt me. And her serious face is as lovely as her smile. She's really quite sweet!"

"She's your future Empress, recruit," Kyros reminded him with a stern smile. He flipped the boy's pistol around and returned the weapon. "Think of her in an honorable way, or you may find yourself in trouble."

The boy blushed brightly enough to blot out his pale skin.

Briescha laughed. "Silver says you are to heal immediately, as she expects you to make use of yourself daily as her sparring partner, since... No, Silver!"

"Since what?" Kyros asked.

She sighed and rubbed her bruised cheek. "Since I don't plan on marring my own sister's perfect face anymore."

"If my future Empress demands it, I will gladly attend," Dirco announced with a deep bow.

The commander shook his head and watched Dirco trod to his post for a long night's watch. "Rank A Lieutenant Kyros, is it?"

"Yes, sir."

"I'm Commander Bridfar of the first Hyperion contingent." He saluted. Kyros returned the gesture. "For Dirco to be so enamored so quickly, and based on what I have learned, I know our future leaders are worthy of their titles and roles. They are exactly what Azela needs. And I assure you, they will be in good hands."

"I'm glad to hear you say it, Commander," Kyros admitted. "I had wondered that all of Hyperion was corrupt and slothful. After today's performance, I was sure of it."

"To hear headquarters tell the story, there was no danger," Bridfar answered.

"Then they've lost their minds with their commission, if I have a word to say about it."

Bridfar nodded. "You have an ally with me, and any man of my contingent knows his place. This reform you mentioned is a long time coming."

Kyros agreed, looking off into the distance. His stomach growled audibly, startling Bridfar and those closeby. "It's nothing."

"I think the lady disagrees," Bridfar whispered, tilting his head toward Briescha, who waited at the door.

Briescha crossed her arms and tapped her

foot. Kyros really was injured! And here he was, acting like nothing was wrong. She raged over details, wondering when he'd last eaten and knowing he was in no shape to stand out there all night.

Trapped and defeated, Kyros turned to her.

"Silver sent me back to bid you all thanks and goodnight." Briescha bowed politely to the guards. "And *you* failed to mention how those ribs aren't just fine like you said."

Her glare wilted him. He held his composure, but the other men knew how he felt.

"Let's go," she said.

And he followed, casting a longsuffering glance back at Bridfar. The good commander shook his head and waved as the door whooshed closed again.

*　　*　　*

"Here." Briescha shoved food into his hand. "Eat this, then we'll take a look at those ribs."

"I am afraid I have guard duty tonight." Kyros protested with a wave of his hand. But he winced in pain.

Briescha shook her head. "You can guard us in here tonight."

"No, I promised I wouldn't." Kyros held up his hands. "It's not appropriate."

Don't care, Silver said with a wave of her hand. *He's not leaving until he's better.* She sat staring out the huge window, past the balcony and across the vast expanse of Xepaqua.

"Not that he could leave if he wanted, Silver." Briescha gave a devilish grin. "That door only opens when we wish it. No protocols in place right now."

"You wouldn't!" Kyros put the food down.

Briescha picked up the food and placed it back in his hand. "We will. Now, eat!"

Silver grabbed her shoulder. *It's time again!*

Silver pressed her hands against her ribs, bearing down against the pain that filled her. *Do you want to use the room?* Briescha asked. Silver nodded. Briescha rushed past Kyros. She pulled Silver toward the door, up the stairs and into the gravity chamber. Kyros skidded in behind them.

Lights flickered on all around them. The huge circular room occupied the whole level, walled in crystal and odd contraptions along the wall. Briescha, with Kyros' help, deposited Silver at the center of the room, in a shallow, cushioned concavity the diameter of Silver's height.

"System initializing! Anomalies detected. System standby," echoed above, an electronic voice that began a countdown. "Multi-point gravity system is online. Danger! Remove anomalies. Danger! Remove anomalies."

"What now?" Kyros eyed the room with confusion.

That's you, guys! Silver said. *Go. I'll be fine.* Silver struggled to her feet, balancing by leaning against her sister's shoulder.

"Now, we get out." Briescha hugged Silver to her chest and then backed toward the door. A siren sounded, ordering all but Silver out of the room. "You know how Silver's body has a rough time holding together as her synchronization nears?"

Kyros nodded.

"This room is designed to provide enough pressure to hold her body together during each session." Briescha shivered. "The Arkayn said it sends out ongoing streams of gravitational force to hold her suspended in the center of the room for the duration, so it envelopes her like a glove."

Briescha exited, staring through the open door as Kyros joined her. Thrumming rattled the walls and vibrated the floor. Light raced in ever-faster rings around the room. The door closed as Silver smiled back at her sister. *Silly-head. Stop worrying!*

"Pressurization in progress. Synchronicity calibration in ten, nine, eight..."

"So does it help with her pain?" Kyros rubbed his chin, his tone doubtful.

Briescha shook her head. "The Arkayn didn't say. But at least she will stay in one piece!"

The thrumming of the gravity chamber reached a fever pitch as the electronic voice announced, "Session 1, in progress."

Briescha wrung her hands so much that Kyros took them in his. "Are you going to stand here waiting the whole time?"

"Yes." Briescha leaned against the wall.

"No." Kyros pulled her toward the stairs. "That system will announce when the session is over, and we'll come back. You'll worry yourself to death! What would Silver say?"

Briescha smiled. "She'd tell me I am being silly."

"She's right."

Silver, he's treating me like you do! Briescha listened over their mental link. There was too much static, and then silence. Briescha panicked. Her heart raced. She wrenched her hands from Kyros' grip and ran back to the door.

"What is it, Briescha?" Kyros headed back out the door, alarmed. "What's wrong?"

"I can't hear her!" Briescha looked all over the door and found a guarded button labeled *ABORT SESSION: NOT RECOMMENDED.*

"Hey! Stop." Kyros grabbed her shoulders. "Stop!" Kyros shook her. "Look."

Kyros read the message below the Abort order, "*Warning: Abrupt depressurization not recommended. Partial or total destruction of pressurized living organisms likely. To continue abort order: enter Arkayn, Hyperion or Bloodline certification code.*"

"Oh, no!" Briescha trembled. "How horrible!"

"Let's go." Kyros pulled her back from the button. "Electronic systems interfere with even the strongest psychic's signal, but the Arkayn Council said the signal would likely terminate."

"She probably had them design it that way." Briescha rapped her knuckles against the wall. "So I couldn't feel the pain with her."

"Then I don't blame her!" Kyros scolded with a stern expression. "Let her protect you for once!"

Briescha allowed Kyros to lead her away from the door, from her sister. Briescha focused on each step to make sure she continued forward. Then Kyros' stomach roared in hunger. His shoulders tensed. He cringed and turned around slowly. She stared at him.

"Come on." She stomped past him and dragged him down the steps.

"You're always going to be grumpy when she's away, aren't you?"

Briescha responded with a glare. But Kyros was right. He was good at being right. She refocused her energy on forcing food down Kyros' throat. She fussed over his tender ribs and, upon medical inspection, verified they were not broken. Her hands on his side, she carefully located the regeneration triggers in the area, and poured her light into each trigger to amplify their effect. Kyros protested for only a moment, but soon gave into her nursing, especially when the pain subsided and he could breathe easier.

As she finished Kyros' treatment, Briescha

heard the chamber's depressurization ann-ouncement sound overhead. They made their way up the stairs and waited by the door. Briescha heard Silver's mind voice weakly at first, then fully as the door slid open. *That was interesting.* Silver leaned heavily against the frame, her face gaunt and the Key birthmark across her chest blazing.

Briescha, a whirlwind of emotion, stood waiting for Silver to admit she was okay. Silver wavered when she stepped forward. Kyros caught her as she fell and hefted her in his arms amid her many protests.

"Silver! Talk to me!" Briescha struggled to keep her composure.

Well, it works. I'm just so tired! I can already tell my recovery time will be improved, Silver told Briescha in a wavering voice. *I don't think I have any physical injuries this time!*

"That's amazing! But don't think I won't check to make sure." She turned to Kyros. "The machine did its job. We'll report to the Council tomorrow with our findings." She followed Kyros up the stairs and hurried past him to turn down the cover on Silver's bed. "How was the pain?"

*It's...*Silver thought better of a lie...*just as bad. Maybe worse, but the end result is better.* Briescha looked so sad at that admission, so Silver told her, *I feel as if I lose less of what I gained.* Silver looked confused for a moment, trying to find the words. *Remember when there were rips and cuts and bruising, I told you some of the power dissipated?*

"And now it doesn't?" Briescha gaped, utterly amazed and filled with joy. She leaned over Silver's chest and focused her power, searching through Silver's muscles, skin and other organs for any issues. Marveling, she leaned back with a smile. She explained to Kyros, "Every time, the synchronizing power is like water, but the vessel is only so big. So some pours over the rim. But if there's a crack in the cup, more gets out until the crack is fixed. Before, she'd get an injury from the overflow. But now, she's perfect! The power stayed in completely, it seems. That is great news!"

Kyros nodded his agreement. "That is amazing! It's also fortunate that Briescha can't feel this new quality of pain."

It is, Silver said. Her eyes filled with childlike mischief. Briescha knew she didn't have to wonder about that design *flaw* anymore, knowing Silver had specifically requested it. Briescha punched Silver in the shoulder. Silver held her arm in a dreamy way and smiled as she drifted off to sleep. Briescha tucked the blanket around her.

"Don't be mad at her." Kyros chuckled. "She just wants to protect you."

Briescha pursed her lips in thought. "I know."

"You do realize," he said, "that the freedom can be used for professional purposes, too."

Briescha looked up at him. "She has freed you to work on matters of state while she's incapacitated. It's your role she protected, as well."

"You're right." Briescha admitted that two incapacitated leaders wouldn't make much sense.

"I know. And you're tired." Kyros dragged Briescha to her feet and gave her a push toward her bedroom. "Sleep. I'll use your office to write my report, with your permission."

"As long as we see you tomorrow, you have my permission," Briescha said with a worn smile.

Kyros bowed formally, but smiled at her before he turned on his heels and headed to the office. Briescha clung to that smile as she wandered into her bedroom, across the floor and collapsed on the bed. So much had transpired that her head spun. But Kyros remained, even smiled for her. She curled up on her bed, exhausted and intrigued, a bundle of feelings she didn't comprehend. She saw his face even as she slept, bringing back emotions she forgot she had.

Silver pounced on Briescha's bed early the next day, shaking her sister awake with such frantic energy that Briescha's heart pounded. She immediately caught the panic in Silver's mind voice. *It's ending!* Silver whimpered in Briescha's head. *This world is ending already!*

"What is it?" She forced her heart to calm down, to detach from Silver's in a way that allowed her to think. "What do you mean?"

I don't want to be a part of this anymore. Silver's anxiety turned to petulant anger. *Let them run their own world. It's not worth it anymore.* She crossed her arms and flopped backward onto the bed.

Briescha stared at the way Silver's lips quivered, how her eyes darkened, and read the meaning behind her words. "What's happening with Kyros?"

Silver turned her head away, sending flowing locks of metallic hair to bob in front of her face. *They're taking him away from us.*

"But he promised!"

A timid knock sounded outside the door. Kyros stood there, his head down, looking gaunt and ghastly. "I'm sorry. I tried so hard to convince them otherwise, but after my report," he gestured weakly to the Hyperion main office, "*they* wouldn't be swayed." He raised his blue and gray streaked eyes to Briescha. "I've been reassigned, ranked up several times for my valor." He spat out that last word.

"Then let me sway them!" Briescha swept within a hairsbreadth from Kyros' face. "Let me explain how you," and she jabbed a finger in his chest, "made a vow to my adopted father and mother, to Jacan, and to my sister that you would be with us, that you would protect us forever. That nothing would come between us. That we would always be okay. With you."

Kyros bit his lips closed and clasped his hands over hers, pressing her fingers against his chest. There she felt an aching alongside the flutter. "My heart still beats for you, Briescha, and for Silver, too." His voice cracked. "Ever since you restarted it."

Briescha felt his great swell of emotion as her own and leaned against his chest. Silver threw her arms around both of them, and there they stood for a long time. Kyros clung to Briescha's hands. He leaned into Silver's warm hair. And Briescha felt her mind flipping through all the possibilities, all the scenarios in which this could not be a disaster. They all hung suspended in this fresh, raw emptiness, this unexpected change that tried to consume them.

"I don't know what to do, Briescha." Kyros, always calm and calculating, shuddered.

As a new realization dawned, Briescha slowly, reluctantly closed her heart to Kyros' ache. She loved this man dearly, but he was not hers to claim. Not with such intensity, not with the desire that tried to penetrate her resolve. The feelings — all the time spent in his presence these many years, all the blushing and joking and attachment — all of it overshadowed one simple fact that she forced her heart to accept. Kyros, no matter how beloved, was a subject of Silver's empire.

Even Silver saw reason and agreed. She still raged maliciously against Hyperion. Then she released her death grip on the two and stared at Kyros as if he were really dying this time.

Briescha gathered her resolve for her next statement. "Then, my dear soldier, my Lieutenant Commander, do what you must."

The shift in Briescha's tone sobered Kyros. He stared at his hands on hers and freed her. Without his heart pounding in her ears, Briescha cleared her mind of his roiling emotions. When she stepped back, Kyros managed to stand at attention. He stood there, trapped by his discipline and still hurting. Yet Briescha knew she couldn't touch him again. When her hand drifted toward his face, she clenched her fists at her sides and gave him his orders.

"You will change Hyperion from the inside." Briescha took a cleansing breath. "Destroy their tyranny and nepotism from the inside, where you'll have priority and poise. Climb the ranks. Be the voice for Silver, your future Empress, inside Hyperion, in all matters. Focus, and plan and learn. Do whatever it takes to protect Azela."

"Yes," and his voice wavered, but he bowed to each in turn, "my dear Empress, my dear Princess."

If you're not going to hug him, I will!

Briescha dropped her head, *You know I can't.* "Silver says there's one more thing." She listened for a long moment. "This is only goodbye for now. You will find moments to visit us." Another order. "When you have brought peace to Azela through Hyperion, and Silver has brought peace to Azela through her ascension, we can be together again, my dear friend, forever, just like we planned."

Silver reached up to Kyros and cupped her hands aside his angular jaw, dragging his face down to her level. She stared into his eyes with the deepest caring and promise, willing him to stare back. When she saw the pain nestled deep within, she threw her arms around his neck, hugging for all she was worth. And he hugged back. For a moment, they were young and carefree again at Forge Mountain.

Briescha, still standing stiffly, avoiding any touch that would shake her resolve, suffered a chuckle to escape. "It's Silver, Kyros. She's screaming *don't die* over and over as she hugs you."

"That's one more promise, my dear Empress, I am determined to keep!"

He set Silver down on the floor again. Suddenly, he was unsure how to act. He tried to stand at attention, tried to turn and leave. Finally, he threw his hands up in the air and settled them on his slim hips.

Briescha watched his confusion and allowed herself a small smile. "Nothing's changed, you know. Not really." She executed the deepest curtsy. "You're still our knight, the protector of our lives and future, no matter your distance or station in this world. Silver is right. Like Forge Mountain, like the meadow grass between my toes, and like the sweet scent of crystal flowers on the breeze, you are here in my heart, in Silver's heart. You are a steady light, a constant, in our flickering world. And when that world stands as steadfast as you, we can be together again."

Kyros took courage from her words, nodding, but the distance in his eyes grew greater. She knew he needed the distance now. Briescha fought the rising panic as Kyros, *her* Kyros, disappeared behind a mask of self-imposed exile to carry out his lofty orders.

8: TIMESPELL

Murmurs and clear voices rose and fell in the sapphire Arkayn Council Hall of Azela. Colorfully tinted spotlights illuminated figures frozen in exquisite grace, humanoid except for hair, skin and eyes formed of various gemstones. The statues emanated faint lights that wavered in unison with their voices. Two very young girls stood in the middle of a mosaic map in the center of the huge blue room. One stood straight, her long ebony hair behind her proud shoulders, her white skin shimmering opal in the odd lighting. The other girl clung to her side, holding tight to a thick shawl that covered her head to foot. She shivered and huddled silently. The pale one began to speak. The fire in the girl's voice echoed in the hall as the scene rippled and faded.

"I am well aware of the past, Arkayn," a strong female voice interjected in the fluttery whispers from the statues dispersed around the room. "The fear of a child does not govern, however. It is the resolute leadership of divine birthright," and she punctuated each word by pounding her fist into her other hand, "that determines how the Empress will manage her Empire. An instance of meekness in a whelp will not bring about the downfall of an Empire as her Empress comes of age!"

Briescha paced barefoot on the same mosaic map from which she'd held Council since childhood, irate at the lingering memory projection. She held her back straight, defiant. Her onyx hair caught the light, the length fully to her ankles. Her skin still sparkled as crushed opal, so pale it reflected the colored light around her. Her large amethyst eyes glared with resolve.

"She is unstable at this time, Princess," spoke a velvet voice to her right. "Nearly four years have passed. How much longer will the people wait for their Empress?"

Briescha turned on the glowing statue. "She will remain unstable until she has reached full synchronicity. This...event...has never occurred before! You admitted it four years ago. Silver's path is not set in stone, not predictable on a scientific level, Science Officer Sladen. Of all people, you should know that one cannot merely expect a set date to achieve something which should be impossible in the eyes of science."

"And yet, the progress should be measurable," Sladen replied, nonplussed. "If we could determine the percentage to which she is linked over the period of time..."

"In four cycles? In four hundred cycles?" an angry voice rang out from across the Hall. "How could anyone know? Her statement is valid and stands, so release her from your barrage, Sladen. All in favor?"

The Hall rang in favor of the scientist's silence. Briescha felt the anger drain from her slowly, like a flame flickering in the darkness. The next breeze would surely drag her down. Such power flooded the Hall when so many were awake! Even someone of her status had trouble withstanding its force.

Into the silence, Briescha sighed. "In four cycles, we do know that my sister has gone from zero control to substantial control. Once she has fully linked, it should be safe for your scientists to infer conclusions. Until then, no one can approach her during sessions. That is all I can offer at this time." Her energy drained with her words. She knew this meeting must end soon.

A melodic female voice rose above the murmuring. "Briescha, your word and fire are all we need to convince us until our heir Salakind Velonsacor Eranklaya takes the throne."

"The rest of the populace is not so easily induced," whispered a sincere male voice. "We query on behalf of them." His tone suggested a warning. "Her absence from these proceedings will no doubt be discussed at length, whether you speak for her or not."

"Silver currently spends all her time mastering control of the forces of this planet!" Briescha mustered a surge of energy to battle her frustration. "That is the only reason she asks me to come without her! Has my sister not brought calmness to this planet's inner workings? Do any of you remember a time as peaceful in your long lives?"

"Hyperion serves well to protect us," another whispered, "and even a select few among them have become suspicious of an Empress who cannot yet run her empire."

"With very few exceptions, Hyperion contributes greatly to such dissent." Silver's disgust arose in Briescha. "Hyperion will know its place before this night ends."

Briescha turned, fueled by Silver's roiling emotions, and strode toward the exit of the Inner Sanctum. Angered also because the Hyperion comment had awoken Silver from the deep unconsciousness that followed her most recent session, Briescha fought hard to discern her anger from her sister's.

"Briescha! Silver!" The voice rang out above the murmuring of the Arkayns. Caslorius glided down the platforms until he stood between Briescha and the closed door.

Silver's mind-voice quieted into a grumbling pout at the sound of their father's voice. She, after all, was not present to glare at the unsettling man.

Briescha, fully his height, stopped an inch from his nose and met his amethyst stare with one of her own.

"Caslorius."

"Father, if you will." He glared at her.

"Father." Briescha's tone crushed the word to dust.

"Daughters." Caslorius worked his jaw, seeking his next words.

"I see no reason for you to stand before me in this private meeting, *Father*." Briescha dropped her chin to glare back at the man, infuriated by his interruption. "As you've made no attempt in two years to be in our presence outside these walls."

"Briescha, I..." Caslorius stumbled across the scolding he intended to impart, taken aback by Briescha's accusation. He opened his mouth to speak, then closed it again. "Diplomacy is required in matters regarding the state."

"Don't worry, Father." Briescha rocked back on her heels. "Perhaps you can minister on more diplomatic methods of teaching those Hyperion dogs their place in this social structure?" Her eyes flashed with mischief.

"Perhaps, if intelligent ears are not deaf to wisdom, I can make that attempt." Caslorius led her by the elbow to a lower tier to sit. "And girls," he began, unacquainted with candid conversation, "I want you to know, your mother would be fairly distressed to learn that you both inherited my temper."

Briescha blinked. Her father's expression remained unreadable, but she was sure he'd attempted a joke. She smiled and then laughed, an echoing sound that bounced all around the hall, dissolving the thick tension in the room.

"It is just as well that you both also inherited her lovely face, her grace, her passion, her intelligence and great capacity for love." Caslorius stroked Briescha's cheek, an awkward gesture from an uncomfortable man.

A smile played at his lips. Briescha suddenly understood why her father stayed away, why he always looked upon them with pain in his eyes—pain she'd mistaken for disdain. Too much, they reminded him of his lost Rascha. But even then, before their births, Arcani spoke of how he was distant, absent, dedicated and seemingly uncaring.

The puzzle peaked her interest, but somewhere in her mind, Silver nestled into her bed and drifted into a deep sleep, unamused. Feeling mildly restored, Briescha stood, knowing nothing she could say to her awkward father about his first admission to her. She returned to the center of the mosaic map. He sat on a tier nearby and ministered for some time between Briescha and the Arkayn Council on matters of state and diplomacy.

"You have my word that this planet will be brought to peace with the Empress' ascension." Briescha felt restored by the vow. She placed her hand against her chest, feeling Silver's pulsing gemstone key where it rested above her heart.

Caslorius cleared his throat nearby.

"And...I'll use diplomacy for as many solutions as I can."

"Then we shall adjourn for the time being," lilted the first voice again.

Briescha lowered herself into deep bows to all the immobile figures around her. Their glimmering lights became more muted as they slipped back into their planet-bound shells. Caslorius excused himself to a back vault of the Arkayn Council Hall, where he focused on secret matters involving his Ministry of Core-Based Theology.

Briescha strode out of the Inner Sanctum through huge double doors. She made her way down the darkening hallway, and then emerged into the sweet, thick air of the glorious courtyard.

Leaning back against those hallowed doors for a long moment, she sought comfort in the beauty around her. Delicate flowers glistened in the paling light. Every petal bloomed faceted and translucent, in full colors of all precious gems the planet produced. Leaves sparkled on manicured branches of ornamental trees. Pathway stones along the sidewalk glowed dimly above phosphorescent minerals mined for the purpose. And the legend statues dwarfed the entire scene.

Mischief arose in Briescha. She glanced around, making sure she was alone. Then she stepped away from the doors, off the glowing path, and sank her bare toes into the cropped garden grass beside the huge statues. Eyes closed, she threw her head back. *Not as soft as the meadow grass.* She sighed. *But close enough for now.*

"Hello, my friend." She rested her pale hand on the Mietina Lord's flank.

Dezul stared in silence, immobile. Briescha didn't fret that he couldn't answer her. Still, she held onto her childhood fancy of awakening him. Her mind returned to that day several years ago when the girls arrived in Xepaqua, to their new home. Silver's mind voice flowed in some language Briescha did not understand, as the future Empress tried to raise Dezul from his slumber. Where had she learned those words? Silver had always known things that were beyond Briescha's understanding, but this was different somehow. The puzzle brought her back to tonight's discussion at Council.

A voice drifted through her mind, very distant. *Rascha would be proud of you, just as Caslorius hides his pride.*

"Darasha?" Briescha, confused, turned back to the Council Hall.

Yes, my dear. The voice crooned, concerned and loving.

"I'm sorry I didn't stay to visit this time." Briescha felt guilty for dismissing her ancestor.

I know how the Council drains energy, child. Whether I am family or not, I would not have you there longer than you could keep yourself upright.

"Well, I'm just so upset, so angry with Hyperion, with the popular view of the citizens considering us a drain." Briescha paced, speaking in a hushed voice. "Even with proof that she is ascending!"

Guard your heart, dear. There are others who may hear you.

Briescha dropped her head. "If someone hearing was the same as someone listening, I'd get my point across."

As an Arkayn, I can't be partial to your situation. I can only provide advice within the context of my singular power. But, as your ancestor, as your family, I can share one very important thing, off the record. Something you can depend on above all else.

Briescha's ancestor was silent for a long

moment. Then Darasha's quiet chuckle rippled through Briescha's mind. *The other Arkayns are reminding me to conserve my planetbound energy. With this glow, they can tell I'm up to something. Poor old dears. I must be keeping them awake.*

The woman's wistful tone jolted Briescha from her melancholy. Smiling, Briescha wrapped Darasha's mental presence in an embrace of energy. "What is that one important thing?"

Love is a master at miracles.

Then Darasha was gone, leaving Briescha wrapped in the warmth from her spiritual embrace. *Love is a master at miracles.* The young Azelan mulled over those words, committing them to the idealistic compartment in her memory, as her hand slid off Dezul's flank and her feet found the glowing pathway once more.

At the arched gate of the Council Hall courtyard, Briescha paused. A small troupe of Azelan Ouranos-in-training marched down the path toward her, their faces shimmering in various shades of gemflesh as they saluted their Princess. She pressed down a flare of anger, as these were innocents. Some may never even rank among the Hyperion faction. Briescha bowed graciously at the display. She smiled as they passed. Outwardly, the unwavering devotion of Azela's Ouranos Organization to the Empire set the moral standard for patriotism. She wished everyone else shared their loyal stance. But with a long-ago assassination attempt linked back to one corrupt Hyperion soldier, Briescha had a difficult time dropping her guard with Hyperion.

"Evenin' *Highness.*"

The sneering voice cooled her blood. She cringed and forced the snarl from her lips. Briescha pressed her lips together, rolling the word *diplomacy* around in her mind, over and over. Bringing up the rear of the group marched Deraddian, still middle-ranked, still a complete jerk. His short, square, stocky body sauntered into her periphery. She plastered a polite smile on her face and met his sarcastic eyes with little emotion in her gaze. She reigned in her harsh tone before she spoke.

"Good evening, Deraddian. Training goes well today?"

"Great, fine. And Council?" His dark eyes flicked all around her, searching for her absent sister. His smile hardened.

"Very well, thank you." Briescha's tone indicated she would not go into detail for *him*. "And good night, *Hyperion*. May your night prove tranquil and productive."

Deraddian harrumphed and nodded, his eyes suddenly distant. He stiffly saluted and loped after his waiting trainees. Briescha glared at his back until he disappeared over a distant rise. She sighed, suppressing her thoughts to keep the Arkayn Council at peace. The fact that Briescha attended Council yet again without her sister could set mouths moving. No doubt, Deraddian would see to that.

From the low rise in the center of town upon which the Council Hall set, Briescha could see the city all around stretch to the distant horizon. The star Paz, a red dwarf, was huge in the sky and sinking into the sea. The red star glimmered behind the amethyst crystal city Xepaqua, glinting off faceted surfaces and fading colors to gray lavender. The thick atmosphere quickly dulled the mountainous background to nothing more than a dim outline. The stillness rang in her ears, perfect and absolute.

She strode through Center Street Park toward her home. She did feel safer over the last years. She glanced over her shoulder. Her constant guards kept their respectful distance. Not one serious incident in almost four years! Kyros, she had heard, spent much of his time cracking down on the crime that had infiltrated the city. His focus and determination had brought small-time and greater criminals to justice. The streets felt safer for his effort. And yet, in the darkness, when the silence rang in her ears, she missed his footsteps beside her and the comforting rhythm of his breathing. His face, its clarity worn by the passage of time and too-little closeness, still smiled in her mind. He was still there, working hard for Silver's cause. He remained so distant, so immured in his Hyperion work, that she felt sure he would achieve his goals even before Silver ascended. And then remained Silver, Briescha's one true calling in life. Perhaps her sister stayed safe from ultimate denial to her throne. *Is she safe from the Azelans themselves?*

"What an unflattering expression on your lovely face, my Princess."

Briescha startled at the soft, rasping all-too-familiar voice to her right. She wheeled around and sought the speaker with longing eyes. Kyros lay sprawled on a carved bench in the center of the midtown garden. He held a glowing crystal ledger and scrawled quickly in it. His long pale hair flowed in streaks of gray and blue, like quartz. He wore dark blue pants and an open pale vest that revealed his chiseled white chest. Briescha froze in her stride, staring at him, unable to remember the last time she had laid eyes on him. Almost a year, at least.

"Kyros!" Briescha rushed over to the bench, leaving her guards far behind. She stared at his lounging form and thrust her hands against her hips. She dug her nails into her palms. She so wanted to hug the life out of him. "You look...well. And relaxed. How dare you act like it hasn't been forever since you've seen me?" She regained control of her volume. "I've missed you." Silver's sleepy agreement sounded in her head. "We've both missed you so much!"

"You seem troubled." His tone wasn't teasing, just observant and a touch apologetic. He gave a shy smile. "And not so much about me as I'd like, if my guess is correct."

Briescha's heart fluttered. *As I'd like*, he said. Her temper flared. "You'd be surprised how much I'm troubled by you right now." Her eyes flashed a warning about his absence. Her mind struggled against her jilted feelings. *He's working so hard, Briescha!* Silver's sleepy scolding voice shut her up.

Kyros eyes flicked to his notes and back to her. "I just ditched Deraddian's bright and shining company to find somewhere quiet to write reports." His sarcasm fell on understanding ears. "He can surely run basic drills by himself."

"Are you sure about that, *Commander* Kyros?" Briescha used his most recent rank. She hid her pride at his climb, and watched him shrug. Then she sighed mightily. "Council presents a case in favor of the people."

"About Silver?" Kyros set aside his tablet and pursed his lips.

"Yes." Briescha scowled. "She's not as close to full synchronicity yet as they'd like. And Caslorius drove home the fact that diplomacy is of utmost importance." She shook her head. "I tried so hard to hide my feelings!"

"Sure." Kyros smiled up at her. "But I know you. Don't worry. It's only obvious because no other topic would upset you as much." Kyros averted his eyes.

"I'm that easy to read?" Briescha blushed, casting a warm glow on his pale face.

Kyros shrugged again. "No need to be a telepath with you regarding Silver." He smiled, still timid and unsure of how formal he should act. He moved several tablet slates and cleared space for her to sit. Briescha and Kyros sat looking at the stars as they emerged in the darkened sky. Several pale moons appeared. She rested her head against Kyros' shoulder. He tensed at first. His heart pounded. But Briescha felt so at ease with him that he quickly relaxed.

"How goes your work in Hyperion?"

"Surprisingly well." Kyros ran his fingers through his hair. "The crime rate has dropped significantly within the city, prompting the rest of Ouranos to employ my new tactics."

"That's amazing!" Briescha patted him on his shoulder and left her hand resting there. "We knew you'd do a great job, Commander."

He nodded, but grew quiet for a long while. When he spoke again, his breath came as a whisper on her face. "I have been studying for all these years, learning from the Archive Arkayns and the scant records that are inscribed." Kyros cast a severe gaze. "I've been trying to get to the heart of the issues within Hyperion."

"What did you find?" Briescha kept her voice low and flat, hidden from her guards, who waited patiently at the edge of the garden.

"That's the problem. I'm still not sure." Kyros fidgeted under her hand. "I discovered an anomaly. Right before Ouranos was founded, and subsequently before Hyperion and the founding of Xepaqua, there are missing years. An entire generation, it seems. Or more."

"Is that even possible?" Briescha frowned. "The Arkayn Council can't willfully omit any knowledge if it's activated correctly. And you reworded your questions to cover gaps?"

Kyros shrugged, jostling Briescha where

she rested. "Every way I could think of doing. The fact of the matter is that, by no fault of the current Arkayn Council, the old records have major gaps. Something happened a long time ago that those with a lot of power didn't want us to know."

"It would take unheard of power to do such a thing." Briescha's heart pounded at the idea of a forced omission from Arkayn minds. "I have trouble considering a time without our military. And whatever happened then resulted in the founding of Ouranos and Hyperion?"

Kyros rested his cheek against her hair. "Yes. Whatever that is, it's the root of corruption. I'm so close to putting the pieces together, but I can't act effectively until I bring it to light."

"I'm sure you'll figure it out. I'll see what I can find out, discreetly, on my own." Briescha buried her face against his arm, breathing in his light, distinctive scent.

"When I figure it out, you'll be among the first to know."

She nodded against his arm. "Now to survive Silver's ascension without this whole society falling around us."

"I wouldn't worry about that." Kyros sat pondering for a long moment. "The planet Azela gave us Silver for a reason. The dissidents are just afraid because her power is so much more expansive than they thought. In reality, Silver could rule by force if she willed it."

Briescha giggled. "I doubt that'll be her style."

"I know it won't be. She's gentle." Kyros chuckled. "She would never abuse her power for that end. She'll win them over with that sweet personality. And a little nudge to the core on occasion!"

Briescha punched him in the arm. He laughed.

"Azela is ready for a powerful leader to show them the way." He rubbed his chin. "The few who complain do not justify condemning all."

"Do you think Silver's ready?"

"Only with the help of her headstrong sister." Kyros grinned. "As long as I've known you..." He shook his head. "You're the only real threat to anyone who would interfere in Silver's destiny."

"You sound so sure of that." She gazed into his unreadable face.

He sighed. "Of late, I take everything into consideration concerning Azela's future." His voice became distant.

"Well, you're right." She smiled brilliantly at him. "I heard you ranked up for all your hard work? Since you won't acknowledge that I'm addressing you using your new rank..." Briescha decided it was time to change the subject.

Kyros harrumphed, acting like himself for a moment. He leaned in, just a hair's breadth from Briescha's face. "I would rather keep a close watch over my two girls, personally, than sit at that horrible, drab desk job day in and day out."

"We certainly miss you," Briescha said in answer, sighing. "The old you, especially."

Kyros chuckled. His breath flowed across her blushing cheeks, making Briescha's heart pound. "I miss you, too. It's a huge cost to me, to be gone from you. That's why this archive issue bothers me so."

"Kyros, you could take a break, if only for a while." Briescha sensed the tension in his voice, in his pounding heart. He needed a break.

"No, I can't. I'd lose what little influence I've gained in Hyperion. The only way is to find the answer." Kyros faced forward, his mind on his quest for knowledge. "I can't be with you two until then. Periods of time don't just disappear. And the omission raises so many questions."

"I know." Briescha looked down at her hands. "I'd be lying if it hasn't peaked my interest as well."

"What happened during those times? War? Rebellion? Something worse? And who could be powerful enough to erase it from our so-called infallible system?"

Briescha shook her head. "I hate to believe in a conspiracy. Is that what you think?" She suppressed the same suspicion he felt.

"I believe that a gem can look perfect on the outside, but close inspection can reveal enough flaws to render it worthless."

"I have never believed that flaws render a gem worthless, Kyros." Briescha's voice turned soft.

She brushed his hair back so she could see his tense face. His streaked eyes were unguarded for the first time since they arrived in Xepaqua. Briescha leaned in and rested her cheek against his.

"I have studied current events as much as you have studied history." She breathed in his light scent again. "I see as much room for improvement in Azela as you see damage. But I hear this planet's heart beating strongly in my sister's chest. I hear her heart beating, and I know that her power will restore peace."

"Is it really possible, in the end?" Kyros dropped his head onto Briescha's shoulder. "For one kind person with power, all alone, to rebuild such a corrupt world with corrupt people? Those same people tried to kill her. Even now they scorn her."

"She isn't alone. And Silver isn't a god, Kyros." Briescha leveled him with a stern gaze. "She is a conduit for power, an example of purity. But she gets angry, she feels hurt. She is very much an Azelan, regardless of how she looks. She, like anyone else, tries."

He shook his head in wonder. "If she's mostly the same, then what's different?"

"You know the difference." Briescha smiled at him. "There's something in her heart that can't be reached by all the...the crap of this world."

"Has she ever asked to give up the power?"

"Wishing for something doesn't make it happen, Kyros."

"Hmmm," he said, dropping his chin in thought. "I...I wonder."

Briescha leaned back and studied his strained expression. What does he mean? He couldn't think someone would try to relieve her of power, could he? "Kyros." Her tone held a note of panic, of warning. "Do you know something about power transferal?"

His eyes went wide, his hands raised in defense. "Nothing of use, I swear!"

"Why would you be researching such a thing?" Briescha's heart sank in dread.

"Isn't it better that I know about it in order to protect you? To protect Silver from it? I just wanted to know if it was possible, just in case." Kyros pleaded with his sincere eyes.

She took a deep breath and closed her eyes, reining in her suspicion and anger. "Forgive me. I just... When Silver is involved, I..."

Kyros laughed. "You prove my point from earlier." He took her hand. "Like I don't understand you after all these years!" He looked into her eyes. His gaze followed the curve of her cheek and settled on her pink lips. Then he closed his eyes. "The Archive Arkayns know nothing of it beyond some vague ancient reference of soul transfer between one Azelan and another vessel, something that...isn't another person. Some vessel that preserves the soul in servitude for a longer period of time. But I asked if there was a danger of controlling the transferred soul, and the Arkayn said that the soul would be like an Arkayn. Infallible, with personality and will intact."

Briescha relaxed against the bench support. "Do you know what kind of vessel?"

Kyros shrugged. "The Archive Arkayns don't know."

"An odd bit of knowledge, though." Briescha let her mind drift with the possibilities. "Makes you wonder if they ever made the attempt. Otherwise, there would simply be no record of such an occurrence."

"I'm positive that the answer rests in the historical gaps, too." The fire dissipated in Kyros' words. He leaned against the backrest, following Briescha's eyes to the stars and several moons. "But it's not for you to worry, Princess. Let me do it for you. The more I learn, the more I worry, the more I plan." He lolled his head to the side, staring at her pale profile. "The safer *you* are."

"Royal obligations being what they are," Briescha answered, "I'm surprised you have time for such loyalty." She smiled a little too openly.

"Rest assured, Princess." Kyros leaned toward her ear. "I'll do what it takes to perform my royal obligations. Anything that is in the best interest of my people. And of you."

He stood to leave and inclined his head in a formal bow.

"I miss you, Kyros."

"Old Kyros?" He smiled.

"Yes."

Kyros nodded again and strode toward his assigned Hyperion barracks. Briescha smiled at his back. He was still a tall lanky man, but his broad shoulders threw off the symmetry of his narrow body. She watched him leave with appreciative eyes when she realized a faint glow on the bench beside her. He'd forgotten the glowing tablet. She glanced down and read by accident:

"The glow of her skin/ And glitter of her eyes/ A heart fast beating in my chest/ Cold and hot sweat upon my brow/ For all I must do in suffering/ Another heart never mine, never mine."

She turned to call to him. "K...Kyros?"

He had returned and stood in front of her, staring down into her face. A flash of panic glinted in his eyes. Then they were unreadable again. He stood still with his arms by his sides. His face glowed with a bright blush.

"Forgive me, Kyros. I didn't mean to..."

"Forgive me, My Lady." His voice came out tight, strained.

"This is a different kind of report." Briescha handed him the notepad. "Poetry suits you."

"Only rarely," he said. He opened his mouth to say something else, then clamped it shut again.

They shared a long, telling glance. Briescha felt his heartbeat through the air with her power, felt his stomach churning in hunger and worry. She opened her mouth to speak.

The ground beneath their feet rumbled. An ear-splitting crack echoed in the distance. Beyond the garden trees and amethyst spires at the heart of the city, a cloud of dense fiery smoke drifted to the heavens, in the direction of the Hyperion base.

Kyros cursed, his fleeting embarrassment forgotten.

"What is it?" Briescha immediately looked toward Silver's tower.

"Are those idiots testing new equipment without authorization?" Kyros fumed. "Or is it some type of attack..." His eyes widened in worry. "Brieschal!" He turned back to her. "She's at home, right?"

Brieschal nodded, dazed.

"Protocol will send Hyperion soldiers straight to Silver." Brieschal stared at him, confused. He grabbed her shoulders. "Can you hear her?"

Brieschal listened. She shook her head, panic gripping her. *Why can't I hear her?*

"Then she's in the chamber." Kyros shook her over and over. Brieschal trembled, realizing what he meant. Hyperion soldiers would try to force open the chamber door to ensure Silver's safety, but the sudden release of gravity would tear her apart. *Would they know that?*

"Can you make it to Silver before Hyperion?" Kyros shook her again.

She nodded and threw her arms around him. "Be careful." Then without a backward glance, she leapt into the air with a telekinetic burst, leaving Kyros to deal with the explosion. The rushing night air burned her face and stung her eyes, shaking her from her paralyzing panic. Her invisible telekinesis sparked and jolted around her, a testament to her hard training over the last several years.

Kyros was right. Azela was ready for a powerful ruler. Silver was near that point. With each crippling episode, Silver gained more control. Without completing the grueling process, the planet would again fall into turmoil, perhaps more violent than before. Brieschal zipped past a small contingent of Hyperion soldiers on their way to the tower and redoubled her pace, leaving the group tousled and confused. She thought she recognized Deraddian's stocky shoulders and slick black hair. She skipped the ground level entrance and headed straight for the high balcony.

The entrance mechanism clicked and, scanning her bloodline credentials, unlocked the door. Briescha barreled into Silver's sleeping chamber and headed for the stairs. A loud vibration rattled the building and dissipated in a long hiss. Briescha collapsed on her knees in relief, as this was the sound of the gravity chamber decompressing. At that moment, the Hyperion contingent spilled into the stairwell, using their authority codes to gain access. Briescha regained her composure and ran to the stairwell. She was just in time to see the last soldier trail past her door.

"Hyperion!" Briescha's bellow echoed up the stairwell. "The chamber just shut down!"

Already, the group had reached the platform leading into the gravity chamber. Deraddian glared back at Briescha, who shoved her way past soldiers who now stood at attention. "Lieutenant Deraddian! You will stand down this instant! It isn't safe!"

"It isn't?" His tone was unconvincing. To Briescha's surprise, the man dropped his hands and managed a proper salute.

"Report on the explosion," she ordered. She climbed the remaining stairs and stood towering over the short man.

"Yes, ma'am. Unauthorized activity in weapons development led to the accidental detonation of a small number of explosive devices. Ill intent is, as of now, unconfirmed."

"Thank you," she said sweetly. "I expect a full report, including suspects and casualties, by tomorrow's city Council. You are dismissed, Hyperion."

"I must respectfully disregard *your* orders, Princess." Deraddian snarled. "Protocol demands that we secure the future Empress at all costs, in case such activity serves a diversionary purpose."

"Not at *this* cost, Deraddian." Briescha leaned down, a hairsbreadth from his face, returning his fierce glare. "And be reminded that in all areas involving the Empress, my say—*her* say—overrides any formal doctrine or protocol Hyperion has developed for this unique situation. Do not mistake your responsibility for power. Consider your team dismissed, and consider your name raised formally for insubordination."

"You have not a single right or reason to claim insubordination!" Deraddian fumed. "I followed protocol."

"Consider it a gift, Deraddian," Briescha whispered, her heart raging against the little man. "Had I been the suspicious type, I would have felt like you knew about the dangers of opening this chamber before decompression. And on those same suspicions, I could report that you were behind the diversion as an attempt on Silver's life."

To Briescha's surprise, Deraddian smiled. "That is an interesting theory," he whispered. "Quite paranoid. Impossible to prove, but..." He shrugged.

"You hateful, spiteful, arrogant piece of garbage!" Briescha grabbed his lapel. In her rage, she easily rocked him backward on his heels. A wave of telekinesis flooded her hands and encapsulated his body, robbing his lungs of air. "You will take insubordination, or you will lose far more than that!"

Stop!

The silent voice rattled Briescha's nerves and clanged through her mind. Silver's voice, often light and calming, shook Briescha to the core. She released Deraddian, who fell against the wall gasping for air. The warm cocoon of her power sparked and fizzled as it dissipated. She stared at her hands for a long moment, appalled by what she could have done.

The gravity chamber door whooshed open. Silver leaned against the wall, feebly clinging to a translucent warming sheet to hide her nudity from the men. The sheet couldn't mask the blazing glow from the Key that spread across her chest. She stared outward with dark-ringed eyes glowing orange with anger. Briescha wilted under her gaze, feeling Silver's intense disappointment at the outburst.

Silver reached for Deraddian. Briescha tensed, ready to hurt him again. Reluctantly, Deraddian pried himself from the wall and offered his stocky shoulder to support her. Briescha took Silver's other side. She turned and gazed into his blue eyes, searching for something she wouldn't voice to Briescha. Deraddian returned her stare until even his eyes softened in conviction. The confusion he experienced silenced him. Together, Briescha and Deraddian settled Silver on her bed.

"Empress is confirmed alive and unharmed," Deraddian announced with a wondering and somehow fearful voice. He coughed once by necessity and again for effect. He brushed past Briescha to the door. "This isn't over. File your report. I have one of my own. Your precious Council, even your father, will hear what I have to say about this night."

Briescha stood in the doorway to Silver's room until she heard the stoic soldiers file out silently. When the door resealed below, she turned to the large room. Inside, a band of lighting fixtures ran the circumference of the room. They glowed softly. Silver's dark sleeping form curled up beneath the translucent warming sheet. Her hand lay limply on the layered silky sheeting that formed her pillow. All of her exposed skin shone with light cast from the wall and mirrored distorted scenes of the room.

Briescha approached, smiling with adoration, trembling as her anger crashed into regret, and brushed back a liquid lock of flowing hair from Silver's face. Briescha saw her distorted reflection smile sweetly. Silver opened her sunken eyes. The molten, swirling irises glowed orange in alarm. The fiery glow subsided to a silver-gray when she recognized her sister. She clasped the translucent fabric to her nude form with one hand and, with great effort, propped up her body with the other. Briescha opened her mouth to apologize, but Silver interrupted.

I don't want you to kill for me.

"I wasn't going to kill him!"

Silver gave her a cold look.

"I didn't start out wanting to kill him." Briescha cowered. "He just made me so angry! And now I've given his cause ammunition before the Council. I'm sorry."

Silver dropped her head. *I don't care about the Council's opinion. I care about you. And you wanted to kill him in that instant.* She placed her hand over her still-glowing heart. *It hurts here when you feel that way.*

"I'm sorry!" Briescha slumped next to Silver on the bed and threw her arms around her shoulders. "I'm so sorry! Forgive me!"

Promise me you won't kill for me! Silver pushed back from Briescha's embrace and pleaded with her eyes. *Please!*

"I promise! Anything you want, just please forgive me."

Silver leaned into Briescha's shoulder and nodded. She told Briescha that she had just recovered from the first surge of power when another tore through her. *I was so scared! I barely made it to the chamber in time!* Briescha clung to her, terrified.

"You're okay now." Briescha smoothed Silver's gleaming hair. "You'll be all right!"

I'm not so sure, Silver said. *I've had a terrible nightmare for the last few weeks.*

"Tell me about it." Briescha tucked her sister's head into the hollow of her shoulder and rocked her gently as Silver showed her the images from her nightmare. Silver, scared and gravely injured, cowered in fear, hands clamped over her ears. Then her body moved against her will. She hurt others and others hurt her and no one would stop it, no matter how hard she cried.

Does it mean something? Silver asked.

Briescha waited a long moment to reply, carefully guarding her worry. "I guess you're afraid that this new power is dangerous?" She hugged her hard. "But you're doing so well! I know you'd never hurt someone!"

Silver sank into silence again. She quietly sifted through the contents of the night's Council meeting, sighing at each redundant point argued by the Council and the citizens. Her heart sank again at their strong words and the threatening undertone of the conversation. She shivered in memory of Caslorius's harsh rebuke. But she hadn't been present for all of Briescha's conversation with Kyros. She politely asked how Kyros was doing.

Briescha felt her face flush. Silver leaned in with a grin. Briescha turned away. "Nothing of the sort!" Briescha gave a short, awkward laugh. "He was talking about some research he did with the Archive Arkayns."

Silver frowned. *What type of research?*

"There's something to do with transferring Azelan souls from the original body to another non-person vessel." Briescha stared at the wall, trying to make sense of it. Silver frowned more severely. "The new vessel would preserve the soul in servitude for a longer time, and the soul would be just like an Arkayn."

So it couldn't be controlled by the one who transferred it? And were you going to tell me about his initial inquiry about the gaps in our history? When Briescha gaped at her in surprise, Silver shrugged. *You can't hide it from me. I'm in here.* She tapped Briescha's temple with a finger. *And you don't have to protect me from all the truth. Especially since it's Kyros we're talking about!*

"You're right." Briescha dropped her shoulders. "I'm sorry."

Did he say how they did it? Silver eyes were bright, her interest piqued. *Erasing parts of history seems impossible, but it would take a miracle to move an Arkayn's soul to another vessel.*

"Sounds about right," Briescha answered in a distant voice.

But your concern made sense, Briescha. Silver took her hand and smiled. *If Kyros doesn't have the answers, then neither does anyone else.*

"Do we have a free slot tomorrow?" Briescha tucked her head against Silver's hair. "We can go ask Darasha what she knows about it."

Silver shrugged again and squinted at a wide bulletin board on her wall. A wide calendar glowed with their many responsibilities. *We do!* One date flashed lazily against the dark background. *But after that, we're booked solid for the annual city council, and everyone is cautious anyway.* She grabbed Briescha's hands and dragged her to her feet, pulling her in a circle. *And then, we'll get to see them again!*

"Arcani! Daddy Ganan..." Briescha's lip quivered. "Jacan," she whispered, a flood of bittersweet agony flooding her heart. "In just two days!"

Silver pulled the ruby flower from Briescha's hair and turned it in the light. *I'd bet he misses you as much as you miss him.*

Briescha traced the inscription lightly with her finger and bit her lower lip. The night she last saw him filled her eyes. She wondered if he had changed his mind since then.

Silly-head!

"I do miss him. I miss the meadow." Briescha closed her eyes, drifting in memories. "I miss Kyros, too. This whole night, I'm just sorry about the whole night!"

This time, it was Silver's turn to hold Briescha. She rested her forehead against Briescha's. *Remember the meadow, Briescha.* Silver pictured the bright light of Paz on the blue grass as it rippled, the ruby flowers as they swayed in the breeze. Forge Mountain loomed in the distance, dwarfing the low building in which they lived their last untroubled days. Silver's memory drew from Briescha's memory and she constructed an illusion so intricate that Briescha could feel the cool meadow grass between her toes. Slowly, her breathing returned to normal and she relaxed in meditation with Silver.

Later, well into the night, Briescha crept back to her room. She settled down with a creeping sense of dread, pulled out her glowpad, and began the full report against Deraddian. With the emotional rage curbed, she composed the document objectively and concisely.

Finally, after a few moments of staring at the completed account leading to her reaction, she recounted her own actions with the same level of objectivity. Her father would be proud of her diplomacy in mentioning both parties' motives and duties leading to the altercation. Her final draft held the full regality trained into her hand. But as she crawled into her bed just shy of dawn, her stomach churned with worry that kept her awake.

Briescha drifted in and out of sleep, imagining the worries that Silver felt in her dreams. She felt her panic and worry. She also saw the meadow in her mind and felt the grass between her toes. She saw the face of Kyros and the face of Jacan, as well. The faces flickered repeatedly in her sight for a long time before she finally fell into a restless sleep.

9: DEADPHASE

With the rising of Paz, Briescha rolled out of bed again. Exhausted and in a foul mood, she forced down her discomfort, unhappy but willing to face the day. Briescha threw on her closest formal longdress, snug and white and flowing with colorful, sheer overlays. She gathered her report and a stylus, and stared a long moment at the ruby flower on her bedside table. Then she pinned up her long black hair with the flower and swept out her door. She nearly collided with Silver, who had dressed in a draping white longdress that hung off her shoulders, pinned at the throat with a ruby brooch. She had gathered her hair high on her head, letting the metallic locks flow down her back, adorned with small ruby flowers that matched Briescha's.

Briescha stared at Silver's regality, smiling in pride. "You look like an Empress today."

Stop that, right now! Silver's cheeks glowed in embarrassment. *We'll be late.*

Feeling suddenly giddy that Silver was attending, Briescha hooked her arm around Silver's elbow and swept out the door, down the steps, and past the Hyperion soldiers who attended the base of their tower. They skipped down the pathway as the guards struggled to keep up.

At the last cross-path before the Council Hall, a short, dark figure emerged from the dawn glow. Deraddian saluted, offering his report. He regarded her silently for a long moment. Then he bowed again.

"I am one unaccustomed to niceties," he began, still bowing deeply. "And if it pleases Her Majesty Salakind Velonsacor Eranklaya and the Princess Briescha, I will gladly go before Council and accept whatever punishment they deem necessary."

At this, he straightened and looked from Silver to Briescha. "I ask only that you please forgive me, even as I go into the uncertain future that an insubordination charge will allow."

Silver looked upon Deraddian with such concern. His eyes pleaded with them both. *I forgive him, Briescha.* She smiled at her sister. *I believe he is sorry. And ignorant or not, he was following protocol.*

So what would you have me do, Silver? Briescha felt the full brunt of her sister's emotions, feeling her mind clear of yesterday's aggravations.

Forgive him. Silver looked into Briescha's eyes, willing her sister to see what she saw in Deraddian's penitence.

Briescha sighed heavily and turned to the man. "Lieutenant Deraddian, by the grace of Silver's generous heart, we forgive you the trespass, intentional or not, against the future Empress' safety. On one condition."

The sudden light in Deraddian's eyes faded quickly. He held his tongue against whatever retort he intended. "Anything you ask of me."

Briescha stared him down. "Formally ask

her forgiveness before Council, and submit to a scan to confirm your innocence."

He blinked several times, but relented. "As you wish." His voice held a note of challenge more than sorrow, but Briescha let it slide when Silver elbowed her in the ribs.

"Then we will see you at Council this afternoon."

He bowed again, then excused himself from their presence and path. The ladies walked on, the Hyperion guards surrounding them.

Is the scan necessary? Silver sounded annoyed. *It doesn't really show our trust in him.*

"I have no trust in him." Briescha shrugged. *And forgiveness is in short supply where Hyperion is involved.* She eyed the soldiers around her.

Silver bristled at the mention of the group. *So is forgiving him a bad idea?*

"Yes." Briescha smiled. "But it is a good show of diplomacy!" She winked at Silver, who smiled and ducked her head. "And we must hurry. Our slot with Darasha is the last calm time we have before we smack into a solid block of work."

The Arkayn Council Hall gate loomed moments later, and the girls ditched their Hyperion guards. They ran past the huge legend statues and through the entry. Regaining their composure, they smoothed their hair and longdresses before opening the doors to the Inner Sanctum. They paused to give a quick but proper greeting to the resting Arkayns. Then they sprinted up the tiers to a place in the top, toward the back and near a curving buttress that jutted inward from the sapphire wall.

Slowing, partly winded, Silver and Briescha beheld their own ancestor, an Arkayn of uncompromising wit and unsurpassed noble beauty. Darasha, nearly identical to Briescha save for emerald eyes, sat with her hands folded on her lap, ankles crossed, and serene face turned to the heavens. Her onyx hair draped across the bench and spread all around her.

Green light welled from deep inside the statue until Darasha's form cast light on the sapphire walls. Then came her voice, like the ringing of bells. "My dear children, the year's business finds you in exceptional spirits! And quite beautiful in your longdresses."

Silver blushed and ducked her head behind Briescha's shoulder. Briescha beamed and sat beside Darasha, leaning her head against her ancestor's shoulder. "We only had one free slot to come see you!" Briescha cried.

Darasha's laughter lilted across the darkened sapphire dome. "I feel so special to be fit into your very busy schedule!"

Silver's face showed such pitiful dismay that both Briescha and Darasha stopped laughing to explain the joke. To punctuate their good-natured chiding, a tinted spotlight flickered on overhead. Spotlights clicked on all over the tiered dome, gleaming on each Arkayn in turn. Darasha chuckled. "They've awakened early today to prepare for the day's many ceremonies. Perhaps time is running out for our meeting."

"Then we'll have to ask you quickly!" Briescha hushed her voice. Silver leaned in from the other side, her face very earnest with her intensity. "We need to know what information you can provide from the gaps in the Arkayns' collective memory."

Darasha was silent for some time, her serene face betraying none of the roiling emotions that silenced her. "The Great Omission," she whispered again, when her green light arose again.

Briescha held her breath in anticipation, waiting for Darasha's next words.

"Legend has it that The Nine, by some unknown power, sealed away certain facts from our collective history," Darasha said in a grave voice. "Our very bare glimmers of memory contain only indications of attempts at Arkayn soul transfer, possibly for the good of extending the power of an Arkayn."

"The Nine?" Briescha furrowed her white brow. "Kyros must have forgotten that detail."

Darasha sighed. "Their reign was quite controversial, as you know. But deposal of The Nine by those of our bloodline triggered The Great Omission. Very important events are skewed or missing, from our full genetic origins to vital details explaining the depletion of a large portion of the population at one point, to why we abandoned star traversal. And even research related to helping the Delvans improve their various...infirmities?"

Silver bristled at the word, even as Darasha regarded it with disgust and confusion.

"What infirmities?" Briescha became incensed. "Eating on occasion? Some vision issues?" She gritted her teeth. "So The Nine are even responsible for the stigma toward those like Kyros!"

"I believe so," Darasha answered absently. She spoke as though reading text. "The words, the history, are there, but when I focus on them, they go blurry. Like they are sealed. I can't retrieve it 'Without the right request'?"

So we have to ask the right questions, Silver offered, *or express the right need.*

Briescha relayed Silver's statement. Darasha agreed, although that brought them little comfort and no further answers. *But now,* Briescha thought, *all we need is the right key!* They sat silently, puzzling over the implications of what they learned.

Tones of low music began in the lower

tiers, interrupting the absolute silence of the sapphire dome. The Elders' lights rose into their earthbound forms, and their auras energized the room with the constant combined hum of intense, singular power.

"And so, our meeting is adjourned for more immediate matters," Darasha said. "Enjoy your day, my dear Princess, my dear future Empress." Her formal voice held a teasing note. The girls bowed briefly before Darasha and rushed down the tiers to their seats on the floor of the Azelan mosaic map.

Paz rode high in the sky before the local business ended. Silver's enthusiasm had waned long since the first business was introduced. Briescha stole a glance at her sister. The many-colored spotlights gleamed on her mirrored skin. Silver sat perfectly still, with perfect posture, staring ahead attentively, responding when prompted, and managing a pleasant and regal expression. Briescha marveled at her. *Stop that, silly!* Silver smiled at her sister when the Council announced the last item of business. Briescha's stomach fluttered.

Deraddian then answered the Council's summons and entered the Inner Sanctum. To Briescha's guarded surprise, he stepped before them with all the decorum and piety afforded the honor of Silver's forgiveness. He executed the most luxurious bows before Briescha and Silver, and to each Arkayn Council member. They gave him the floor to plead his case.

"If protocol has brought me so close to dishonoring myself, by accident, in a deplorable act of treason, then I beg the forgiveness of my future Empress and her imminent and kind sister, the Princess Briescha." His palpable remorse flowed through the room. He bowed again, then submitted to the Council's full scan.

"The Arkayn Council finds this man not guilty by reason of following vague protocol."

The magnetic thrum from the Council reached a fever pitch of agreement. "What absolute judgment does our future Empress make in this case?"

Deraddian rocked on his feet against the power. He held his ground, pressing his lips and eyes shut to concentrate. Silver glided across the floor in her white dress and stood towering over the man. She crossed her palms and placed them outward against his chest, a gesture that was Azela's universal symbol of forgiveness. The Council hummed its approval of the action.

Meanwhile, Silver stared intently into Deraddian's wide blue eyes. Briescha felt the fear there, even from several feet away. The man finally cupped his hands and placed them over Silver's, the action that symbolized his acceptance and gratitude for her forgiveness.

"Be advised, soldier. A leader of the future Empress' level has chosen to forgive you. To forgive shows kindness that must not be misinterpreted. Have you anything final on this matter to bring before Council, Lieutenant Deraddian of Hyperion?"

The Councilman let the formal question hang in the air a long moment, knowing the Council's power and Silver's presence had affected the man. Silver pulled her hands out of his, gave him a curt nod and beaming smile, and resumed her seat beside Briescha. Deraddian regained his composure for a final request. "I formally move that protocol be revised with such situations in mind, that Hyperion may serve more effectively in its one true purpose, that of securing the throne for Azela's *rightful* heir."

The Arkayn Council rang out in agreement, pleased at the patriotic showing. But they in their singular innocence missed his tone, his blatant implication that the rightful ruler wouldn't be a deserving Silver. Briescha seethed beside Silver, ready to strangle the man where he stood.

He's just scared of me, like so many of the others. Silver took Briescha's hand. *I've forgiven him, and maybe you're just being paranoid.*

No, not this time. Briescha had a whirlwind of thoughts and a catch in her gut, a lingering hunch that something didn't fit. Did he lie to the Council? How in the world could he have deceived them? What would he gain from his actions?

He would gain a great deal if you strangle him before the Council. Silver glared at her. *Calm down and guard your thoughts. They're a jumbled mess anyway.* She patted Briescha's hand and gave it a squeeze. *We'll sort it out tonight.*

With that came the adjournment for their noonday break. Briescha scowled at Deraddian's back until he faced her. Then she plastered on her best smile. "Long live our *rightful* Empress, Deraddian, and a long life to you as well."

Deraddian forced a proper reply. He couldn't even meet her eyes. She read the dark splotches on his face and perspiration. The Arkayn scan must have drained his energy more than Briescha realized. Briescha tried to hide her smug smile when he staggered out the door, shaking after the full brunt of the Arkayn Council's power.

After two hasty curtsies, Silver took Briescha's hand and sped out of the hall, beyond the Inner Sanctum, and along a narrow passage hidden by the great outdoor columns and ornate topiaries.

"Why the rush?" Briescha laughed despite the vines slapping her in the face.

Shhh! Silver grinned back to her. *It's a surprise, but we have to hurry!*

Briescha stifled her laugh and ran through the manicured courtyard, climbed the wall by hiking her longdress to her hips, and landed lithely on the glowing cobbled path. Silver pulled her into a lush planted alley and up the winding steps that led to a private residence. At the carved door, she stopped and smoothed her hair and dress. Briescha followed suit, wondering whose house would have such a lovely balcony in the heart of town.

A familiar voice pierced the air, making her heart skip a beat. Kyros answered his landline on the other side of the door, even as Silver's hand paused above the doorbell.

"What do you mean you thought it wouldn't hurt to try it out?" Kyros pounded some surface on the other side of that door. "I can't believe you used the device without my permission! It's not even cleared for controlled testing yet!"

What is he talking about? Silver cocked her head to one side and listened to the silence. Briescha shrugged. *I'll give him a minute, but the clock's ticking!*

Briescha nodded. Her heart pounded. What a great surprise, to see Kyros today of all days! However, angry Kyros did not interest her in the least. And what device had been tested without his permission? An uneasy knot twisted in her stomach. She shivered, though it was quite warm on the little balcony.

"Absolutely not!" Kyros pounded his fist on the poor counter or floor or wall again. "I can't believe you could be so stupid. That is most certainly not the way that device is intended to be used. You could've killed yourself, but at least that would save me the trouble of disciplining you..."

This time, the tirade lasted so long that Silver finally rang the doorbell.

"Just a minute!" Kyros lowered his voice. "Keep making excuses, Lieutenant. I'm listening to every last one. And I expect you to meet me immediately following your shift tonight, in the lab. And every last spec had better be in place on that thing when I get there!"

Silence.

"Absolutely not!" Kyros banged on something again. "You screwed up. You make it right. The right way. Now get back to work. I have something far more important to do right now."

The door cracked open seconds later. Kyros waved them inside and bolted the door behind them. "I'm sorry. With these things," he gestured to his tablet, "I don't get a break from work, even when I'm hiding."

There he was! The Old Kyros, fretting over work and feigning disinterest in the highly intricate technology spawned in the last twenty years — technology that he took an active role to incorporate within Ouranos, namely Hyperion. Under his eyes, dark circles etched a work-wise path. His gaunt cheeks mirrored the same dark shadows.

"What in the world has you so upset?" Briescha fussed over his face and lack of sleep while she dug food out of the cabinets to force on him. "What's this about a device?"

He faltered. She gave him a stern glare. Then he waved his hand to dismiss it. "It's barely in development. All I can say is it's meant to help with crowd-control in a high-risk situation. And some idiot just flipped the switch! It killed power in half of Research and Development and still didn't operate like it should have."

"We have an ongoing theory about that

idiot's identity." Briescha and Silver shared a glance.

Kyros sighed, clutching the mug placed in his hands and eyeing the rehydrated soup Briescha set before him. "I'll take care of it, of him. Don't worry. When I figure it out, I'll report back to you guys. That's my job."

"Then let's talk about anything but work for the rest of our noonday." Briescha placed her hand on his. "We have so much catching up to do, and I don't want to squander this gift Silver arranged!"

"I've missed you both so much," he said. He stared from his mug to the girls and back again. Then Briescha cast him another severe look. He obediently ate while they chatted, until they made him eat his fill and were sure to be quite late returning from their noonday break.

"Well, then." Kyros stood from the table, scooting his chair across the floor. "Let's get you back to the festivities! I'll be your escort this time, finally."

They danced around Kyros and looped their hands through his elbows and gaily retraced their secretive steps back to the courtyard, with their many visitors none the wiser.

10: DARKSIGHT

Craftspeople, their families and visitors filled the tiers of the Arkayn Council Hall, prepared to witness Azela's yearly business. Tinted spotlights glowed over many Arkayn statues, many dampening their power to benefit their less powerful visitors. Silver and Briescha assumed their seats of honor at the center of the mosaic map. Briescha forced her eyes forward, a regal and bland expression on her face. She clasped her hands in her lap, giving a squeeze every time her gaze wandered in search of Jacan.

We'll visit them soon, silly. Silver smiled at her sister, her face far too open, too knowing.

Briescha nodded, allowing a small smile. Her hearing drifted over the many conversations echoing in the dome. One in particular caught her attention — a heated debate between a retired Warbound soldier and, by his distinct accent, a young man from an island in the Distral Seas.

The young man scoffed in protest. "But isn't it silly to think we're superior, like our very race is important in some way? I mean, this whole planet is Azelan, right? Whether we're Warbound or Forgebound. Even the Delvans are still Azelan!"

Briescha's neck prickled. That old racist undertone. She sighed. The soldier gave a grunt, preparing his protest.

"Then why is it so hard to accept a human living on Unata?"

"Because we're Azelan, no matter what! We're not mutts like those nasty Unatans!" The soldier coughed in his laughter, his shoulders creaking with old age. "What a joke! Garyn Kei and her new pet human."

Why do they hate Unata so much? Silver picked up on Briescha's interest. Briescha shrugged, intending to ask Darasha later.

"Surely you've heard stories about that human? His name is Rowan Jun, and he's far from a pet. News carries of his training in war, and his success on the battlefield." The young man paused, forcing his voice back down to a whisper. "However barbaric we consider Unata, the great Fear Planet, we mustn't discount a single citizen of that world. And why the age-old hatred anyway? Does anyone have a clue why you older folks hate an entire planet full of people you've never met?"

"Well, you see..." Briescha and Silver strained their hearing. "It's because, well. Huh!" The old man harrumphed, then broke into another rasping cough of laughter. "To think I'd live to see the day when a souther-seaman would chastise me. I hope death takes me soon, so I don't have to live with the shame!"

The younger man laughed alongside him. Briescha tuned out the conversation after that, focusing on a spot in the mosaic floor. Briescha shook her head, mulling over the implications of the odd conversation. *Rowan Jun must be something special if Unata welcomes him.* Silver's wonder caught Briescha off-guard. *Queen Garyn is known for her brutality, and she didn't kill him or let him die.* In her periphery, Briescha saw Silver's dismissive shrug.

Briescha agreed. *Maybe humans aren't as weak as we've heard.*

"Would you like to share your business on Unata, Master Warbound? Young Dutybound?" Sladen shrieked to quell the conversation Briescha had recently ignored. He hated off-subject discussion unless he was the instigator. "Something of relevance, perhaps."

All eyes fell on the two men. They shared a glance. Both stood, the old soldier with more effort that the seaman. The soldier nodded his agreement to the young man, who stepped forward.

Giving a deep courtly bow to Silver and Briescha, he stood before them on the great mosaic map of Azela. In the glowing spotlights, Briescha noticed the square cut of his jaw and how his long amethyst hair hung to his waist. His pale skin reflected the colored light around him, but held no shimmer of gemstone. The young man was Delvan.

"My greetings to our future Empress Salakind, to the Princess Briescha, and to the esteemed members of the Arkayn Council." He bowed to each in turn. "My younger brother is named Kranton." A much younger man with vivid amethyst hair and sparkling skin waved from the tier they had occupied. "My name is Drastin, and we travel to glorious Xepaqua from the Distral Seas in search of acceptance into the fold of Ouranos, with our particular desire to be counted among the Hyperion Faction." He bowed again.

"A fitting introduction. Even taking into account your youth, we can appeal to Ouranos on your behalf," said another Councilman. "From what family do you hail?"

"Our innumerable thanks to you, honorable Councilman. As for our family... From an unknown father, I hate to admit, as Mother, ah, enjoyed much company in her younger years." Drastin ducked his head at the smattering of laughter afforded his joke. "But our mother is from the finest fishermen stock in the whole Distral Seas."

As the laughter died down, Sladen reiterated his initial question. "And what view on Unata have you to share?"

"We heard that Unata was brutally attacked by the Gangre-tan slavers nearly two years ago." Drastin paused for the mixed crowd response. "Did we send aid to our closest neighbors? No."

The vicious crowd response shocked Briescha.

"We take care of our own!"

"They never sent help to us, the dogs."

"Let them fight like savages."

"Our lives are far more important than theirs."

That last one irked Silver, who was on her feet before Briescha realized. The visitors stared at the imposing figure of Silver and were stunned to silence. Silver stared at the speaker, a nihilistic aristocrat by the pretentious clothing she wore. Clenching her fists by her sides, she stepped with full regality to where the woman gaped up at her. Briescha stood, ready to relay Silver's words, her racing heart matching that of her sister. As she listened to her sister's thoughts, she felt such pride.

Silver gestured to the woman as Briescha began to speak.

"Your future Empress renounces this woman's claim — an assertion that compromises

Azela's very soul of social compassion across all societies and worlds — and appeals to the good citizens of Azela to reconsider their ill-conceived hatred. War destroys home, life and spirit. To lightly cast off anyone locked in a cycle of battle and preparation for battle is to abandon the foundation of Azela's peace-seeking society."

Silver whirled on the woman once more, seeing the glow of embarrassment in her haughty face. "And you, a woman of culture and a proper upbringing..." Briescha paused for a long moment. *No, Silver. Don't stoop to name calling.* Silver reworded her statement for Briescha. "A woman of privilege? You would represent the arrogant hatred of the masses, with no other justification but your own self-indulgent, inadequate assumptions."

A noise like thunder rumbled all around the Arkayn Council Hall. Silver's molten orange eyes glowed from her dark face, challenging the woman to speak ill of any creature having life. The gemstone key blazed with light. The ground beneath the Hall shook just a bit. Fearful voices arose from the visitors. *Silver!* Briescha turned to her sister. *Rein it in!*

Silver sighed in her head. *You're right.* The shaking stopped.

Oh, no! Silver glanced around the huge room. If the gaping faces around the Council Hall were any indication, more than just the ground had been shaken with Silver's display of power. *They're scared, too.*

Give them the high note, Silver. Briescha sent a warm mental embrace to her sister. *It's okay. Fret later. They needed to see that you can control it.*

"Do not allow the absence of war on this planet to blind you. Each Azelan must remember that we struggle to maintain peace. The path is a hairsbreadth wide. We are just one conflict away from losing peace to complacency. Do not continue making the same mistakes of the past. Move forward with a heart full of the goodness in this world, and let go of these unfounded prejudices. Your hearts are full to the brim with kindness, if only you polish away the stain of bitterness. That is what the Great Peace Unequalled requires of its inhabitants, and that is the peace I will bring to you."

Silver smiled at Drastin, who had plastered himself against a pillar in fear, before she took her seat once more. The Hall filled with applause, slow at first, then building to a fever pitch. She ducked her head in confusion, but maintained her placid expression as her anger subsided.

Briescha resumed her seat beside her sister, brimming with pride.

"Then it is settled," rang a voice from among the Arkayn. "As we move forward with our commitment to peace, so too shall we seek to gain and share knowledge, wisdom and camaraderie with our closest neighbors on Unata!"

The applause that followed that ruling sounded rather sporadic and died off quickly into muttering, segmented conversations.

The same Arkayn called for silence. "Now, we shall commence with our annual business."

Azela's Annual Business commenced with a loud bell, jarring them from their gossip to more pressing matters of state. Briescha made appropriate, structured statements and relayed Silver's appropriate replies to out-of-towners. Then another bell decreed the ceremony for Confirmation of Inheritance. Both girls felt their hearts pounding in their ears.

Ganan and Jacan descended from a high tier in the back of the Hall and stepped forward at the Council's beckoning. Briescha stared as

Jacan's broad shoulders and warm topaz skin came into view before her. She felt the fluttering deep in her belly. Jacan and Ganan turned to Briescha and Silver. Ganan beamed at the girls, and gave them the most embarrassing flourish of a bow. His greeting was quite proper, but full of the bubbling fatherly love that made their chests hurt and their cheeks burn.

Jacan stood before them — stooping, for he was even taller than before — and reached for Silver's hand. "Dearest Empress Salakind. You have grown into quite the lovely and powerful woman. I salute your great accomplishments and grow excited to bask in your Great Peace Unequalled." She grumbled in her head, dying of embarrassment and wilting under his kindness.

Then Jacan took Briescha's hand. She felt his pulse caress her hand, then her mind and heart. His mind had a calmness on the surface, but churned beneath with his excitement. She pulled back her power to stay out of his thoughts. The press of his flesh remained and brought back an intense whirlwind of emotion she expected time to extinguish. She could not suppress her quickened breath, pounding heart or manic thoughts.

When she raised her head to gaze into his red eyes, she saw her terrified face in the reflection. She fell into those eyes, felt like they'd hold her forever, and was quite content to allow it. His heart pounded with hers until the sound rendered her deaf to any outside sounds. Then he spoke.

"*My* Princess Briescha." Jacan's eyes glinted with the fire Briescha avoided sensing. "By your exquisite grace and generosity, and that of our Empress, I stand before the Arkayn Council for the Confirmation of Inheritance initiated by my father Ganan. I humbly request permission and the blessing of my dear Empress and my cherished Princess."

Briescha stared at him for a long moment. His words didn't match what his heart cried out. She sat dazed for a long moment. Then she smiled at Jacan. Her heart matched the pace of his heart, and she drifted in her mind, longing for whatever it was he silently offered.

Silly head. Silver elbowed her hard in the ribs. *Tell him yes.*

Briescha cringed more in embarrassment than pain. "I, ah, we give our blessing for your inheritance, Jacan, son of Ganan. May you honor the title of Master of the Forge."

"Step forward for the skills and knowledge demonstration, Jacan."

"Yes, Science Officer Sladen." Jacan leaned toward her. She felt his breath against her face. "May I borrow your ruby flower?"

She tilted her head in confusion. She nodded and released her hair from the large pin. He gave her hand a quick press and turned back to Sladen. He offered his greeting to the Council, and then submitted to their intense scrutiny.

The Arkayn Council scanned Briescha's perfect ruby hairpin with many exclamations and much positive feedback. Jacan turned to wink at her and said something quietly that caused an approving ripple of agreement through the attentive Arkayns. Briescha blushed though she hadn't heard the comment. Her heart fluttered again.

Silver chuckled in Briescha's head. *Silly.*

Hush. Briescha tried a sharp tone, but wilted under Silver's teasing.

Jacan wove the full history of Forge Mountain and all the previous heirs, their great works and sworn duties. He presented newer and impressive works to prove his skill in joining crystals. Ganan stood nearby, beaming his smile from Jacan to Briescha. The Confirmation of Inheritance for Azela's most important Master dragged on. Heads lolled all around the room. As Paz swung low on the horizon, glinting through sapphire walls, Sladen announced an end to the interrogation and inspection.

The Arkayn Science Officer projected his voice in the large dome. "Jacan, son of Ganan, present yourself."

Jacan clasped his hands behind his back, awaiting their judgment.

"We find you worthy in heart, mind and tongue to continue your indispensable work as apprentice to the Master of the Forge. With the blessing of our future Empress Salakind Velonsacor Eranklaya and our esteemed Princess Briescha, the Arkayn Council of Azela confirms your inheritance before all your kinsman. You shall for the rest of your life remain Forgebound, and receive all titles, honors and properties afforded your position. Azela, welcome your future Forgemaster!"

The visiting townsfolk from Forge Mountain whistled and cheered, startling the other visitors from their stupor. The others snapped awake in batches, elbowed one another into standing, and applauded out of synch. When the Xepaquan citizens joined in with their polite clapping, the momentous occasion received an appropriate fanfare from all the assembled countrymen.

I guess this's a bigger deal than we thought. Briescha stared wide-eyed as everyone vacated their seats in jubilation. She gave Silver a hand up from her seat and cheered along — in an appropriate, demure way permitted by her status. Her heart soared for Jacan, though. *I knew he was apprenticing, but he just seemed kind of laid back about it to me.*

It's because they're family. He got really serious after we left, though. Silver nodded in the direction of a sapphire platform before them. *Look at that sphere! He's really improved since your ruby flower.*

I rather prefer my flower above all other trinkets. Briescha pouted.

Silver scoffed in her head. *We'll see about that, silly head!*

Oh, you know what I mean! Briescha turned away from Jacan to stare at her sister. *Your trinkets are obviously the most precious of all!*

Silver pretended to ignore her.

Jacan received the applause with humility, bowing and smiling and even blushing. From a sparkling pillow on the sapphire pedestal, Ganan lifted one perfect, smooth and clear diamond sphere the size of his head. Jacan cradled two beautiful ruby filigree cylinders in one large hand and Briescha's sparkling ruby flower in the other.

The dismissal bell rang three times. Briescha and Silver bowed to those assembled and to the Arkayn Council, both glad to see the proceedings end at last. Azelans cried out their joy and congratulations from all over the Hall. Most filed out in a grateful rush, eager to remove themselves from the slow proceedings and the constant drain of energy caused by the immense Arkayn power, since most outlying provinces rarely had more than a few Arkayn Council members in their Halls. Xepaqua's Council Hall held over a hundred at any given time.

Briescha saw the press of visitors descend on Jacan and Ganan, recognized a few miners from Forge Mountain, and even saw the thick red braid of Arcani bobbing in the flowing sea of gemstone hair.

Having been dismissed, she dropped her

air of decorum and wanted to throw her arms around Arcani, Daddy Ganan and Jacan. A throng of foreign visitors diverted their path to offer well-wishes to Briescha and Silver. They stayed at a respectful distance, but soon formed a solid wall between Briescha and what she wanted more than anything that day.

Briescha behaved, hiding her annoyance behind the mask of duty. She answered their questions with eloquent grace and relayed Silver's answers with equal bearing. There was no end to them. Most wouldn't leave until they'd touched Silver's hand or studied their distorted faces reflected on her arms and face. When she felt ready to burst in anger at their continued freakshow treatment, the last few filed past her out of the Inner Sanctum and toward the courtyard.

Drastin and Kranton, the Hyperion hopefuls, dragged their feet. They smiled at Briescha and her sister with the most curious mixture of lasciviousness and mischief. Briescha sent her telepathy outward, trying to see beyond their outward display. The Hyperion emblem blazed in the forefront, far too crisp for normal ambition. Intentionally projected. *Hiding something.*

Silver, hearing Briescha's assertion, scowled. She inclined her head to them in farewell. *They're just kids, though. And they had many chances to hurt us the whole time at Council.*

Maybe they didn't want to hurt us, but something is definitely off about them now. I didn't see it before. Briescha narrowed her eyes, angry she didn't sense the façade before. She made no attempt to hide the suspicion and anger rising in her heart. Kranton's bottom lip quivered in fear at the face she made. He pushed his older brother out of the Inner Sanctum in a hurry, barely clearing the door before it swung shut behind them.

We'll tell Kyros to keep an eye on them later. Silver patted her arm. *It'll be okay.*

Briescha nodded, fighting to push down the violent feelings those boys dragged out of her. Standing alone on the mosaic map with Silver, she breathed a sigh of relief. She glanced to the small Forge Mountain group, aware that only her friends and family remained at last.

Finally, Jacan turned to face her. His grin was a ray of warmth to her aching heart. His ruby eyes seared her blushing face. She stared, her mouth hanging open. He stopped short of where they stood and dropped to his knees before her. He tore his gaze from her face and bowed his head. She took the red flower from his hand, letting her fingers brush his palm and feeling his strong, quick heartbeat. Briescha swept her hair into the pin and smiled down at him.

"Dearest Empress, *my* Princess," he whispered. "Will you honor me with an evening of your time, or even the briefest stroll in your garden? I'd very much love to hear about your four years of reform and economic growth, or anything else that pleases you."

He's a silly head, too. Silver poked him with her toe. *Get up!*

"Hey!" Jacan rubbed his knee where she poked him. "I'm trying to be respectful here!"

Ah. I see you're not mad at me anymore, Briescha teased Silver. *We'll put a stop to this right now!*

Silver drew her body up to its full height. She glared at Jacan.

"Only if you get up and stop treating us weird." Briescha leaned forward in a whisper. "Otherwise, Silver is going to go from toe poke to kick in a second. And trust me, she hits rather hard these days, when she needs to."

A shadow passed through his eyes. "It's a shame she needed to hit anything. Ever." Jacan towered above her, just a tad shorter than his kid brother Fagan, with shoulders almost as wide. He stopped his hand from scratching his ruby hair and pinned his wrist at his side.

"Silver insisted on making us an asset more than a liability." Briescha smiled at Jacan, though her mind swam with suspicion at those boys. Her heart shook the longer she looked at her one-time brother. "And she's learned quite a bit beyond her civic duties in the time we've spent here. I have learned, too."

Briescha rolled her eyes at his bleak expression.

"We'll have to speak of that, too, then." Jacan offered the crook of his elbow first to Silver, then to Briescha. "And everything else we can fit into your busy schedule!"

He guided the girls to their waiting family and Forge citizens. Arcani dropped the big diamond ball she took from Ganan. He snatched it out of the air with a loud, laughing complaint before it hit the stone floor.

"This has to make it to the Arkayn Vault, woman!" Then he settled an arm around Arcani's shoulders.

Ganan's eyes sparkled at his Arcani with such love. Briescha's heart soared. She missed the looks they exchanged. Arcani dropped her formal front and ran to greet her foster children. She stood on her tiptoes and squeezed the life out of Silver and Briescha, exclaiming all the while how much they'd grown. Briescha squeezed back until they all groaned from cut off circulation.

Ganan swept the girls from Arcani's embrace and cradled their heads against the concavity of his throat on each side, as he held them when they were children. "Far as I'm concerned, my girls, you still fit right here, near my heart." He kissed their foreheads and held tight to them for the longest time.

Then Fagan burst in, fresh from his duties under Kyros' close supervision. Fagan snatched up Jacan into a crushing hug and swung him back and forth. Jacan gasped for the air to laugh, thumping his big little brother on his back. Kyros was nowhere to be seen, which was the norm lately. He was a busy man, after all, but his absence reeked of his hate for Jacan. Briescha smiled at the family-proper's reunion with a mix of joy and grief, knowing it would draw to a close all too soon.

I think my face is gonna crack. Silver pressed her grinning cheeks with her fingers.

Mine, too. Briescha threw her arm around Silver's waist. *I'm even happier to see you smile so much!* They stumbled into the group of Forge workers and townsfolk they had known and loved since youth, so happy to chat and hug and see them after so many years. *It's almost like we're back home.*

Silver's heart soared. *I miss them, too. I miss the meadow now. Can you smell it on their hair, in their skin? It's amazing!* She audibly sniffed the next visitor's hair. He was the short Foreman who worked under Ganan. He laughed and shook his head. She squeeze-hugged him again. They knew this Silver child had always been a little odd.

Briescha breathed deep of the next person as she turned around, her eyes closed. She had to agree with Silver. "We probably smell like Arcani's medicine crate from living in this city so long!" Silver's mind voice giggled from her right. This person's scent tugged at a different part of her memory. The meadow and warmth of Paz, the fires of the Forge, and something even more familiar that she couldn't place. When her nose bumped into that someone, her eyes snapped open. Warm topaz skin dazzled her for a confusing moment that quickly melted into mortification.

"Don't worry." The rasp in his voice dropped low. "You smell wonderful to me, too, *my* Princess."

Jacan stared down at his dear Princess, his crimson gaze smoldering just for her. The fire in her face glowed from her cheeks. She couldn't muster a single witty retort, and that perplexed her more. Her heart fluttered. Her breathing hitched. The pit of her stomach trembled with something akin to hunger. She wavered on her feet. His large hands snapped out to steady her. The new scars on his thick forearms glowed pink in the varied lighting of the Council Hall. His chest rose and fell in a rhythm that tugged at her gaze. She felt safe, even as her ears rang with dizziness, her eyes grew dark and she pitched forward against his inviting, broad, scarred chest.

11: PLANETBOUND

You big dummy! You silly head! Silver's scolding held an edge of worry.

"I can't believe how long it has been since you ate, Briescha!" Arcani fretted and fluttered over Briescha. "As much as you work, you should at least be taking some extra nutrients a couple times a month."

"The light is too bright." Briescha's head throbbed.

"Oh, much brighter than my precious daughter, apparently!" Arcani didn't like being ignored, even by a patient. "Were you trying to get sick?"

"Just really busy." Briescha waited for her head to clear before opening her eyes.

"Ah, an excuse! That makes everything okay." Sarcasm from Arcani sliced at Briescha's heart. Briescha watched Arcani flail her arms in frustration. Arcani tapped Briescha's forehead with two fingers. "When are you going to take care of yourself, huh?"

Briescha had no answer and no reason Arcani would accept. She tucked her head down and curled onto her side, against a warm body.

Then she noticed Jacan's strong, warm arms around her, cradling her across his lap on a low tier in the Arkayn Council Hall. She crumpled in embarrassment, drinking in the sensation of her body pressed to his and trying to find her bearings and the strength to scramble to her feet.

"Oh no you don't, young lady." Arcani placed her hands on Briescha's arms, clamping her waving arms against her belly. "In light of your collapse and hard work these many years without a vacation, the Arkayn Council just approved some mandatory rest for you, lasting the remainder of the week. You and Silver won't be permitted to leave the city just yet, but you are to relax within Xepaqua. And until we set foot on that longboat back to Forge Mountain, we will ensure that you take this assignment as seriously as your last four years' work."

Briescha opened and closed her mouth several times, sure that she would fail whatever attempt she made against these orders. Arcani stalked away, digging through her bag for something. Then Briescha noticed the silence in her head. She found Silver staring over Jacan's back, a few inches from her face. Silver pressed her forehead against Briescha's, sighing in exhaustion and worry, with muddled, incoherent thoughts shaking her core. Silver hadn't been silenced by worry in a long while. *I'm sorry, Silver. I'll try harder now, and I'll still be able to take care of you.*

Silver shook her head, her eyes a mask of continued fretting, her mind-voice silent with whatever demons she wrestled. She dropped her eyes to her chest and ran her fingers over the gemstone Key.

You don't want me to?

Darasha's consciousness drifted into Briescha's mind, sending a calming aura of love and peace through Briescha, and by effect, through Silver. Silver gave her a ghost of a smile. *Silly-head.* Then she tugged on Briescha's hair before turning away and retreating to the high tier, in answer to Darasha's summons. Far up the tiers, Briescha saw Silver sit beside Darasha's immobile form. She laid her head on the woman's shoulder and sighed again, allowing her mind to flow through all the stressful events of the day.

Feeling faint again, she settled her head against Jacan's broad, hard chest. His heart thumped against her ear, sending tremors through her body in a rhythm she couldn't ignore. He pulled her tighter and whispered that she would be okay. She nodded, snuggling her face against his warm skin, glad of an embrace that wasn't cold and foreign and emotionless. The last four years made her feel quite jaded. But in Jacan's arms, she drifted from the worries of her world for just a while.

"Here, you great silly bumbling brat!" Her foster mother's voice had calmed to a loving grumble. Arcani shoved a bottle of some vivid red liquid and a pouch of food in Briescha's hand. "Eat, drink. Before you die for sure." She slid her thumb down the side of Briescha's cheek.

Then Briescha saw the real worry in Arcani's eyes. She regretted her preventable collapse even more. Cramming the food in her mouth and chasing it with the sweet drink, she choked twice with emotion. *Why am I such a fool?* The nutrients flooded her system over the next minutes. *This is something so small that I overlooked. And now I feel better.* Her clarity built a wall around her self-pity in no time. *Yes, I've been a fool in more ways than one.*

Briescha was loathe to leave Jacan's arms as much as Jacan regretted releasing her. She still felt his heat along the whole right side of her body for several long moments after she dragged herself upright again. Or perhaps she imagined that part. He did stand closeby, with his large hands out to steady her, until he was sure she could stand unaided.

Taking a cleansing breath, Briescha heard the clamor of visitors outside as they made their way out of the courtyard and toward the Inner City Garden of Xepaqua for the planned festivities.

"If you're quite yourself again..." Arcani fussed over Briescha's messy hair, "they'll want to gawk at you for a bit." Arcani glanced up the long tiers. "You, too, girl!"

Silver perked up, lifting her head from Darasha's shoulder, and took the tier steps two at a time. She hugged Arcani again and slugged Jacan in the shoulder, and pinched Briescha for good measure.

Briescha rubbed her arm. "I guess I deserve that. Now stop with the silent treatment!"

Silver smiled around at her Forge family. *Maybe soon. We'll see.*

"Petulant child!" Briescha scolded Silver, but smiled anyway, glad that her sister acted more like herself.

The Forge workers gathered around. Fagan stood at the door, peering out to see who waited. Arm in arm, the sisters led their family toward the great outdoors and the scrutiny of a thousand visitors. Their constant Hyperion guard — this contingent led by the decorated Commander Bridfar — met them outside the Inner Sanctum and fell in line at the front and back of their group as they made their way out the courtyard and toward the garden.

"It's a pleasure to see my dear Empress

and Princess in such high spirits!" Bridfar inclined his head to Silver, who waved him off. "They've spoken often and fondly of their Forge family, and I've heard many impressive reports otherwise about your great accomplishments, Forgemaster Ganan." He gave a curt nod to Ganan, who returned the gesture. "And congratulations are in order for the future Forgemaster! Jacan, is it?"

"Yes, Commander, sir." Jacan beamed. "I cannot venture to imagine a greater honor as one Forgebound."

Briescha blushed. She felt his eyes on her neck, the side of her face, the back of her head. She twisted her head to look up at him. "Except what?" Her whisper was just for his ears.

His eyes went wide. "I didn't say 'except'."

"But I heard it."

Jacan smiled. "Perhaps you did, but I didn't say it."

Confused, her mind bouncing about in confusion, Briescha tore her eyes away from him and focused on the path. She felt the heat emanating from his chest just inches behind her. *Why does he have this effect on me?* Silver elbowed her, gave one of those knowing looks Briescha hated sometimes, and laughed in her head.

Halfway to the park, the crowd split ahead. A lone figure lurched out of the press of people and disappeared down an alley. Briescha stared after the person, uncomprehending. One of Bridfar's men headed after him, but too late.

The amethyst spire to their right erupted with blinding light and a deafening drone of vibration that rattled the ground. Then, halfway up the building, the walls shattered in a rippling shockwave. Shards of crystal shrapnel flew in all directions, raining down on the unarmed civilians and Hyperion alike.

Briescha threw her body in front of Silver. Silver's hands moved like lightning. She shoved Briescha into Jacan's arms and moved her right arm in a long arc. Flipping her other hand toward the sky, she raked her fingers up with some great effort. Her eyes blazed yellow and her Key cast searing light even in broad daylight. Then she stumbled to regain her footing.

Jacan pulled Briescha away and turned his back to Silver. Something hard thumped against his back. Once. Twice. Five times. Briescha couldn't catch her breath. Even the screaming of Xepaqua's visitors didn't return the air to her lungs. She looked up into Jacan's pained face. He smiled at her. The idiot smiled!

"Jacan!" Briescha forced her hands up and to his cheeks. "Stop it! You're getting hurt!" She shook him. "Stop it now! Or I'll..."

"No." Jacan coughed. Then he smiled again. "You are more important than a little pain."

Jacan's grip loosened when he dropped to his knees. Briescha pried herself from his huge arms and spun around to his back. Crystal blood flowed from cuts and glowing bruises that ran the breadth of his broad shoulders. He heaved in deep breaths. Briescha held out her stupid, unskilled hands to help him. Her heart pounded. *Why did I forget everything? I can heal.*

"Go!" Arcani stepped in and, with the voice of habitual authority in such situations, shoved Briescha aside. "She needs you."

Briescha froze, staring down at her dear Jacan.

"He'll be fine, and thanks to him, so will you!" Arcani waved her away. "Go!"

"Silver!" Briescha uncluttered her thoughts with a sharp shake of her head. *I'm an idiot.* She gave a frantic glance all around and looked for Silver. She lurched to where Silver stared at her hands. Silver swayed on her feet. Briescha gripped her shoulders and steadied her.

Are you okay? Silver's voice shook with exhaustion.

Of course! Briescha mustered all the confidence she could manage. *But you! Are you okay?* She inspected every visible inch of her sister.

Of course. Silver offered a weak smile, but heaved in and out.

Then look at me! Briescha shook her. Silver stared at her hands again. *What's wrong? What are you doing?*

Crushing and building mountains, like you said when we were little. Her smile wavered. She gazed beyond Briescha, who turned for the first time since the explosion.

The entire top half of the tower fell at a right angle across the center street. A few loose stones rumbled impotently down a huge wall of glowing yellow spikes that braced the building and stopped it from crashing into the ground. A higher half-dome of the same crystal stone encased the entire city block, the surface studded with shards of amethyst from the initial explosion.

The realization took a lot longer to dawn on Briescha. *You're amazing, Silver.*

I didn't catch them all, though. The shards. Some got through. Silver's aching worry etched across her face. *Please ask Bridfar to count the wounded and report them to me. And check on Jacan. I tried, but couldn't cover them all in time.*

Sound erupted all around Briescha for the first time. Azelans were panicking, rejoicing, and crying out in confusion. Some cried out in pain. Hyperion soldiers were barking orders and making a use of themselves in helping the wounded. Somewhere behind her, Arcani's commanding voice rose above all as she took control of the healers.

Briescha threw her arms around Silver. *I can't process this right now, but it's something amazing.* Then as an afterthought, Briescha kissed her sister's cheek. *And don't you dare try to feel bad about it.* The yellow glow of Silver's eyes faded. The Key's glow faded back to a normal pulsing heartbeat. Then Briescha led her over to Arcani for a quick once-over.

Arcani pulled her hands away from Silver's ribcage and opened her eyes. As she refocused her mind, she sighed. "You're just exhausted from your exertion, thank the great Golden Seer!"

Briescha wrung her hands still. Arcani gave her a stern look. "Jacan'll be fine, too. Now off with you! Make a use of yourself."

Briescha stole a glance at Jacan. He laid on his belly, looking bored. He'd been ordered still by Arcani. He always hated being still. He caught her staring and smiled at her, giving a dismissive gesture that he would be okay. She heaved a sigh of relief.

Briescha pushed her way through the double line of Hyperion soldiers that flanked them as soon as they confirmed Silver's safety. She spoke to a very grim-faced Bridfar, relaying Silver's request for an injury count. Then she headed toward the nearest medical setup to see how she could help.

"Princess Briescha! You'll need a guard, please." It was Dirco who spoke — Silver's long-time training partner and, lately, willing punching bag.

She paused, making a show of staring all around her. "There are more Hyperion soldiers around here than citizens. I feel quite safe. But if

Commander Bridfar permits it, I could use an assistant." She waited for Bridfar's hurried affirmative, then whisked away Dirco to help.

Many of the next hours, Briescha spent in medical setups, patching up or psy-healing minor injuries. Bridfar delivered a favorable casualty report of zero deaths and two hundred minor to moderate injuries. Silver's relief flooded Briescha, even as her mind-voice weakened in need of rest. Briescha patted the arm of her current patient — a feisty boy who suffered a dislocated shoulder from a big falling rock — and released him to his gracious souther-seas mother.

She nodded to the dogged Dirco, who gathered her makeshift healing kit. "Have you found any evidence of the ones who set up this disaster?"

"Not exactly, though we have detained some suspects, thanks to Forgemaster Ganan's quick action." Bridfar waited until Briescha joined him in a walk back to Silver's cot.

"Daddy Ganan?" Briescha frowned. "What did he do?"

"Ah, ummm...It appears he has a knack for finding people, and finding out things." He lowered his voice. "There are dissidents all over. You know this. Hired assassins and entire organizations that want you both dead. But today's demonstration may add fuel to their arguments."

Silver grumbled in Briescha's head. *Stop that, Silver! You can't help what they think. You did a great thing!*

"Or it may help the citizens rally around her?"

"Quite a few, maybe. Hopefully." Bridfar saluted Briescha, then bowed. They'd arrived at Silver's cluster of soldiers. "The alert level is high for now, though. Until further notice, your guard contingent is tripled. We've sent one contingent to The Tower to check for bombs or other security breaches. They'll get a building access manifest and cross-reference it against Hyperion records. You'll be quite safe in your own home, at least."

"I feel better knowing you will be around, Commander." Briescha curtsied with an elegant flourish. Then an odd thought occurred to her. She turned to Bridfar with her eyes dancing. "I'm trying to determine how death threats and assassination attempts became a part of my daily routine."

"As long as you both survive, there will be threats and attempts. That's why we're here, the ones you can trust." He winked at Briescha. "And that's why Kyros works so hard for you both!"

She smiled, rolled her eyes and excused herself to prepare her exhausted sister for the trip back to The Tower. Silver had her eyes closed, both her body and mind nearly asleep. Making small talk with Arcani, who just finished with her last patient, Briescha asked about Ganan and his finding people and things.

"Oh, you know Ganan!" Arcani waved her hand. "He wasn't always the Forgemaster. Well, he always trained toward that. But he did a great deal of work, ah, outside Ouranos back in the day. He doesn't choose to talk about it often. Some rough stuff." She shrugged.

"Well, now I'm even more curious!" Briescha laughed, but it sounded tired. "I'll have to chat when he gets back."

"He'll be back before you know it." Arcani's face was rarely so wistful. "And I'm sure he'll answer whatever questions you want him to, if he can! But you, young lady, need to take Silver and both of you need to go rest."

"I know, I know." Briescha hesitated. "But

what about you guys?"

"Special accommodations were made for the Forge crew. We'll be safe, and I'll let you know when Ganan gets back."

Briescha nodded, her thoughts muddled with her long day and yet another attempt on the life of her sister. "I'll head out now. I love each and every one of you!"

"I know, my dear children. I know!" Arcani pulled Briescha's face down for a kiss on the forehead, then stooped to kiss Silver. "Now go and feel better."

"I'm going, too." Jacan stood and stretched his rippling back. The wounds had faded, but still looked discolored.

"Oh, no you're not!" Arcani stood toe to toe with him, poking a finger into his chest. "I didn't spend my last bit of the day's healing to let you go off and reopen your wounds!"

Jacan grunted, then laughed. "Ouch! I'm just taking a walk, and then creeper-staring at these two precious women every minute I can for the rest of the night. And probably tomorrow night, too."

"Oh, no you're not!" Briescha cried out this time. Her face flushed in a bright glow.

"Please." His imploring eyes cut into her soul. "I'll be a perfect gentleman. Except for the staring thing."

Oh, let him, Briescha! Silver smiled up at him, rolling her eyes. *He's just worried about us.*

"Well, Silver says it's okay." Briescha narrowed her eyes at him. "So I guess you can come."

Jacan cupped his mother's face in his large hand and kissed her on the cheek. "See you and Father tomorrow."

"Yeah, yeah. Goodnight, guys!"

Hyperion insisted on carrying Silver on her

makeshift cot all the way to The Tower. Her protests to Briescha fell on deaf ears. "Who's the silly-head now, huh? You," and she poked at her cheek, "need rest. And no one defies Arcani's orders except this guy who has to live with his decision." She jerked a thumb toward Jacan.

They only waited a few more minutes when they arrived at The Tower. The first contingent completed their sweep of the area and cleared it for entry. Silver grumbled again when Hyperion soldiers carried her up the stairs and deposited her on the floor of her room. She flounced over to the bed and flopped down.

"What she means is thank you! Regards to the Commander and to Dirco!" Briescha shut the door, waiting for the security device to register a closed system. When the system beeped and set the alarm, she relaxed.

"You have to fake it a lot here, don't you?" Jacan's voice warmed her with its sincerity. He watched her, intent on her every move.

"Most of the time." Briescha sighed. "But I'm not always good at it."

"Well, you don't have to be fake around me. You know that."

Briescha smiled. "Yes, I know."

"Hey, brat!" Jacan flopped down on the bed near Silver and snatched her up in a hug. "You're more than just a shiny hunk of metal, y'know? That stuff was pretty impressive out there today."

Silver pretended to snub him, but her face broke into a grin as he rubbed his stubbly face against hers. She pushed him away, tickled so much she couldn't stand it. Briescha stared, awestruck. *It's just like when we were kids.*

He's a jerk. I hate that. Silver laughed anyway. Her eyes drooped and she yawned.

Jacan ruffled her hair and stood up.

"Can I have a few minutes with my sister?" Briescha's grin was apologetic.

Jacan excused himself with a gracious bow and a quick wink. He wandered downstairs and through the first door he found. He must've glanced around the interior for a moment. Then he laughed, full of mischief, and closed the door.

Briescha frowned for a moment, then sighed. *He's in my bedroom.*

Is that a bad thing? Silver yawned again, this time not bothering to put her hand over her mouth. *I mean, why're you acting all standoffish with him. You've wanted to spend time with him for four years. So spend time!*

Briescha wanted to hate sleepy matter of fact, Silver. She even laughed at Briescha's blushing face and poked it with a finger. Then she shirked her clothes, pulled a loose, wispy nightgown over her head, and slipped under her covers. *You take care of the company tonight,* Silver mumbled. *I'll visit tomorrow.*

Briescha hugged Silver and kissed her forehead, feeling her light warmth. The abrupt movement pushed the warming sheet from Silver's shoulder. The light from Silver's Key pulsed in time with the internal heartbeat of Azela. Silver's thoughts grew somber and reflective.

"You got quiet again."

Will they really try harder to kill me now, like Bridfar said? Anguish filled her peaceful face. She slumped over on the bed and curled up. Briescha wouldn't lie to Silver. In silence, she curled next to her sister.

They'll protect us. Briescha squeezed her. *Kyros is with us, and all of Hyperion. Well, at least the good ones. And Jacan is here tonight. Do you want him to come sit with us?*

Silver shook her head.

Then how can I help you feel better?

Silver stared up at her with her face twisted in sorrow. *It's so hard to just hold it in. It hurts for so long, and I can't fix it. I couldn't even keep everyone safe today. I couldn't even protect you. The one person who can't die in my life! I couldn't even keep you safe myself!*

But you did!

I was lucky. They'll keep coming. Silver twisted out of Briescha's embrace. *They'll win one of these days.*

No, they won't!

As long as I have this, and Silver pulled down the blanket, *they will try.*

Hey! Briescha grabbed her by the shoulders and shook her. Silver tried to pull away. "No! Listen to me. You do your job. I'll do my job. I'll do it better than ever. We're a team, and we won't fail."

Briescha held Silver at arms' length and stared into her eyes and at her quivering bottom lip. "It's okay to hurt. I can't help you if you don't let me in, though. So hurt and cry if you need to, but let me be here for you."

Silver cried then, for the very first time. Her tears fell as blood rubies, spilling over her cheeks in a torrent that overflowed the bed and mounded up on the hard floor. Never before had Briescha's sister let a single tear fall. Briescha stared at her for a moment, shocked, and then threw her arms around Silver. Sometime later, when at last Silver's sobs slowed and ceased, Briescha touched her forehead to Silver's.

"I love you, my dear sister. Call to me if ever you need my help." Briescha smiled, infusing the words with her love. *And I will be there: across the city, across the planet, across space itself.* She grinned. *I will come to you.* She flooded her words with all the passion she could suffuse into them.

Briescha smiled into Silver's trusting,

loving face and placed her hands on either side of her shining cheeks. Briescha pushed back Silver's hair. Each molten lock slipped behind Silver's ears and flowed in a reflective cascade to drown out the light of her Key. Briescha kissed her sister's forehead and moved to stand.

Her bare feet slipped in the mounds of tear-rubies that covered the floor at Silver's bedside. Each perfect gem sparkled in the low lighting. Briescha maneuvered a foothold and eased her sister back onto her folded headrest. Briescha pulled the translucent sheet up around Silver's shoulders. She kissed her beloved sister once more, and then skirted the tear-rubies and walked down the steps to the next floor and through the door leading into her bedroom.

12: FLAMEHEART

Briescha looked up toward the floor where her sister slept as the lights went down and the door whooshed closed. Darkness enveloped her. She breathed deeply of the cool air flowing through her room. She bit off the torrent of worried thoughts that tore through her mind. She ran her hand along the wall, casting warm light into her room.

"Is she okay?"

Briescha clamped her hand over her mouth, stifling a shriek. "Jacan!"

He chuckled, a low sound deep in his throat. Her neck prickled at the sound. "Forget about me already?"

Jacan lounged across her bed, his weight propped up on an elbow.

"Only for a moment." Briescha fidgeted in the doorway. "Glad you got comfortable while you waited."

"Well, it is a soft bed." He bounced on his hip. The bed rippled in response. The corner of his mouth turned up in mischief. "See?"

With a mighty effort contrary to her fluttering heart, Briescha rolled her eyes. "I'm aware."

He sat up and patted the bed. Briescha sat down, stiff-backed and formal, willing her heart to slow down. Jacan scratched his head. Then he leaned back against the headboard, closing his eyes.

"Let's get the small talk out of the way." He sighed. "I have something to tell you."

Briescha stared at him as he rested there. His closed eyes crinkled in some private joke. His lips held a pleasant curve. The gentle rise and fall of his chest drew her eyes. Her mind drifted to a time so many years ago. Jacan napped in the meadow back then, the warmth of Paz beating down on his glistening topaz skin. In the meadow far away, Briescha, missing his closeness, had leaned in to kiss his cheek and brushed his lips instead. In her room now, sitting right beside him, she trembled. Her breath hitched.

He peered out of one squinted eye, his grin growing wider.

"You know me well enough already. I doubt anything has changed." Briescha felt the heat radiating from her cheeks as her voice wavered. She clamped her hands together in her lap.

"Fair enough." Jacan perked up, pitching forward in excitement. "I have a secret."

She blinked at him, forgetting her embarrassment for the moment. "Well?"

"I can't tell you, Briescha!" He fidgeted, sounding too giddy for his hulking size. He leaned in to deliver a harsh whisper. "It's a literal trade secret. You remember when we were young, we wondered why we didn't have space travel like other planets? Well, we don't know why they stopped." He gave a nervous chuckle, choosing his words wisely to keep his secret. "All I can say is Azelans really did try space travel in the past! The legends are true!"

She stared at him, her mouth agape. "Well, did they succeed?" She remembered her conversation with Kyros about Arkayn history gaps, sure that Jacan's knowledge would help.

Jacan opened his mouth to answer her, then pressed his lips together and rolled his eyes.

"Really? You're not telling?"

"Can't." His eyes still gleamed. "I probably already said too much. Silly me."

Brieschta bit her lip, forcing her scolding tone into something more manageable. "And I wonder why you're being so silly around me?"

Jacan blushed in response.

Brieschta pursed her lips and lifted an eyebrow. "All I have to do is touch you to learn everything."

He laughed then, a light, teasing, nervous sound that made the hairs on the back of her neck stand up again. He rubbed the nape of his neck with his hand and raised his eyebrows. "How true that is, *my* Princess!"

Brieschta gaped at him, a dozen awkward emotions freezing her in place. Then she giggled to alleviate that nervous churning in her gut. Jacan laughed with her until they were gasping to catch their breath. They spoke in hushed, excited voices through the night, catching up on every moment they'd missed.

Jacan grew quiet as Brieschta told him about the attempts on their lives, and various grumblings from citizens trying to denounce Silver. His jaw clenched and teeth grinded. Then she had to find another happy thing to share about their lives in Xepaqua to bring him out of his dark mindset of self-blame. He couldn't be in Xepaqua all the time! His work took him back to Forge Mountain. He was officially Forgebound.

Briescha couldn't allow him to dwell on things he couldn't remedy.

In the end, Briescha had more to say, since Jacan admitted his training and work grew monotonous and his focus single-minded. She didn't dare push further to get Jacan to reveal his secret. She was careful to close her mind to each innocent, teasing touch — a slap on his knee, a poke to his chest, a pinch of his cheek — so that she did not pull his secret by accident.

When at last Briescha's eyelids grew too heavy, she drifted against Jacan's chest and felt his strong arms encircle her. His heart pounded against her cheek, against the psychic barrier she erected to stay out of his head. He may have said something to her in those next moments. She may have mumbled an incoherent response, sighing at the sweetness that pulled her into a deep, comfortable sleep.

Briescha gasped, waking up to her door sliding open in the dim light. Who? Her stomach churned. Then she focused on the figure silhouetted in the doorway and breathed a sigh of relief.

"Kyros! Hello!" Briescha rubbed her eyes and looked with some confusion to where Jacan stirred beside her. When did she fall asleep? Her face burned with her proximity to Jacan and having been caught asleep by Kyros. "To what do we owe the honor?"

Kyros cast his dark, brooding gaze from Briescha, to Jacan and back again. "I came here to make sure you were safe. I heard the explosion from my office. Seems like you are...fine."

"Oh, we are quite safe! Hyperion performed an admirable service today, err, yesterday. You'd be proud of Silver, too." Briescha leapt to her feet, her embarrassment fading into doting pride over her sister. "She saved all those people!"

"You're incredibly late. And here I was," Jacan yawned mightily, a languid smile settling on his face, "thinking Kyros was the one who vowed to protect you guys!"

Kyros tensed, his hatred for Jacan unchanged, palpable.

"Jacan, don't pick a fight!" Briescha stepped between them. "Kyros is just protecting us in a different way now."

Kyros regarded Jacan for a long moment. His teeth grinded. "No." He sneered. "He's right. I should've been there for you."

"You have been!" Briescha clamped her hand on his arm. A swirl of conflicting emotions tore through her, incoherent and overwhelming. She pried her hand away and fell back against the wall, her chest heaving. Her psychic barrier had fallen as she awoke.

"What in the world did you do to her, Kyros?" Jacan spat venom, spanning the space between them in an instant.

"Nothing!" Kyros fussed over Briescha, alarm draining the acid from his voice. "This isn't the first time she's touched me!"

Jacan cursed, making no attempt to hide his distaste at that last statement. He shoved Kyros aside, swept Briescha off her feet and deposited her in the center of her bed. Her head reeled from half-emotions and fragmented images. The senseless barrage continued for some time. Since her brain couldn't process the contact, she fought to suppress it. Briescha struggled a long time to clear her mind of whatever troubled Kyros. When at last she could breathe, Briescha became aware of too much heat too close to her face.

Briescha waved them away. "It's not his fault. I was just sleepy and forgot to shield myself. Part of my training. It's been happening for over a year." Her waving hand slapped against another outstretched palm. "Silver! I'm sorry I woke you!"

Over a year. Silver's mind voice sounded sleepy, but concerned. *It still hurts you, though.*

Briescha blinked up at Silver. *Yeah, but don't tell them.*

I didn't have to tell them. She hauled Briescha up to a sitting position.

Both men stared back at her with haunted eyes full of worry.

Briescha sighed. "Stop that! I'm perfectly fine." She presented her unharmed limbs and face for their inspection.

Beyond them, the first rays of Paz shone behind the amethyst spires of Xepaqua. The warm glow raised her spirits. Briescha carefully erected her psychic barrier and snatched Kyros up in a big hug. He stiffened in her embrace, still too formal to give in. Silver jumped in and squeezed them both. Jacan sighed behind them.

Briescha released Kyros and stood beaming. "Thank you for taking time to check on us!" When he opened his mouth to apologize, she gave him a stern glare. He closed his mouth again and executed a deep bow.

"It is my duty," he whispered. "I'd like to report before I leave, if you have the time." Kyros glanced back and forth between Jacan and Briescha.

Jacan laughed when he caught the implication. Briescha blushed profusely. How did she manage to fall asleep in the same bed as Jacan? How irresponsible of her!

"I was just heading out, anyway." Jacan rested his hand on Briescha's shoulder. "I feel incredibly well rested for the small amount of sleeping we did."

Briescha pinched him hard on the soft

skin of his inner arm. He yelped. The brightness of Briescha's cheeks lit up the room. Yes, irresponsible indeed!

"Briescha here isn't accustomed to such vigorous late nights of activity, you see." That fake gloating tone! Another pinch from Briescha, another yelp. "Alright, I'll stop!" He laughed heartily.

"You may go on with your report, Kyros." Briescha smiled. "Ignore this idiot."

Kyros glared at Jacan a long time, his roiling emotions transparent in his pale eyes. Then he pulled his shoulders back and cleared his throat for the report. "We have suspects in custody who are likely involved in the bombing near the garden. They are currently under interrogation."

"Oh? That's great! Will they submit to a telepathic scan?"

"That's possible." Kyros glanced at Jacan. "The man who caught them is none other than the Master of the Forge himself, Ganan. He's currently part of the interrogation committee."

"Then you'll get your scans, Kyros." Jacan drew back his shoulders and grinned. "He's not just a dabbler in Forgecraft. He's known for his skills in persuasion."

"So I've noticed." Kyros wiped his expression and continued. "Repairs are underway on structures damaged in the attacks, and the Arkayn Council will meet once cleanup is concluded to determine how best to utilize the demolished building lot."

"How long until everything is set to rights?"

"Less than a week, if all goes as planned." Kyros stood at ease. "Permission to speak?"

"Always." Briescha wondered at his change of tone.

"Our future leaders were targeted only a

short distance from their place of business, on an auspicious day of celebration." His eyes pleaded with Silver, then Briescha. "It is possible that everything won't be set to rights, as you say. They involved your citizens, giving no regard for their safety. If they'll attack on such a large scale, you're not safe anywhere, with anyone." And with that statement, he gave a dismissive wave to Jacan, who worked his jaw. "We need to work harder to keep you safe."

"With the security measures of this building, the constant security detail all around shadowing our every step, and the security of the Arkayn Council Hall, what could we possibly do?" Briescha became incensed. "This new showing of power by Silver should prove that we don't need as much protection as even that. Is the other option more seclusion? I'll not have us chained and locked away like beasts. Silver would endure it at the expense of her free spirit if I told her it was necessary, but I'll not require such a fate of her. Yes, until we are immobile, gracing the Arkayn Council Hall ourselves, we will not live in chains. The Key is with Silver and I am with her, and as long as she is the possessor of the Key, we will be in danger. We may struggle, but we will prevail."

"I would rather that another carried the burden, to keep you both safe." Kyros lowered his voice to an anguished murmur.

Briescha cupped his face with her hands and willed him to gaze into her eyes. "I wouldn't wish such a burden on another, just as I told Deraddian years ago. Such astounding power belongs in the hands of someone born for it, or built for it. Silver is bound to this power, at the core of her soul, and she will live to bring the Great Peace Unequalled to Azela. She will release us from vice and avarice."

"You speak like Silver's place is a

prophecy rather than an unforeseen birthright." Kyros shifted his eyes from hers to Silver.

"No. But since she created the phrase 'The Great Peace Unequalled', folks have been deifying her for some reason, by some long forgotten theology theorem." Briescha felt Silver's disapproval in her mind. "Silver doesn't like it."

"Then why use it that way?"

"Because I'm only sure of one thing, and that one thing is standing next to us, wishing for all she's worth that I would shut up and let her go back to sleep."

Briescha released Kyros and kissed Silver on the cheek.

Kyros stood in stunned silence, emotions churning in his eyes again. Briescha didn't reach out to him again. Her shield held steady for that long, but with emotions that strong, she wasn't sure about touching him again.

Jacan laughed and hugged Silver. "That's my cue. Goodnight, er, good morning, little Empress. The rest of the family and Forgebound folks may be wondering about me. I'll head out and let you both recover!" His long gaze into Briescha's eyes left her stomach fluttering again. He took her hand and bowed to kiss it. Then he extended his hand to Kyros, who solemnly grasped it like a vice. "The lady has spoken. Let's show ourselves out. Besides, I'm pretty much a prisoner in here without one of them or Hyperion coming to my rescue."

Kyros bowed with a flourish, his jaw tense and his eyes unfathomable and transparent at the same time. Then he led the way into the hallway and down the stairs. Jacan grinned back at Briescha, then disappeared out the door.

She hissed, "Be good!" and heard a chuckle in response. Then she sighed, glad that Kyros wasn't prone to the shady side of his authority. Otherwise, Jacan could be in trouble.

Silly-head. Silver giggled. *You worry too much.*

That I do, she mused. She turned to her tousled bed and felt a tingle go up her spine.

Silver's mental link sparked with warmth and sweetness. *You slept well?*

Briescha blushed again. She remembered every word, every breath, and each little teasing touch that left her wanting more than she could rightfully take. The rhythm of his heart lingered in her mind at last, joining the past to the present in a constant thrum of desire. *Yes.*

She managed to meet Silver's eyes finally. Her cheeks hurt from their constant smiling and hot blushing. Silver's pensive expression stalled Briescha's rising guilt and tugged at her soaring heart. Briescha went to her, stretching out her arms.

Silver hugged her for a long time, squeezing until Briescha groaned. *I'm just so happy.*

I'm glad, but why? Briescha pulled back and gazed into Silver's gray eyes. Tears gathered at the corners but did not fall.

Because you have these wonderful feelings. Silver grinned. *You care about both of them so much, and your heart is fit to burst with your emotions. I mean, I love them, too, but it's not the same nature. That sweet feeling, I'd have you seek it out.*

Briescha stared, uncomprehending. *You know I can't pursue such a thing. I'd never leave you for a man!*

Silly! Silver pinched her cheeks hard, making Briescha wince. *This is just our job. Granted, it's an important job that takes up much of our lives. But I'd trade it all to see your face this happy!*

You were really listening to my rant, huh? Briescha stared again, regretting the weight she placed on Silver's shoulders. *If only it were that easy.*

Kyros just wants us safe. Silver shrugged and waved off his concerns. *But I have an order for you, my dear sister.*

Briescha laughed. *Oh? And what's that?*

When this big peace comes along, Silver drew her shoulders back regally, *and all the crap is laid to rest, you will follow your heart to the man you love and allow him to fill your days with those smiles for the rest of your life.*

Look who's the silly-head, now! Briescha tucked her face against Silver's neck and willed her tears not to fall. *If any man loves me half as much as you, I'll gladly follow your orders.* Silver squeezed her. Then she yawned into the stillness of their silent conversation.

We are on vacation, you know. Briescha hugged her. *Let's sleep in.*

Silver mumbled an agreement in Briescha's head and stumbled toward her bed in the next room. Briescha listened for the warm static in her head that meant Silver was asleep. She wondered at the selflessness of her sister. Knowing the road ahead was perilous, she smiled despite her fears.

Silver, bit by bit, showed how suited she is to be Empress. But to order Briescha to love someone else? Briescha couldn't see beyond the present, beyond each struggle toward an ultimate goal. She could feel her face grow warm, her heart flutter, the fine hair rise on the back of her neck. Allowing love in her life beyond her sister seemed impossible.

Briescha changed into a filmy camisole and underwear, kicking her sleep-wrinkled dress into a corner. She stared again at the twisted cover on her bed, at the impression Jacan's head had left in the folded pillow where he slept. Her heartrate quickened. A gorgeous, kind, sweet, funny and absolutely wonderful man had slept here, flesh to flesh with Briescha. *And I put up the barrier like some prude.* Her heart pounding, she looked toward the door. It was closed tight. Feeling foolish, she shrugged out of the camisole and slid her underwear to the floor. Now fully nude, she slid her hands down her sides, noticing how sensitive her skin felt. She stole a glance at the light streaming through the window and ordered the wall solid again.

She removed the barrier in her mind, desiring to hold onto her experience with Jacan, if just for a moment longer. Her breathing picked up as she sat on the bed. Her buttocks tingled as unseen fingers caressed her backside. Briescha whimpered, rolling her bottom harder against the sensation.

She slid her fingers across the silken sheet. Fragments of Jacan's emotions flooded her senses. She gasped and pulled away her hands. Then, braver still, she plunged her hands into the folds of the sheet and blanket. Jacan's heartbeat caressed her face again, sending a flush of warmth across her body that settled and flared in the unexplored depths of her anatomy.

Briescha closed her eyes and fell back into the embrace of Jacan's essence, an imprint made even stronger by the depth of his emotions. She pulled the sheet around her shoulders and raked it tight across her hard, sensitive nipples. She stifled a low cry and bit her lips together, allowing her power to draw out each desire and memory Jacan left for her.

Briescha writhed in his phantom embrace, her bare skin prickling and heated under his work-roughened hands, her back arching to meet his toned torso, her legs groping to encircle his lean hips. The blanket twisted and twined between her squirming legs and she rocked against the firmness it formed. Her breathing came faster, in time with the thrusting of her hips. *Harder*, she pleaded in her mind. *Oh, please, deeper!* His low growl sounded in her mind and thrilled her as phantom Jacan met each thrust with a force and depth that left her aching for more. One final push and her body stiffened in ecstasy, sending ripples of pleasure through her body in waves that lasted an hour. She panted his name in a soul-rattling whisper. Trembling and spent, she drifted off to sleep, feeling his arms around her as if he were more than an apparition conjured by her telepathy. Even the kiss he left on her forehead felt real.

13: DREAMSCAPE

Briescha paced before the chamber door, wringing her hands. A deep dread filled her belly. The silence of Silver's absence settled like a dome of senseless reverberation.

"She's been in there too long, Arcani."

She reflected on her tantric episode with Jacan's residual essence. Shame choked her. Outwardly, her cheeks burned with anger and frustration. Her unusual deep sleep had kept her from hearing Silver wake and enter the chamber.

"Paz is setting." Arcani set down her medical bag and leaned against the wall, crossing her arms over her chest. "She went in before dawn. That's her longest session yet. But to be fair, she spent a lifetime without actively using her power."

Briescha cast a nervous smile at Arcani. "Thank you for coming here. I don't mean to be a pest. You're probably right. I just can't shake the worry until I see her."

The console signaled an end to Silver's session, at long last. Briescha cried out in relief, embracing Arcani. The corridor rattled as the huge machine began its lengthy decompression cycle. Her aching head eased with each pulse from the chamber.

Her link with Silver sparked and prickled in Briescha's mind like long-dormant nerves awakening. The tingling gave way to pain — sharp, deafening jolts. Abnormal psychic pain, and what felt like an incomplete reconnection. Briescha fought for each breath, clamping her hands on her head.

"Briescha?" Arcani shook her, had been shaking her for some time. "Stay with me! Hey!"

Briescha felt a hard pinch on her cheek. That sharp physical ache drew her out of the psychic agony of the unusual reconnection. "The machine didn't keep me blocked until the pain subsided this time, for some reason. And there's something else missing."

"What in the world could be missing?"

Briescha shook her head and breathed easier, trying to calm her mind and sure that having Silver in her arms would reassure her. She focused on the blinking light that would turn green when Silver could stagger out, into her waiting arms. Arcani, ever confident and supportive, steadied Briescha on her feet.

When the door finally rolled open, Silver lay still on the floor's concave center. Static filled Briescha's mind. She rushed across the floor and dove at Silver's prone, unconscious body.

"Silver!" Briescha reached for her.

"Briescha, don't! Remember the last time you rejoined too quickly!" Arcani cried out in frustration. Briescha already touched Silver's shoulder. A kinetic crack sounded where their skin touched. Briescha fell limp over her sister.

The jolt to Briescha's brain jarred her through and through. Silver's disjointed dream flooded her eyes with horrors she had never witnessed. Pain and chains and slashing creatures. Monsters! A horde of monsters crawled out of a blackened lake of fire. The creatures took on shifting, grotesque shapes. Her heart pounded. *Is this the world she visits during her sessions?* Briescha turned to run.

Then Silver's pale hand flashed in the darkness, tearing through the inky surface. Briescha cried out. The soundless reverberation roared in her ears. She leapt toward the beacon of Silver's hand and pulled her from the dark, scorching lake. With her fingers and arms burning, Briescha pulled her sister far away from the fire, across the charred earth. The monsters followed. Then Silver dug in her heels. Briescha pulled again, but Silver would not budge. Terror gripped Briescha's heart. She turned to Silver. Her sister's face distorted in a hideous smirk. Silver opened her mouth. The ground trembled beneath her feet. The monsters halted their pursuit. Briescha pushed her way out of the dream as Silver's hot breath seared her face.

Briescha fell to the floor, heaving and coughing and screaming. She clutched her hands to her chest, unable to suppress the shrillness of her voice. She flailed when Arcani came near.

"Stop it this instant!" Arcani's order rang in the air. She snatched Briescha's flailing hands in her own. "Briescha! What happened?"

Arcani's alarmed voice made Briescha's stomach churn. She followed her foster mother's gaze to her hands. Still steaming and striped in white bands the width of Silver's fingers, Briescha's arms ached in the cool room. The splattering of black during the dream had seared oddly swirling scalds up her forearms.

"By the Golden Seer, child! What happened in there?" Arcani soaked a fine, smooth cloth with a red-tinged liquid and applied the compress to Briescha's injuries. The burning feeling died down. Arcani turned Briescha's wrists this way and that, inspecting the edges of her wounds. "Well, the burns didn't hit muscle. That's fortunate. But you'll have some scars to show for your effort. This skin," and Arcani traced the edges of Silver's handprint, "shows the worst damage. No need to worry, though. We'll force some food down your throat and you'll be feeling better in no time." She wrapped Briescha's wounds in shimmering white fabric, giving her a winning smile and a pat on the hand.

Briescha turned and focused on treating Silver. Briescha stared in horror at the routine checks Arcani conducted on Silver. Arcani's touch didn't bond the two into a hellish world of death and suffering. Then Briescha realized she was hysterical and forced her pulse into a regular rhythm. Of course, it wouldn't rub off on Arcani! Silver's voice only flowed through Briescha. And it was that voice Briescha longed to hear more than anything in her small world.

Static answered her again. Briescha drifted, focusing hard on speaking to Silver. But after a session so long, she was sure to be worn out.

"Hey, Briescha!" Arcani tugged on a lock of her hair. "Help me for a minute, will you?"

Arcani shouldered Silver's weight on one side and gestured that Briescha should take the other. "She's exhausted, and her body has claimed her in sleep. I'd say she feels no different than any other day after a trying ordeal. She won't wake up, but her switch isn't as easy for me to access. She's in no immediate danger from sleep." Arcani shrugged. "How's her brain?"

Briescha focused on the all-too-normal

sounding static. "Quiet, but here again." She sighed, partly in frustration and partly in relief. "When she sleeps, I can only hear when she dreams. And what I saw tonight! She has never dreamed like that before."

"You think it's what she deals with in the chamber?" Arcani knew Briescha's worrying mind all too well.

"Of course." Briescha felt the flutter of normal, mundane frustration rise in her belly. "She wouldn't have told me, of course, no matter how bad it hurt her."

"No, she wouldn't." Arcani grunted. Settling Silver on her bed downstairs, she straightened and stretched her back. "But you'd protect her the same way if you could."

Briescha hung her head.

"Let me keep an eye on Silver. You've been sequestered in here all day, and your doctor orders you to relax." Arcani pulled the cover up around Silver's chin. "I think I tucked her in often enough in the past to know what I'm doing. And I'll monitor her vitals and get in touch if anything changes."

Briescha shook her head in defiance.

Arcani gave her a stern look and shoved a meal bar in her hand. "I don't care how much influence you have in this city. You're still my patient. You will eat this. You will leave. You will come back when you have learned the meaning of rest. And I'll stay right here by her side. Someone is waiting for you down there."

"What? How did you know?"

"You wouldn't have heard him." Arcani dismissed Briescha's confusion. "You were too busy screaming to hear him trying to beat down the door."

Briescha gasped at Arcani's caustic remark. She hoped her blush to be mistaken for her comment, not her memory of last night's psychic event.

"Get out of here." Arcani laughed. "Do what's best for you right now."

Briescha threw her arms around Arcani's neck. She brushed her fingers against Silver's cheek. She did feel normal again, just sleepy. And when Briescha pushed beyond her fingers and into Silver's chest, she felt the switch there. There was plenty of light there, so she would follow Arcani's orders.

Having settled her sister to rest under Arcani's expert supervision, Briescha ordered the window open. She slowed her descent with telekinesis. Jacan waited, chatting with far too much exuberance among Bridfar's attending Hyperion guards. Jacan ducked his head when Briescha arrived, a light blush glowing on his cheeks. Dirco laughed at him. Briescha's heart fluttered with joy. She forgot for a moment about Silver's unsettling session in the chamber. She scolded the soldiers soundly for their gossip, in good spirits that Jacan had found friends among her favorite guards.

"Guard and gossip go hand in hand, Princess Briescha." Bridfar tucked his chin and saluted her. "But luckily, Lady Arcani stopped this guy from breaking down your door."

Jacan's stricken eyes peered down at her. "I was just trying to keep a promise." His smile hid none of his distress.

"I wasn't in any real danger, after all." Briescha tucked her hand into the bend of his elbow. She smiled to show him her relief. "I just reconnected a little too abruptly."

His jaw worked in silence.

"Really." She squeezed his arm. "Silver was having this horrible dream."

He dropped his chin and nodded. *Is he blushing?* Briescha led Jacan to the mid-city garden, with Dirco and Bridfar's other guards a respectful distance behind them. Ganan and the Forge crew teamed with local craftspeople to repair the damaged buildings and clear rubble from the lot. The city buildings stood strong and straight again, with plans underway to rebuild the destroyed tower.

The garden was a lower priority. Some structures had a few cracks left on them, with bits of amethyst sticking out at odd angles. Briescha felt her stomach churn. She clenched her fists, forcing down the fear that rose up. Static filled her mind with disjointed images and confusing sounds. Silver called out in her sleep. Her vision dimmed. She dropped her hands from Jacan's arm.

Briescha turned in the balmy night air in a slow circle that made the ends of her hair flow out, and then listened over her mental link for Silver. A dim nightmare rose in Silver's mind. She felt pain from an unseen injury. She flailed and accidentally hurt faceless people in an unending void. She cried out in her heart for someone to stop the pain! Briescha reined in her panic and sent out a wave of love and caring to her sister. Briescha pushed away the ones who laughed and comforted the ones who hurt. In Silver's dream, Briescha herself stopped the pain and soothed her sister into a peaceful, happy dream. Static sparked soon afterward. Silver sank back into a dreamless sleep.

Briescha pulled back her mind and propped her face on her fingers, wrapping the other arm across her chest against a sudden chill. The blurry nightmare followed Briescha. *At least this one is just a blurry mess!* But Briescha tried to shake off the feeling of despair her sister had projected.

Briescha shivered, unable to shake the

ominous feeling from Silver's dream. Jacan took her trembling hand and pulled her close. She couldn't stop shaking, even in the comfort of Jacan's embrace. He led her to the bench and bade her sit.

"Silver again?"

Briescha refocused her eyes. "I can feel it swimming around in here. Just take my mind off it. I'll be fine."

"What would you like to talk about?" He stroked her long hair with a calloused hand, tucking her cheek against his neck.

"Anything."

"I had a vivid daydream you might like to discuss."

Briescha felt the heat rise in her face. She pulled away from her safe place at his neck. Her eyes snapped intently to him. Her stomach fluttered.

"Okay. Ummm..." Jacan looked past her and lowered his voice. "I had a remarkably interesting daydream when I last left you to sleep. You were in it. And..." He blushed. "Let's just say it was very realistic."

Briescha's jaw dropped. "Did you? Did we...?"

From far away, a resonating hum drew her attention. She searched for the source, choosing to look anywhere but into Jacan's searching eyes until she gathered her thoughts. She dismissed the sound, sure that the laser cutting equipment was just cooling down.

"Briescha?" His voice cracked.

"I just heard something."

"Me, too. The sound of you evading a subject." Jacan leaned in to whisper in her ear. "And yes, I did. We did. And I've never felt more alive. Although it was rather awkward walking back with Kyros.

"Oh no," Briescha said, keenly embarrassed.

Yet still, the rasping of his voice quickened her pulse. His warm breath caressed her throat and flowed across her thinly-clad breasts, arousing her body to unfamiliar desires. She peered up at her warm, sweet Jacan. *I must tell him what we shared last night!* Her body trembled in emotion, sending waves of tension through her belly.

"What if I told you I had a similar dream?" She frowned, searching for the right way to tell him.

"I'd say I doubt it was as good as mine!" Jacan glanced to the guards in the distance, and then leaned in close. "The way we moved together..." He closed his eyes and reveled in the memory.

Briescha stared at him in awe, trying to control her pounding heart. "What if I told you it wasn't a daydream?" She traced his jawline with a light touch.

"Are you teasing me?" His breathing doubled. "Pretty sure I'd know if you really popped in for that kind of visit!"

"No." She pressed her lips to his ear. "What if I subconsciously wanted you to feel that way, and I may have wanted you so much that I projected this daydream?"

The hum in the distance returned, louder than before, thrumming in time with the beating of their hearts. The sound irritated Briescha's inner ear and canceled out the churning in her stomach.

He blinked several times. "Then we'd have a lon..."

Jacan's eyes clouded. He worked his jaw several times and couldn't force out the rest of his sentence. Then he collapsed against her chest. Briescha cried out in surprise. Her searching eyes found her guards crumpled in a motionless pile. Placing her hands over Jacan's chest, she tried to force light into his switch, to no avail. Everything she heard or felt faded from his body until even the switch disappeared in her mind.

All the while, the thrumming increased to a fever pitch. Her ears ached. Her mind fell away into an abyss of fear. The vibration in the air overtook her sight and she collapsed blindly into the dream. Faceless people shoved her toward a violent creature. She sought escape and found none. Even her screams disappeared into the formless void. She turned to face the monster, a desperate measure of prey attacking predator. The savage creature overpowered her. She saw her flesh slashed by hate-sharpened claws and screamed in horror, feeling her strength flow out of her body with each drop of blood.

She startled awake at the moment she faced death. A shudder jarred through the cold gemstone bench. The ground shook and hanging vases swung on their chains. Large crystal urns rattled off their pedestals and shattered on the luminescent pathway stones. Then, just as suddenly as it began, the shaking stopped.

Briescha reeled, her head still foggy with a horrific headache. She stared down at fresh blood dripping from her bandaged arms. The pain didn't register enough to rouse her. She gripped the soggy bandages and squeezed with all her might, using the pain to sober her mind. Her senses sharpened from the gloominess and terror of her nightmare. *An earthquake? With Silver nearing absolute power?* She forced her trembling body upright, pressing her hand to her head to temper the pain. She jostled Jacan at her side.

Jacan slumped to his side on the bench,

sprawling motionless with an arm and a leg drooping to the ground. Briescha cried out in fear, shaking him with all her strength. Still, she couldn't rouse him from some deep slumber. She leaned closer, touching his face with her fingers and concentrating hard on her diagnostic power, but a harsh static repelled her power. He was alive, she could tell, but unable to move, to hear, or to awaken. Terror gripped her, and she turned to the city, toward the tower she shared with Silver. Silence answered her summons. She trembled in fear. *Where is Silver?*

With a final regretful glance at Jacan's still body, she leapt into the air and toward her home, toward Silver. Beneath her, narrow fissures broke through Azela's crust, revealing thin lines of the glowing life force beneath. Her heart and mind ablaze at some treachery that caused Azela to turn against itself, Briescha descended to the balcony of the one place she feared to enter: Silver's fortified bedchamber.

A moment passed before Briescha could step forward on the ledge. A flutter in her chest prevented her from going in. An odd premonition stunned her. *What disturbs me about the doors?* Her hands rose of their own accord and traced the door seam. The amethyst edges were perfect, not a nick or chip to be found. Briescha somehow expected destruction of the doors, or at least some damage. Otherwise, how would anyone get in to hurt her?

A wave of realization flooded her and froze her hands on the door seam. Then the doors slid open by the power mechanism that acknowledged her bloodline. *By the Seer!* Had the future Empress let in her assailants? Did she know them?

"Arcani!" The midwife sprawled across the floor. Briescha stooped to check her vitals. She lived, albeit under the same static that affected Jacan. Briescha's hands trembled as they touched Arcani's throat. "It's far too quiet. No one else is here."

She could not decide which worried her more — finding Silver hurt in some way or not finding her at all. Who else had been in the tower? Only Hyperion had access to the building, and only answered to protocol in case of danger to the Empress. But they surely wouldn't have enough time to respond? Briescha felt furious. Her stomach knotted in worry. *I have no idea how long I've been unconscious!*

Her blood froze in her veins. The chamber! She took the curving steps three at a time until she reached the landing before the chamber door. Punching in an access code, she read a usage log. The chamber was inactive and had been since Silver's long session that left her unconscious. She opened the door and peered all around the empty circular room. Nothing caught her eye, so she turned to the computer again.

A snippet above that log drew Briescha's attention. Before Silver's long session, there was a very brief access session during which the machine wasn't even activated. Maintenance hadn't been scheduled at that time. Cameras hadn't been deemed necessary in the area — or Silver had forbidden them in order to protect Briescha — so Briescha commanded the computer to provide whatever specifics it could.

The sensitive floor registered the weight of two individuals, and by weight distribution estimated two adult men had entered the chamber and left within a half hour. The computer knew nothing else of the visit except the time. The fine hair raised on the back of Briescha's neck. That window of time occurred when Hyperion had searched the Tower, after the bomb attack!

Rage filled her.

She rushed back down to Silver's bedroom and pulled Arcani's limp body to a more comfortable position. Then she leaned into the scene of Silver's disappearance.

"Lights!"

The undamaged globes shone warm light from the perimeter of the bedroom. Writhing evident from her nightmare, Silver had wrinkled the top cover to her firm underbed. Silver's translucent warming blanket was nowhere to be found. Briescha looked for it beneath the bed and all around the room to no avail. She decided Silver had probably been wrapped in it at the point of departure. *Why would kidnappers take the time to make her comfortable? Were they merely hiding her conspicuous skin?*

She saw little evidence of any type of struggle. The only remaining item was the many-times folded bolt of a similar fabric that Silver used as a pillow. Briescha's brows furrowed her perfect opal forehead in desperation. She knelt across the bed and grabbed the pillow. Her outstretched bare foot slipped in the rubies Silver had cried. Briescha stopped her forward plunge. Still, her face brushed against the folded pillow before she had caught herself.

A torrent of mixed emotions flowed through her: love, trust, fear, worry, pain and numbness. She grasped the pillow with both clenched fists and fell to her side on the bed, letting the feelings course through her head and flow down her limbs. Her teeth clamped shut with the intensity of it. Then she was limp. Sobs tore through her throat, a wrenching pain so deep it shook her soul. The fabric, for so long the place where her sister's head rested, had retained her essence in her final moments before she was taken. Again, oddly, she saw no clear pictures of the struggle. Only muddled shadows. What power affected even Silver's acute abilities? Briescha clutched the cloth to her breast as she swung her legs down and sat upright.

Her feet rested on the layer of rubies again. The tears of the Silver Empress — so full of sadness and pain! Briescha leaned forward to see them twinkle in the dim light. Something amid the stones caught her eye. She spun to kneel on the floor.

"Brighter!" she commanded. The wall lights flooded the room with glaring light.

Her sparkling eyes closed halfway in adjustment to the light. Then she clearly observed the curious substance covering several rubies. Blood, perhaps. Probably Azelan blood. Someone cut his or her foot here in pursuit of the Empress. After all, Azelans wore foot coverings sparingly, as making their gemmed skin less visible to their comrades was distasteful in their tradition. Someone was barefoot when kidnapping Silver. She reached to touch the blood. Only a dull ache of guilt remained for her powers to pick up. It was too old a sample to get a name or a face. The scattering of rubies suggested a larger Azelan, perhaps one of the giants. Smaller concavities pointed toward someone who possessed smaller feet. Briescha looked closer at these narrow indentions. They appeared deeper toward the toe with a space for the instep, and a sharply delineated heel depression. That person wore a heeled boot — more a foot protection than decoration.

Silver? She cried out in her mind. *Where are you? Why won't you answer me?*

Briescha unfolded Silver's pillow near the bed. She knelt and cupped her hands around the pile of ruby tears and began sweeping them into a mound, clamping her lips to push back the confusion and fear she felt. Her unsteady hands gathered them onto Silver's unfolded pillow, ignoring the strong emotions tied to each small gem. She dug through a drawer and found a fine silken cord to tie off the pouch she made and a pair of shears to trim away the excess fabric.

Briescha, grim-faced, rose to her feet and looked around the room. She placed a kiss on Arcani's cheek. Then Briescha stepped out of the room, onto the balcony. She stared back and forth between the ledge and the room, her gut churning with some revelation she missed. On the banister that circled the balcony, she noticed scrapes and scuffs. She touched the surface and received a strong impression of something mechanical, a hulking machine churning the air outside the tower. Then she gasped. They arrived and left by the balcony! But what machine had she seen? She screamed in frustration. *What's going on here?*

14: WORMWOOD

From the tower's vantage point, she viewed Xepaqua glowing serenely violet in the light from Paz. Her hands clutched the banister, over the scuffed mark. She focused on what little information she could glean from that contact. Finding little of use there, she leaned forward to view buildings beyond the tower to get her bearings. By the arriving dawn, she knew she'd lost almost half a day, not just mere moments as she thought. Darkness had not yet passed, but the predawn gleam of Paz revealed the extent of damage to surrounding structures.

Some of Xepaqua's peripheral structures fractured; others had collapsed completely. The silence bore evidence to further problems. *Where are the Sentients?* Not even the Avians rustled the breeze with their gleaming wings or pierced the quiet with their clear voices. Briescha listened, with both ears and mind.

She closed her eyes on the sight beyond, and opened her other senses. She dug her fingers into the handrail and concentrated. A faint light emanated from her tense body, flowing like a shimmering smoke until it swirled back around her. Briescha felt the air vibrate, bringing her vital knowledge. Deep beneath the surface, the planet groaned. Briescha reached deeper, farther; the pale light both emanated from her and permeated her body, returning wisps of feeling and emotion.

Her power as yet unrealized, she pushed beyond experience to find the others. Then a fading, wavering strength approached her mind. Someone's consciousness touched hers with a single plea — *help!* Low pulses of life sprang up in the vicinity of the first, each weaker than the last. She immersed herself in the feelings — fear, confusion, helplessness, and betrayal — until she was a part of their suffering. *Who, where?* Their fear became her own. Still, she couldn't locate them, her mind muddled again. A strong force interfered with her power. The pain came in waves, wracking Briescha mentally with a physically realized agony so overpowering that she could not tear away her consciousness. Someone, something was killing them all!

Sentients cried out and writhed on a cold, foreign floor. Briescha felt the hard floor beneath her as if she laid there and tried to look up through eyes not her own. Backlit and cast in shadows, a large figure with a sharp-edged club grunted as he swung the big weapon with a loud crack outside her line of vision. He mumbled almost in sorrow at her mental host. A heaviness in the way he spoke felt familiar to her. Pain filled his voice, some sadness she couldn't discern through ringing ears. She saw dim visions where several of her fellow Sentients lay mangled and dead or dying in expanding pools of their own pale, glowing blood. The light of life dissipated as it cooled and crusted around them. She lifted her host's head slightly, painfully — for something was broken in his neck — and glimpsed a slender figure silhouetted in a bright corridor. The figure was a man, for all his graceful manner and flowing hair, who turned from his departure to gaze at her host. He tilted his head to one side and spoke in a velvet Azelan dialect.

"Impressive that you've awakened, Sentient." His low voice brimmed with quiet purpose. "But for all your power, you have no dominion here." He paused. She felt his close scrutiny and realized too late what he implied.

"Your sister will never rule Azela. She is too gentle for such a fate. I will ensure Azela's future, and where I take her, you cannot follow." His last words rasped in his throat. He gestured to the large figure with the club, who raised his weapon over the dying body of Briescha's host and comrade.

The larger man looked back without acting. Briescha saw the other shake his head. He then tilted his chin sharply, indicating his wishes to the giant.

"Who...?" she choked out through blood soaked lips.

She couldn't place the familiar voices through that body's damaged hearing. She began to doubt she recognized them. But the club fell. The speaker turned toward the light. She thought his hands clenched in fists at his sides. She saw his head drop forward. The eyes through which she saw began to cloud over and numbness crept across her body.

Briescha ripped herself from that body and returned to her own at the moment when death could have taken them both. Her own body ravaged by psychic agonies, she collapsed into spasms of new pain and mental torment. Her tears fell as diamonds of unprecedented anguish; her blood felt cold within her. She curled up stiffly on the balcony, her entire being disgusted with her helplessness.

"I allowed them to take you away. Blindly! In a cursed spaceship!" She beat the floor with her fists. "By the Golden Seer, I've failed. Forgive me, my dear Silver! I failed in my promise to you!" Briescha screamed, her voice hoarse. A numbness born of apathy crept into her mind, echoing in the silence of Silver's absence.

Then Briescha felt the full brunt of her sister's mental presence. Silver cried out across the expanse of space between them. The scream reverberated through Briescha's skull. *They're hurting her!* The numbness in Briescha's heart burnt away in the fire of her anger. She scrambled to her knees, eyeing the mound of teardiamonds she had cried for her sister. She pulled a handful toward her, then the scream came again.

Silver's screaming cry gave way to terrified mumbling. She pleaded with Briescha. *Sister! Sister! Come! Please! Come! They hurt me!*

Just as quickly, Silver was gone. The silence left Briescha trembling as much from the shock of Silver's absence as the aching of her body. Silver's terrifying plea a catalyst, the fact that Silver lived an empowerment, Briescha clawed her way to standing, bracing herself on trembling legs. "They hurt you. They stole you away from me. That fool plots your fate." Her free hand grasped the silken bag of rubies from the floor, into which she shoved the handful of teardiamonds. She knelt to gather every last stone into the pouch. "I have just decided his fate." Briescha cinched the bag closed and rose to her full height. "I don't know how, Silver, but I'll come for you. Endure. I'll soon be there!"

Coldness arose in her breast at the arrogance of that man, and his bold foolishness at taking Silver away. All Silver's hard work would dissipate. All of Azela would return to the tumult of bygone days, perhaps even worse. And no one knew how that may affect Silver! But why the clenched fists and drooping head as he walked away? *Is it remorse he feels?*

Briescha's blood boiled in her chest. *I'll make sure he regrets every single moment!* She cleared the handrail with a single bound and watched the crumbling city blur while she made her way to the Arkayn Council Hall.

She dropped to the glowing paving stones that lined the courtyard. All the fragile flowers had been crushed and trampled. Someone tried to defile the legendary statues, cutting away at dear Dezul's twining lapis lazuli horn, cracking the wings on the great ruby Avian of the Forge, and the Draklian's sparkling diamond eyes had deep gouges all around. Each was desecrated at the center of power: the Mietina his magical horn, the Avian her wings and the Draklian his all-seeing eyes. Surrounding structures had much more crushing damage that hadn't occurred during the quake. Someone had reacted with rage when the statues weren't as fragile as he or she hoped.

"Serves you right, monsters." Briescha turned to the entryway of the Hall. A flutter of memory — Silver speaking in an unknown tongue to Dezul — left her wondering how right they were about the statues through the years. "If those creatures are real and their parts that important, you don't deserve them."

Shoving her way through the entrance, Briescha barreled down the corridor. Her bare feet slipped in some moisture on the slick crystal floor. She pitched forward, stubbing her wrists and knees when she caught her weight. Beneath her hands, blood cooled and crusted, making the floor slick. Her hands trembled. The substance sent a flood of terror and pain through her addled mind.

Groaning, she gazed out and into the face of another Sentient. The man's eyes had clouded and the light had gone from his skin some time ago. Briescha cried out and scrambled back. She crawled and stumbled over lifeless arms and legs. Contorted faces of slain Azelans lined her path, their blood crusting and caking all around their bodies.

She screamed and compelled her body to rise. She focused on the gigantic double doors leading into the Inner Sanctum, to safety. Her legs propelled her down the hall. She glanced neither left nor right. She knew those people, recognized their mouths and eyes, twisted though they were. She knew they had screamed and screamed, then died in agony. Then she stopped cold at the entrance to her destination. In huge, ambling letters of crusted blood was emblazoned a phrase that curdled her blood.

The Golden Seer's corpse rots in the soil. A long death to the Silver!

Briescha uttered under her breath every foul Azelan curse she had heard. When she turned, the dead stared back at her. So many had died, but to what end? Head lowered in dread, she pulled open the desecrated double doors. As the warm interior air of the Inner Sanctum rushed over her face, she opened her eyes on a terrible, dark stillness. The Arkayn Council's energizing effect on the huge oval room, the kinetic atmosphere that drained even Briescha, had dissipated. She sensed only a very faint thrumming pulse here and there, some fading with each breath she took.

Briescha frowned. Each Arkayn had a distinctive backlit shadow even in the dark. Often a Council attendee, Briescha knew their familiar arrangement throughout the Hall had been upturned. The statuesque figures that once throbbed with power and vitality were no longer in place. Her heart twisted in fear. Briescha stepped forward across the inlaid floor with a mosaic map of Azela, her feet finding a familiar path. She gazed with growing uneasiness all around the many-tiered sapphire room.

"Spotlights! Now!" Briescha ordered, her voice barely a whisper.

The soft, tinted light filtered through thin sheets of precious gems to illuminate each Arkayn. Not one of the lights struck its subject. Briescha saw mounds and chunks of crystals and gemstones scattered across the floor around each special setup, each corresponding to the Arkayn who occupied the area.

"No, please!" Briescha's stomach churned. She clutched her trembling hands to her chest. Briescha rushed to the closest Arkayn. His long ruby hair and blue-topaz skin had slowly crystallized, but were distinctive to identify. Briescha clenched her teeth and fought back tears. She stroked the smooth exterior that had been the surface of his shoulder and parts of his internal anatomy that she knew to be gem-flesh.

"Oh, Sladen! You poor fool!" She knelt and touched the remainder of his destroyed face. His bitterness, his essence, flowed from his flesh into her fingers, and then faded into nothing. There was no deception. Sladen lay in pieces at her feet. "Irritating though you were, you didn't deserve this."

"Who would do this?" No one answered. The raw silence of Silver's absence blended with the terrifying stillness of the Inner Sanctum. Briescha carried her denial around the dome to each of the shattered Arkayns. She wavered with each step. Then she stumbled over the feet and long robes of a visitor who had fallen in the corridor.

"Caslorius!" Briescha knelt and rolled him

onto his back. She prodded his gaunt face with clumsy, trembling fingers. Her heart raced as she pressed her forehead to his. She sought his switch, but found it encompassed by the same darkness as the others. Briescha cried out in her spirit, so thankful at least that he lived. *Father!* She forced her light into the darkness around his switch, channeling all her will into the single, desperate act. The jolt cleared his consciousness of the enshrouding fog and shook Briescha to the core.

Caslorius opened his amethyst eyes on his grief-stricken daughter, and pushed his body upright. Briescha rocked back on her heels, trying hard to regain her composure. The neural connection to her father sparked. For a moment, he gazed into the eyes of Rascha. A great swell of sorrow arose in his core and flooded outward, past the turmoil of his abrupt awakening and into the mind of his daughter. Caslorius took her hand, closed his eyes and gently severed the connection. His calculated façade returned.

"Father?" A title she never used for Caslorius. Her quivering lip turned down in an uncharacteristic pout. Her father's sorrow ached in her chest. She clutched his hand to her face, holding back tears that threatened to fall. The events of the past few hours — the past few years — rushed to ensnare her. She tried to form the words she needed to say, but nothing came out when she tried to speak.

Caslorius pulled Briescha to his chest in a long embrace. "Your mother would be proud of you two." He squeezed her shoulders and held her at arms' length, reading her face.

One long look into Briescha's eyes and he knew. "Silver's gone?" Something akin to rage billowed in his quiet tone. Briescha nodded and bit her lips together.

Then the words spilled out. She told him how the kidnappers had come into Silver's room without damaging the entry. She told him about the dying Azelans on the metal floor. She sputtered and clamped her hand over her mouth, her throat tight with emotion. Caslorius held her tight.

"I remember someone entering the Hall, then the fog settled over the whole place." Caslorius glanced around him. "I struggled to move, but made it this far before it — whatever it was — shut me down. I saw Azelans with clubs." Caslorius clenched his jaw and pressed his lips in a tight line. "They attacked them! The whole bottom row of the Arkayn Council, defenseless, shattered before my eyes. I couldn't cry out. I couldn't stop them. I was useless."

"Stop." Briescha found her voice. "Silver would scold us for saying we were useless!"

"So she would." Caslorius rubbed his eyes with his fine, long fingers.

Briescha forced a terrifying subject. "What happens if the Arkayns die? What will happen to the Archives if the Arkayns die?"

Caslorius wracked his brain for a long moment. "Centuries of wisdom would dissipate if they all perish. But we will have to confirm if they've orchestrated an extensive destruction by attacking the outlying Council Halls." He dug his fingers into his scalp and groaned with the implications of a wide-scale attack. "All Arkayn Council members can access the Archives, though some specialize in the Archives. But as each Arkayn dies, the others absorb their connection. It's usually balanced by new Azelans with Power Traits reaching Arkayn status."

"But if many Arkayns die suddenly, those who remain would suffer physical pain and psychic trauma beyond our understanding." Briescha glanced around the room at piles of rubble that represented her precious Council. Her heart hurt. Their suffering doubled as they died.

Caslorius sighed. "Yes. It would be rather gruesome. And those who remained would most likely be overwhelmed to the point of a psychic break."

A familiar but tired voice echoed in the stillness of the Hall. "You have little faith, dear Caslorius, in my bloodline's legendary determination."

Briescha's heart sprang high with hope. "Darasha!" She scrambled to her feet and went hurtling up the tiers with Caslorius on her heels.

As she ran up the tiers, she noticed that other Councilmembers had sustained minor damage. She stepped warily around larger chunks of gem-flesh. The energies from those Arkayns ebbed and flowed, dissipating with each cycle until they died. Even minor damage forced them to lose hold of their physical bodies. Briescha's one hope, Darasha, lay ahead.

"They lost their zeal about halfway up." Caslorius spat out the observation. He mumbled a prayer over each dead Arkayn, committing their sacrifice to memory for the ceremonies that would follow.

Other faint whispers of life echoed within the dying statues as Briescha rushed along the upper tier. Briescha saw Darasha—a vision of perfection sitting primly on the sapphire bench beside a pillar, her hands clasped serenely on her lap, ankles crossed, and her head turned slightly to the left and her chin tilted up as she gazed toward the heavens with her last physical breath. The great waves of her long ebony hair spread out all around her on the bench, perfectly framing her pale opalescent skin. Sparkling eyes of emerald gazed outward and upward, into the cosmos itself, searching out deep secrets and storing them in her essence. Definitely a relation of Briescha's, even their small noses had a similar tilt. Relief spilled out of her in a gusty sigh shaken with sobs.

She fell into Darasha's lap with a guttural flood of joy. Darasha's glow arose as if in hiding, growing brighter with each moment.

"Briescha, Caslorius." Darasha's immobile form shone light all around, brighter than Briescha had ever remembered. "They dulled our senses somehow. But they destroyed my brethren, my fellow Arkayns!"

"It appears, by my count, you are the last left alive in Xepaqua." Caslorius managed a reverent bow, then retreated into the scathing fury Briescha sensed from him. "We don't know about the outlying Halls yet."

"Yes." Darasha grew quiet. Briescha knew she was counting and found wanting. "With each death, I felt the flood of power. I had to focus on harnessing the power. It nearly drove me mad. I managed enough to drive them away before they completed their work! But the power has settled for the moment. Yet so many have perished!"

Briescha shuddered, remembering the mangled bodies of her countrymen in the corridor. *They were just visitors who got in the way!*

"But as they killed more and more, I felt the power flow into me. I regained my consciousness. I couldn't stop them by the time I was in control." Darasha's placid face betrayed none of the guilt she felt. "But I belicve I drove them away before they could finish everything they set out to do." A tone of sorrow welled in Darasha's voice as her consciousness drifted around the Council Hall once more. "Not in enough time for the Arkayns, though."

Briescha laid a hand on the cool hard

surface of the lady's shoulder. Darasha sounded weary but energized. "They took our dear Silver from Azela?"

"Yes." Briescha coughed, her voice barely audible over the tightness in her throat. "I can't hear her anymore! I haven't even the power to follow her. I need to find her and bring her home, at whatever cost!"

"Nonsense," Darasha began. Her internal light flickered rapidly as she sifted through centuries of information. "Remember when we realized that certain information has to be unlocked with the right request? Something just opened up with your intent. The right request, a soulful, sincere request."

"You know how to find her?" Briescha's heart gave a leap of hope. "Please, quickly!"

"You know the rumor regarding failed space travel? At great risk, we built a ship. All of diamond and crystal, powered by the heart of Azela and guided by a Sentient Azelan with uncharted power," Darasha recounted.

Briescha stared at her in shock. "What does all that mean? That we did travel before?"

"No. They couldn't find a suitable Sentient." She focused in silence again. "They couldn't develop artificial intelligence advanced enough to serve as core processor. Their resolution was to infuse the vessel with an Arkayn soul, our most advanced processing system on Azela. The heart of Azela is likely a chunk of the planet's core for a power source."

"That's what Kyros meant by transfer of power." Briescha glanced up at Caslorius, past the shadows that danced in his eyes. "They've attempted it before, into a ship!"

"Yes, but this little corner of the archives comes with a warning. All involved died."

Briescha sobered at that revelation, burying her face in her hands. "Then what can we do?"

"We shall do what our family does. Overcome." Darasha's pride arose in the pulsing green light that emanated from her. Once again, Briescha felt the thrumming power of the Council's presence. She took heart from Darasha's confidence.

"You must know, dear Briescha, they will be relieved Silver is gone." Caslorius choked on those vile words. "They'll welcome you in her place." He included the Inner Sanctum in his expansive gesture. "And then they will beg you to stay." Caslorius laid a thin hand on Briescha's shoulder. "I myself have half a mind to beg you."

"Then I am being selfish?"

"By standards of a ruler and due protocol, yes." Her father drew her to him once more. "But you are Silver's one true protector. If anyone can find her and bring her back, you can."

"What should I do?" Briescha trembled all over. "The planet will turn on itself. People will die."

"If your concern is for us, Azela will survive. It has survived far worse in the past, I venture to claim." Caslorius turned to Darasha, who confirmed his statement. "And if my suspicions are correct," and his eyes grew dark again, "Silver will suffer far worse for what they are planning."

"They'll break her down, and then they'll try to take her power?" Darasha's voice trembled in rage. "There's no way she could survive that!"

"If they succeed," Caslorius clenched his fists at Briescha's side, "they'll return to Azela to claim Silver's place as ruler."

"I'll die first." Briescha felt her own rage well up, roiling and seething in her chest. "Selfish or not, I've made my choice. I'll go to her, wherever she is."

"Then it is decided." Darasha spoke with an air of finality. "I'll get ready."

"Is that wise?" Caslorius slumped forward. Briescha noticed the habit was identical to Silver's. Her chest hurt again.

Darasha scoffed at his apprehension. "Wisdom has done little to prevent this situation. I'd rather do something useful than rot in this shell when my family needs me! And don't start on me over risk and danger and loss. You may be horrible at showing it, but you miss your little girl as much as I!"

Caslorius dropped his head, defeated. "Holding back is something I've done too long."

Though her mind reeled in confusion, Briescha struggled to process her next step. "The people will be so scared, even if they are relieved. They'll trade one fear for another."

"I will speak to them." Her father's soft voice broke on the last word. He touched her shoulder, an urgency in his eyes. "I want you to know how much I love you both."

"Oh, hush." Briescha waved off his affection. *That's enough cryptic references and all-too-late emotions!* "There'll be time for that when we've sorted this out and my sister is back. Also, you guys are acting like I can just hop on a passing comet and ride my way out of this place! I need some answers before I can function in this plan." She pounded her fist into her hand to emphasize each point she made.

He stared at her with his mouth agape.

Darasha gave a dark chuckle. "There's that no-nonsense temper! She reminds you of Rascha even more now, yes?"

"She does." Caslorius grinned past the sadness on his face. "I'm so sorry I stayed away all this time, my dear daughter. If only I could..."

"Enough. You're already talking like

there's a definite way for me to follow her! I don't like offers of possibility. I want something solid and real."

Darasha unfiltered her power long enough to calm Briescha's emotions. "Your friend with the Forge secret? In light of these recent developments, he'll be granted permission to share his secret. That will be your solid, real answer. By the time he's made preparations on his end, I'll be ready here. I'm going with you."

"Are you sure we can make this happen?" Her rage curbed by Darasha's flow of love, Briescha settled for wringing her hands. "I mean, do you really think we can go to her?"

"We will, by whatever means necessary."

Briescha breathed deeply. She forced down her hope until she could deal with another pressing matter. "Father, would you be able to rule them in our absence? With Ganan's help?"

"I will." Caslorius glanced around the Council Hall. "But I have concern over matters of government. If our kidnappers so easily infiltrated the Tower, and left no damage as you said, then my personal trust in Hyperion has fallen."

Briescha considered the possibility that Hyperion could be behind the kidnapping. Her heart sank. "Kyros will let us know who can be trusted."

"Then we'll worry about that when we speak to Kyros. If you want to take any companions on your journey, I recommend leaving anyone associated with Hyperion here, in case they're in on this coup. Those who remain would be of little use in a conflict. You'll need experienced warriors."

"I'll need Unatans, then." Briescha nodded, steeling her mind for the first stop she would make on her journey.

"If they can look beyond whatever caused

our age-old hatred."

"If they can't, I'll have to make them."

"I've no doubt that you will." Darasha's glow flickered. "I must prepare now, and you both have much to accomplish. I will serve Azela in this small way, and may one day have the opportunity to look down from our Star, hand in hand with the Golden Seer, and see that my sacrifice has served its purpose."

"But Darasha, is this the right path?" Brieścha couldn't calm the frantic beating of her heart. "I have so many responsibilities."

"Yet only one truly rules your heart."

That crushed Brieścha's line of thought. Silver's face, her essence flooded Brieścha's mind and memory. The aching absence engulfed her spirit in despair. "It'll take a miracle to get to her!"

"Don't you remember what I told you? Love, my dear child, is a master at miracles." She nudged Brieścha on her way in a wave of bittersweet tenderness. "Now go with your father and see this atrocious work laid to rest."

Brieścha forced each foot to move forward, encumbered though they were by the weight of the sin around her and the undertaking that lay before her. Caslorius mumbled behind her as he committed names of victims to memory. Brieścha stared again at the carnage outside the horrific Inner Sanctum, at the curse on the blood-smeared doors, and stepped into the bright morning.

"They've awoken." Caslorius gestured to the Sentients who had stirred, shaking and clutching their heads in confusion, pain and grogginess. "We can't let them into the Inner Sanctum until we've processed the scene."

"Agreed." Brieścha stared across the group that gathered. Her stomach flipped when a contingent of Hyperion appeared on scene. Then she breathed a sigh of relief. "Commander Bridfar!"

Bridfar led his group through the center of the trampled courtyard. Deep blue encircled his eyes. A long gash split his cheek. The blood had dried and the wound sealed with a long scab. But he and Dirco and many of his other troops arrived. Their heavy breathing and damaged uniforms alluded to a struggle in the lost moments or hours past.

"Princess Briescha!" Bridfar bowed.

"Report, Commander!" Her voice broke. She already knew his first news.

"Per protocol, we could not locate and secure our future Empress at your dwelling." He stared into her eyes and therein saw the many sorrows she tried to hide. "I left several men to process the Tower scene, because we do suspect foul play." Then his voice softened. "We won't find her inside the Hall?"

Briescha shook her head. She lost her voice to the pain inside and bit her lips closed until she could speak clearly again. "She is no longer in Xepaqua, nor any other place on Azela."

Bridfar's eyes darkened yet further. "At the very least, we have secured our Princess." He ran his long, work-roughened fingers through his tousled hair. He glanced around at the Sentients who gathered. His voice dropped. "Our second protocol is the safety of the Arkayn Council. What lies beyond those doors?"

"A scene you must process, yet with great care." Caslorius gripped Bridfar's arm when he stepped toward them. "Do not betray my daughter's trust, Commander."

"I'm not your average soldier, Minister Caslorius." Bridfar jerked his arm from his grip. "Their safety is my one true goal, by an oath that I failed to uphold, because some spineless coward put us to sleep rather than facing me with honor." He brushed past Caslorius. "I am in no mood for posturing regarding my sworn duty as you now posture in the role of fatherhood."

Caslorius opened and closed his mouth, having thought better of his response.

"Now tell me what happened?" Bridfar leaned in to Briescha's distraught face.

"They're dead, Commander." Her eyes glazed over as she saw each face, each contorted look of horror, each scattering of gemflesh. "Only Darasha remains, because she drove them off with her increased power."

Bridfar made no attempt to hide the shock in his eyes. "They must've set out to destroy our Council from the beginning. Silver, but forgive me... Silver alone would've been sufficient for some type of ransom. We'll overturn every rock if we must to make sure she's not still here. I swear it."

"I'm certain she is gone."

Bridfar stared into her alarmed eyes and heard the tremor in her voice. His voice came out softly. "Until we know for sure, we must determine who is behind this horrible attack. And we must gather as much evidence as possible before anyone enters this place."

Briescha's mind drifted back to the death in the Hall, the desecration in the Inner Sanctum. She shuddered. "Have you seen Kyros? He must be informed when he is found!"

"That's a problem." Bridfar narrowed his eyes. "I haven't seen even his shadow since I've awoken! But keep your wits about you, and take care who you trust. The kidnapper may still be present and may wish you harm. I'll leave you in Dirco's capable hands while we prepare the scene for forensics. I'll be right on the other side of those doors if you need me, okay?"

Briescha bit her lips to keep from crying.

Bridfar clapped his hand on her shoulder and gave it a comforting squeeze. Then he swept past her into the horror she had left.

Dirco joined her. He tensed at her side. Feeling eyes on her back, Briescha turned to face the crowd. Their low mumbling rose to a fever pitch. The group pressed in on all sides, hemming Briescha, Dirco and Caslorius onto the small platform leading into the Sanctum. The anger and nervousness and whirling confusion flowed in waves.

Briescha raised her hands in a placatory gesture and called for order so she could speak. The group droned on, their panicked chatter growing louder. Briescha suppressed her rising panic. She searched in her mind for the purest feeling of love and calm she could muster, a bittersweet moment in the meadow back home at Forge Mountain with all her favorite people in the whole world. Then Briescha focused that one pure emotion into a soothing wave of calmness. The air sparked with invisible psychological shields, both from mechanical devices attached to belts and armbands and reflexive natural barriers throughout the assembly. The Sentients could not be reached by her well-intentioned manipulation.

"Listen to me!" Briescha shut down the fount of calm and unleashed her frustration. "The Silver Empress is gone!"

Tense quietness fell on the group. Then the tumult returned. Amid cheers, gasps of shock and a smattering of outrage, Caslorius stepped forward.

"Silence!" He raised both hands and leveled those who cheered with a piercing stare. Stillness returned. "The Silver Empress has been kidnapped and taken from our dear planet. We have reason to believe the same perpetrators have committed the unthinkable atrocities that have befallen those who lie beyond the doors to the Arkayn Council Hall. This horrible travesty will be investigated and anyone found involved will be prosecuted to the fullest extent of the law."

"Is my father still in there?" a gentleman cried from the group. "He left for Council last evening and hasn't returned."

"We are currently processing the crime scene and will release full reports later. However, I regret that his name is among those in the Farewell Song."

Caslorius patiently provided the same answer to a score of other citizens in attendance. He called for order again amidst the outcry. He recounted the events of the lost hours in minute detail, sparing certain details privy to the investigation.

With Caslorius handling the citizens, Briescha scanned the gathering. One of Bridfar's men skirted the large crowd, pushing past those close to the entry platform to where Briescha and Caslorius stood. Noticing the young man's arrival, Caslorius bowed his apology to the crowd. Briescha stepped back as the man mounted the steps in a bound. He executed a hurried bow to Briescha and Caslorius. Then he saluted Dirco, who had intercepted him.

Dirco acknowledged the recruit's gesture. "Report, recruit." He glanced over the soldier's shoulder. "And discreetly."

"Sir!" He paused to catch his breath, placing the glow tablet report in Dirco's hands. "There is news from the Tower, and more."

"Give us the summary." Dirco's soft voice rasped with cautionary authority.

"Our investigators found a device in the Tower's compression chamber room." His fingers outlined a cube in the air. "It was hidden in the central pressurization node and had a remote bypass circuit wired directly into the system's mainframe."

"Function?" Dirco ventured, his brow furrowed.

"Speculative, right now." The recruit flailed in frustration. "The investigators can only ascertain that it was activated recently and continued functioning until late last night. Some sort of amplification. The timestamp indicates an overlap that coincides with our Empress' last session."

Briescha's stomach fluttered and knotted into a tight ball. "Oh no! Silver was unconscious after the last session, and I felt it was unnatural. But they targeted her so she'd be weak?"

"It appears so, our Princess." The soldier cleared his throat and pressed his lips together.

Briescha peered at him. He faltered. "What else?"

"Kyros is missing."

Briescha stared, uncomprehending. She wavered on her feet. Dirco caught her shoulders, keeping her upright. Her head spun with a dozen explanations, all of which left her reeling.

"I'm sure there's a perfectly good explanation for his absence." Caslorius lifted Briescha's drooping chin with a finger. "We'll sort it all out."

"None of this adds up. Is he dead? Is he wounded somewhere?" In her memory, Kyros laid nearly dead in the meadow as Silver had found him. She shuddered at the possibilities this time, given the state of the Inner Sanctum, and Kyros' revolutionary stint in Hyperion. He could've easily made enemies.

"We know nothing more about Kyros at this time. But conjecture would lead us to several unsettling conclusions." The recruit stared for a long moment at the Council doors. Then he shared a meaningful glance with Dirco.

"We'll try to avoid conjecture for the moment, recruit." Dirco eyed the preliminary report he'd provided, swiping through the contents with a wave of his hand. He squinted on occasion at some detail that caught his attention. His mouth closed in a tight line.

The recruit bowed to Briescha and saluted Bridfar. "We will notify you of any additional intelligence we gather."

Dirco dismissed him. "Minister." Caslorius bent his ear low to the soldier's words. "There is much to be discussed, and much more to discover. Please, give the rites so that we can take action in this horrible incident."

Caslorius stepped forward in the stance of one well-versed in delivering horrible news with grace. "Our blessed and prosperous world has been infiltrated and attacked. Each of us is a victim. We have all been violated in the most cowardly way possible. And worse still, our own Arkayn Council has suffered most for the actions of those monsters involved." The ever-increasing group of Azelans cried out in outrage and horror and confusion. "Those beacons of wisdom, intelligence, in both order and chaos, have ever been our guiding illumination in the darkness. Those dear souls who sacrificed their eternity for their fellow countrymen, have fallen to appalling destruction. Together, we shall find a path in this sudden nightfall, and a new light for our ways."

The crowd shuddered with sadness, each person realizing what Caslorius had revealed.

"Let us honor those who have joined the Seer of the Light. She welcomes them in the light of Paz, as it is written. May we open your hearts to remember their names."

A man stepped forward, near crippled with age and the hardening of his joints near death. He pushed through the crowd, past the attentive mourners.

"What right have you, Caslorius, to conduct such rites without convening a council of peers?" His voice trembled in sorrow and with the rasp of advanced years. "And you, *Princess* Briescha. Did you want that freakish power for yourself so much that you destroyed them?" His eyes were glazed mirrors of accusation and anguish. "And how convenient that this happens so close to that metallic monster's inauguration! You disgrace us!" He spat on the ground and stood beneath them, at the bottom of the steps, heaving in lungsful of air.

Caslorius stepped forward, a snarl on his lips. Dirco bridged the gap between them with his outstretched arms. Then Briescha stepped around both of her defenders. She descended the steps and stood before the ancient man. She recognized him.

"The loss is mine as much as yours, friend Disor. Did I not grow to adulthood with your children? Am I not of the same flesh as all of you?" Briescha reined in the fury that threatened to erupt at his display. But he hurt. He was hurting. She couldn't hurt him further. But she couldn't allow them to take Silver's purpose in vain. The murmurs rose and died. "The coming of the Silver Empress was shocking even to those who lived long before you walked Azela's fertile land. Your sorrow is valid, but your anger misplaced. Do not insult my sister, your future Empress. Insolence will not be tolerated in the face of such disaster, and your challenge will not disrupt what is deserved of the dead."

Several young Azelans gasped, wide-eyed, at the spectacle. Older Azelans came to themselves and berated the man for his vast insults to the Princess, future Empress, and the departed Council. He grew silent, but his anger melted into wave after wave of heart-wrenching cries. "My wife is in there. But my wife. My children." He broke down before her. She laid a soothing hand on his shoulder as the same folks who berated him led him away. Briescha mounted the steps and held her father's hand when he began the rites.

Silence reigned as Caslorius spoke, weaving a respectful and beautiful history of each Arkayn Council member. He even found the most elegant words for the departed Science Officer Sladen. Briescha's heart had a brief flicker of pride in the way her father conducted the rites. Sometime later, he finished. At last all heads tilted toward the star Paz, all hands spread outward in admiration and respect, and the haunting melody of the Farewell song rose through the thick atmosphere toward the heavens.

As the last note of music drifted away on the breeze, Briescha told them everything she knew. They learned all: the reason for the earthquake, the experience of body-sharing Briescha had stumbled upon, the dead Azelans on the cold foreign floor. They discovered those in charge were Azelan. They found out for the first time about the spaceship and its past failed attempt. They learned about Briescha's plan to search for their Empress.

Then came the questions: "Who took the Empress?" "How will we govern ourselves?" "What if the ship doesn't work?" "Why risk the last Arkayn?" "Is there any way to stop the planet's problem here?" "How are you going to get a piece of the Core to power the ship?"

"Allow me to help with that, my Princess."

From the edge of the gathering came Jacan, the grim pain evident in his ruby eyes. He stretched his neck and rotated his massive arms until they popped in their sockets. Gently, he moved aside his comrades to reach Briescha. She stared down at his broad shoulders and forearms, all welted in scars, each crystallized pink on his warm yellow topaz skin. Her face flooded with relief.

Jacan scowled, working his square jaw in thinly veiled rage and sorrow. He gazed up at her through locks of long crimson hair dampened by the morning dew. He reached for her hands and lowered his lips to her palms.

"Forgive me." His voice broke as he whispered into her open hands. "I couldn't protect you. Or Silver."

Briescha twined her fingers into his. "Don't you dare do that to yourself."

He clung to her hands, his own trembling. "So many are lost, and I couldn't save a single one, not even one who I see as a sister."

She had nothing to say to him. She felt the same.

When he lifted his head, Briescha saw liquid crystal tears threatening to fall. Drawing himself to his full height, still maintaining a light touch on Briescha's palm, he turned to the gathering.

"The future Empress is a patroness of my special jewelling. Most are gifts to her sister, the Princess Briescha. One such gift was to outshine all others with its unique beauty."

Jacan presented an ornately carved amethyst box that filled even his large hand. A pulse emanated from within. "She wished you to have it the day she took the throne, Princess. The Silver Empress herself left with me to the mines seven full moons ago, and asked her planet Azela for a gem of exquisite beauty, more so than any have seen. She wanted something as lovely to the world as her sister is to her."

His wavering smile and look of wonder

warmed Briescha's face. "And the ground opened for Azela's Empress, and from that glowing crevice, she withdrew a stone from the core of the planet that pulsed with every beat of Silver's heart." He removed the lid and knelt again before Briescha, his ruby eyes deep and brimming with respect and love.

The crowd muttered among themselves.

Briescha bit her lips closed to keep from crying at her sister's loving gesture. She faltered. She closed her eyes, remembering her sister's cries for help. Briescha froze where she stood, the feelings of the day rushing to overwhelm her. A hand on her arm jerked her out of the horror. Jacan still knelt before her, and the others stood around her. The warm hand pressed higher, and she met his concerned eyes with a stronger resolve.

For the first time, she looked down at the gift her sister would have bestowed upon her. A necklace shone from within the box, a large solitaire gem more gorgeous than any Azela offered, faceted to perfection by the very hand that gripped her arm now. Strands of fine silver wove a perfect web around the gemstone that swirled and pulsed with each beat of Silver's heart. The light pulsed too dim for Briescha's comfort.

Briescha touched the necklace. The web-chain brought a whirlwind of memories back to her. Silver as a child played in Daddy Ganan's workshop while Jacan made a ring for her. Then a flash-forward to another gift, and another. Then Silver stood with Jacan, pulling a lock of her shining hair forward and cutting it to make the web-chain that now held the corestone. The swirling hair in her hand lost its liquid form and became as metal, then Silver smiled broadly at Jacan. Briescha pulled her mind back to the present. Jacan smiled, the tears still brimming in his eyes.

"She wanted you to hold her heart with you always, and have something so you could always see her face when you missed her." Jacan stood and lifted the necklace from Briescha's trembling fingers. He pushed aside her ebony tresses and fastened the clasp with strong gentle fingers that lingered ever so briefly on her throat. He pulled her hair back behind her shoulders, again lingering, and stepped back with great ceremony before her, clenching his hands behind his back. The silver on her throat felt alive, felt like her sister, like a stream of consciousness that flowed with the energy from the gem to rejuvenate her spirit.

Briescha, buoyed by the obvious love of her sister and the support of Jacan, whirled to face the crowd. "The planet is reverting to a state that predates Silver. We can bring the planet back under control. I am willing to risk a great deal to reverse the damage done, and I'm willing to risk everything I am to bring my baby sister back home!"

The crowd churned with mixed reactions.

"I need you now, my dear brethren." Briescha placed her hand on the amulet at her throat. The light flared in response. "We both need you. I know many of you have hated us. You have been afraid of us. Some of you even wanted us dead. And on more than one occasion, you almost succeeded. But my dear sister has suffered for you, continues to suffer because of who she is. Silver loves this world, even with its hate and bigotry. She loves the Azelans though they often fear her. Would you, in Silver's any action, ever find fault in her loving and pure intentions?"

The crowd murmured like a gentle wave.

The gemstone on Briescha's throat thrummed and pulsed. Briescha felt the love of her sister in its gentle flow. "Then please, give me leave to find my dearest, and set right the heart of Azela once more!"

The desperate and affirmative outcry reverberated throughout the city. Several older Azelans assisted with delegating tasks in preparation for the ultimate voyage in known Azelan history. All hurried toward their new responsibilities. Buoyed by their hope, the Azelans unified in the face of planetary upheaval and loss.

Briescha watched as they all hurried about with their great purposes. She glanced to her father, who gestured with great authority in his own delegations. Bridfar and Dirco moved among their ranks issuing commands. Wave upon wave of Hyperion soldiers arrived at her location, and she didn't have the heart to suspect any of them of wrongdoing.

Watching so many Azelans work together from such varied echelons, she stared with renewed hope. Briescha's heart fluttered even as it ached. *Hope and faith will keep them together in my absence, if I even succeed in my attempt to leave. If I succeed in returning with Silver.*

So many unknown variables threatened her resolve. Yet she stared on, plotting her own next step in this risky endeavor. The deepest part of Briescha's heart knew that hers was a fool's errand and that her selfishness knew no bounds. Yet she would stare down any obstacle for her sister, for her very soul's core. For her dear Silver. And not even the Golden Seer could stop her. Love, after all, is a master at miracles.

15: HEARTSICK

The following moon cycle passed in a sickening wave. Bridfar's investigation expanded from the Arkayn Hall and the twins' tower home to the halls of Hyperion in Xepaqua. He kept conjecture from Briescha, but soon she pieced together the stark evidence placed before her. On this, the final day before she set sail for Forge Mountain and the unearthing of the great ship that held her future, Bridfar made a final report and his full disclosure.

"We have purged an entire company of low to mid ranks, and many officers have been severely demoted or purged. Dozens await hearings in the military judicial system, which has also been, ah, refreshed in recent years. It seems that Kyros accomplished much of what he set out to do, and quite sincerely. For him to have done so much for the good of Azela, then sink so far is unfathomable. Yet, it is an absolute shame and with great trepidation that he has been named a suspect in Silver's kidnapping."

Jacan, ever in Briescha's presence of late, scowled at the Commander. "Are you certain?"

Even Jacan, hate Kyros though he may, seemed to have trouble accusing him of such an act.

Briescha paced in her small room, packing the remaining items she thought she would need on her journey. "I would assume the worst of anyone but Kyros!" She busied her trembling hands with ties and cables on her bags and boxes. Her conscience had already named him at least suspicious in her heart.

Bridfar settled on the edge of her bed, elbows on his knees. He scrubbed his face for a long moment, then leveled her with the full authority of his gaze. "Kyros, Deraddian, and two new recruits are unaccounted for, as well as a handful of military engineers of unknown alliance. All others are found alive or dead. The engineering on that machine planted in the gravity room matches Kyros' skillset perfectly, utilizing his signature welds and arrangements, a pattern as accurate as a retinal scan. And the machine was made to amplify his innate Power Trait of influence."

"Influence?" *Since when did Kyros exhibit a Power Trait? He'd never mentioned it before, she was sure of it!* Briescha's temper flared and she turned on the man. "Silver was not merely influenced to leave her home and family at the risk of everything she loved! The planet is tearing itself apart as we speak, everyone in the city was comatose, and you would call it *influence?*"

Bridfar guarded his expression and sighed. "Your past and relationship with Kyros aside, Princess, the facts are before us. Directly or not, he is involved."

Her quivering lip turned down in a pitiable pout. She shook her head over and over. "With Kyros gone, in whatever capacity, you are the one I trust most in the military now. I apologize for questioning your research. But please understand, any person I have nursed to health from death's door and loved...like a...like a brother...could not possibly hurt my sister."

"I hope, for your sake and hers, you are right, my Princess." He sighed, rising wearily to his feet. He then turned to Jacan. "My men have still found no substantial information on the whereabouts of your father Ganan or brother Fagan. With radio communications finally reestablished in the city, where the damage was worse, we are now repairing outlying communications systems in our outposts. But Ganan and Fagan were confirmed in the city at the time of attack. My regards to Arcani, as I understand she finally is sleeping."

"She's exhausted, asleep aboard the longboat. My father's continued absence has worn on her. It was all we could do to get her to agree to leave this place." Jacan's mouth formed a tight line. Then he nodded his gratitude and shook the man's hand. "We are all in your debt for your diligence, Commander. In light of this information, I'll have to resume forge duties in my father's stead, and get this ship excavated for our Princess. I've sent ahead instructions for their preparation, and will see to the matter personally."

Briescha sucked in a breath and slammed the lid on a box she had packed.

"Princess?" Bridfar extended a hand to her.

She bypassed his hand and threw her arms around his neck. "We couldn't have done so much without you. I'm so sorry I've been angry. You and Caslorius and Jacan will do a wonderful job of governing while I'm gone. And do give Caslorius my regards."

In her peripherals, Jacan hid the look of sorrow on his face. She wondered at his strength. He'd been her rock these last stages of preparation, and tried to bury his heart in duty. She released Bridfar and respectfully dismissed the man to his other pressing duties.

"You have some heart, Princess." Bridfar bowed and kissed her hand. "I will see you at the launch, if I can get away from Xepaqua. But I want you to promise me one thing."

Briescha inclined her head.

"If you run into Kyros out there, know that he isn't the same man you remember. Promise me that you will see him for who he is, at that moment, and act accordingly." His eyes flashed a warning. His voice echoed in the room, full of experience and authority. "Don't hesitate, or you will never get your sister back to Azela. Be as cold and unforgiving as the vacuum of space, or you may yet live to regret it."

The warning sent a shiver down her spine. Bridfar met her gaze as a decorated officer of war. She understood then that he had suffered immeasurable horrors for the honor of protecting the capital. She knew that he was right. "I promise."

He bid farewell to Briescha and Jacan, then headed out the door and down the steps of the tower. Briescha stared after him until the external door whooshed closed with a distant buzz. Jacan touched her shoulder.

"You know he wouldn't mislead you."

"Who?" Briescha's mind was distant, somewhere among the stars.

"Bridfar, of course."

She nodded. "But Kyros is my friend. It was always Silver, Fagan, Kyros and you. My family. My whole world. I will keep my promise. But I won't carry that bitterness in my heart. It's too heavy to bear."

Jacan's mouth pressed into a tight line again, and he was lost in his thoughts. "Let's head to the docks. Your faithful ol' blue is down there waiting by now."

Briescha glanced around her room, at the scant five compressed packages of personal items she planned on taking with her for a journey of indeterminate duration. She lifted the ruby flower from her nightstand, her fingers tracing the delicate edges, and pinned her hair back to one side. The Heart of Azela pulsed at her throat, a constant reminder of Silver's absence and ever-expanding distance. No other object in this room mattered to her quite so much. Jacan gathered her boxes and bags under one arm. Briescha turned and allowed Jacan to lead her into hall. She stared up the steps toward the expanse of Silver's bedchamber.

She paused only a moment there, then swept out the door and out into the light of morning, ready to face the biggest challenge in her young life.

*   *   *

Descending to the docks with a full Hyperion contingent flanking them, they heard the singing and chanting of a multitude of people before they arrived. Xepaquan citizens lined the road and every surface, a living sea of people that threatened to flood into the ocean. Briescha's steps slowed. She remembered her arrival with Silver, and how so many citizens stood in silent protest. Now they cheered and screamed encouragement. Their emotions were tangible in the air, sincere and hopeful. Such a horrible occurrence had an amazing outcome.

Briescha paused, bowing graciously to accept their acknowledgement. Then she boarded the blue topaz longboat she'd loved at first sight. Dirco and Jacan filed in behind her, along with a small group of Hyperion soldiers serving as escort. The same kind crew piloted the boat. They wore grimness behind their bright eyes, determined as they were to cheer up their princess.

The crowd blurred in her eyes. Even the disappointed dot on the edge of the pier named Caslorius blended with the others. How could she tell her father goodbye when it may be forever? Their droning cheers faded into monotony. Mechanically, she raised her arms to wave to them. But something important was missing. Silver's exuberance. Briescha followed each curve of the intricate dock carved by Daddy Ganan to resemble the ocean. And she watched it fade into soft blue and disappear. Her heart calmed with the gentle rocking of the longboat. Jacan tugged her toward her cabin, away from the liquid crystal that ebbed and flowed around them.

Briescha peeked in on Arcani, who had one knee propped against the smooth wall of the ship and one arm dangling off the edge of her cot. Her lips twitched with silent, worrying words. Briescha kissed her adoptive mother's forehead. Wordless images of pain and loss and fear crossed the barrier of their flesh. The bittersweet feelings unnerved her. She gently separated her emotions from Arcani, pushing a sweet, calming aura through Arcani's troubled mind. Arcani relaxed into peaceful slumber. Briescha slid the cabin door closed behind her, feeling a heavy melancholy drift into her heart.

She leaned heavily on Jacan's shoulder, all the way up the steps and into the aft cabin. She glanced at the blue walls through which she could just see the light of day. So much had changed since their youth aboard this familiar longboat. In this very room, she had spent time drilling protocol and discussing distant futures with Arcani and Silver.

Briescha's chest ached remembering how she told Silver she could crush mountains. She sat down hard on the bed, her head swimming. Jacan sighed and turned to leave. Briescha reached for his hand, gripping it in a vice of fear and worry. He stared down into her face. Coldly, for he'd blanked his expression to protect her.

"Will you please?" Briescha pressed her lips into a thin line. "There is no safe place in this world right now except with you. Can I rest in your arms? I want you to hold me now, for as long as you can."

Jacan regarded Briescha for many long moments, his brow furrowed in contemplation. She pulled his hand and his body followed, settling firmly against her side. Briescha rested against his chest, felt his heart flutter beneath her fingers, and sighed into the warm pulse of his emotions as they flowed past his flesh into her cheek. He quickly suppressed the flow, but even that was telling.

For once, Briescha settled her mind into simple relaxation. She could consider what she felt from him at length when there was more time. But now, for this short time, he leaned back against her pillows and she rested against him. His warmth arose to envelop her. And his arms soon followed, shyly at first but then with renewed tenderness. He dropped his lips to her hair, whispering soothing words as he held her. As she drifted off to sleep, she sighed again, safe and content in his arms with the crystal ocean ebbing and flowing around them.

Briescha awoke at sunrise, her opal hand clenched upon Jacan's warmly bronzed skin. His fingers left trails of warmth where they glided up and down her shoulders, sending a shiver up her spine. Feeling her stir, he stilled his hands.

"Apologies, my Princess." Jacan scrambled upright and set Briescha gently against her pillows. "I didn't mean to awaken you."

"Nonsense." Briescha stretched her arms high overhead, driving away the ghosts of nightmares with the light of Paz streaming through the topaz walls. "Paz beckons. We must be near Forge Mountain by now."

In the distance, the greeting tone sounded. Briescha's heart soared at the memory of the sound. Wearing their same travel clothes from the day prior, the two rushed out the door to lay eyes upon their homeland. There, upon the prow, leaned Arcani. They joined her.

"You're late to rise, my dear children." Arcani turned weary eyes to them and gazed back across the water.

Briescha settled her hand in the crook of Arcani's elbow. She placed a quick kiss on the woman's temple. "And you, as ever, are the earliest to rise. And with your color returning with much needed sleep."

"Oddly silent, it proved." She turned a challenging gaze up at Jacan. "Save for the constant sighs and murmurings of unrequited emotions from my boy here. As if such things weren't evident."

"Mother!" Jacan wore an expression of pure shock and embarrassment at her blunt revelation. He began stammering a string of excuses that no one in their right mind would entertain as truth. Jacan's face bore the brightness of a childlike blush.

Briescha felt her face burning. What did he say while she was sound asleep? She could only guess, and the guessing made her blush so much deeper. Jacan avoided her eyes. Arcani met them with good humor despite all that happened, and resolve.

"Your home has missed you, my dear girl." Arcani squeezed Briescha to her side. "The revelations of these many events have stripped away what little finesse and tact I chose to employ in the past. There is no time for such sentiments. Though I yearn for a long-lost time when you, Silver, Jacan and Fagan were scrambling underfoot in the mines until I would send you to the meadow. Even Kyros is there in my memory, skulking about, rolling around training stats in his head."

Briescha bit her lip against a tide of accusations recently brought against a man she had known and nurtured since youth. Tones sounded to announce their arrival at the forced water channel that would speed them toward the Bay. Arcani was unapologetic. Briescha caught the welling of tears in Arcani's eyes before she blinked them away. How selfish I have been, disregarding Arcani's fostering of Kyros and raising him as a son.

The mountain closed around them and opened onto the huge Forge Bay. Briescha saw it all as in a dream. The throng of people greeting them. The trees blooming in all colors. The dull roar of their voices blending and echoing in the bay. And she even imagined Daddy Ganan standing at the edge of the pier, dressed in his work pants, covered in the grit, soot and dirt of the mines, waving both arms in the air like a maniac. A huge grin across his face. She ached missing him, and for her mind to play such a trick in the light of tragedy saddened her.

"Ganan?!" Arcani's cry jarred Briescha back to sharp wits. "Ganan..."

"Father?" Jacan's voice wavered, uncertain and confused. His hands dropped to the railing for steadiness, as his knees appeared to shake.

Briescha stared back and forth between those two, then returned her attention to the pier. The man she thought an apparition of memory stood there in life! Waving, grinning, jumping up and down like a child. Scarce had the little blue ship glided to a stop before Arcani dove from the rail into his waiting arms. Jacan cleared the rail and stood next to the man. He appeared unsure of whether to hug the man or pat him on the back. So he stood there with his hands outstretched.

Briescha stood unmoving, shocked, filled to the brim with a dozen emotions that she couldn't identify. He lives! After this long cycle, he lives! Finally, Jacan tired of the confusion in his arms and hugged both the man and Arcani, who showered his face with kisses and clung to him in tears. Then Jacan came aboard to lead Briescha, who was still in a daze, to disembark. Standing in front of Daddy Ganan, she stared ahead, disbelieving her eyes and fighting the relief that tried to rise.

"My girl." He shifted Arcani to one side. Then he laid his warm, calloused fingers on the side of Briescha's face. She cried out finally, shaking with tearless sobs as she fell forward and clung to his side. "My dear, sweet girl."

Ganan greeted the rest with a cursory glance over the ship's remaining crew and a quick salute to Dirco. Dirco's jaw dropped. He scrambled to return the salute. He stammered a title that Briescha's ears missed, then corrected himself to address the Forgemaster. Briescha stared at Dirco, trying to figure out his flustered demeanor. He was often friendly and shy, but also quick of wit and rarely stumbled over his words. She resolved to ask him later, after the debrief, if everything wasn't made clear.

With Arcani and Briescha clinging to each side, Ganan led their small entourage to a tiny shop carved into the mountain, just off the pier. Down an aisle and through a cleverly hidden door at the back, he brought them all. Briescha's heart fluttered and seemed to sing a long, wavering note. He's here. He's alive. His heart beat under her clasped hand. Daddy Ganan made her feel safe in a way she didn't think could happen anymore. But his presence raised many questions, and her mind teetered on the precipice of loss. What else could possibly happen? She shook her head to close that line of thinking.

"Lights!" Ancient glowing orbs above did Ganan's bidding.

The walls looked darkest down the sides, a deep amethyst, while the top wall glowed warmly pink in the globes of light. In the center of the floor rested a huge oval amethyst table with well-worn chairs of the same material.

Jacan reveled. "I didn't know such a place existed!" He ran his hands across the smooth table edge. "No way this fit through that door! Did they carve it out of the stone when they made this room?"

"No doubt," answered Ganan. "The chairs, too, most likely, cut from exactly where they slide under the table. You'll notice the same marbling and color of amethyst, and everything matches up." He squeezed Arcani and Briescha, then released them. "The old folks proved ambitious even about the things that would never be seen by most of the outside world. True Masters of the Craft."

"But why did I know nothing of this room?" Jacan stared around. No accusation arose in his voice. Only curiosity.

"Many things, you do not learn about this job until it is time." He gave his son a warm smile and a reassuring clap on the shoulder. "I'm glad I survived to complete your training."

Jacan, rendered speechless and fighting some deep emotion, nodded his agreement.

"Dirco, would you be so kind as to lock that door and secure our perimeter?" Ganan spoke as a man with authority beyond his rank, but then again, he always spoke this way. "These deep cut rooms are quite effective for meetings of a confidential nature. They're old. Free of prying technology because of the signal dampening effect of thick rock."

Dirco called back, "Yes, Forgemaster." He pulled a heavy bolt across the door and proceeded to a sheer curtained hole in the back, confirming it a closet before taking his position beside Jacan, behind Briescha.

"Our Princess will preside over this confidential meeting." Ganan stood at the second seat. He gestured for Briescha to sit at the head of the table. When she hesitated, Ganan inclined his head to someone standing behind her. Jacan leaned in and pulled the seat out. Glowing with embarrassment, she sat. Smiling with pride, Ganan gestured to Briescha. "Princess?"

Briescha pouted, but acquiesced. "Move to open the floor for discussion of confidential matters. All in attendance shall be considered hereby Forgebound in word and deed to the secure handling of any information presented and discussed in this meeting. Do any in attendance disagree to be bound?"

Silence greeted her.

"Who in attendance agrees to be bound?"

All those in the room answered an affirmative.

"Excellent." Briescha gave Daddy Ganan a scolding stare, but he was grinning ear to ear.

"I know, Ganan." Arcani spoke up, her voice still elevated in joy. "She reminds me more of our dear Rascha every day."

"That she does, love."

Briescha glowed again in embarrassment. This time as she stared from under her long black lashes, she saw thin scars across Ganan's face. *Those aren't Forge scars. They weren't there before. What happened?*

"Well, I'll answer that look in your eyes, my girl. And I'll take questions at the end, please." Ganan rubbed his broad jaw and traced the edges of a long scar. "The first half of the last month, I spent in the wilderness near the Forge, where I'd been taken by our enemy while I was unconscious, from whom I escaped when I woke up." He chuckled. "A few of our hostiles landed with me in tow, behind the Forge in an ancient contraption, pitiful really, not even sure it'll travel well in space..."

"Dear," Arcani sighed, "stop fixing the thing in your head and get on with what matters right now."

"Yeah, but I can't imagine what heap they found that thing in!" He shook his head. "Anyway, I have a personal protocol in place that gives me certain authority over a small group of individuals set aside for this type of scenario."

"A small group of individuals?" Briescha leaned into the story.

"Not important now. Just espionage stuff, as needed. From my service in younger years. Well, my team showed up to..."

"You served?" Briescha threw her hands in the air. "Since when is that part of your Master training?" Dirco coughed or laughed. Briescha turned on him. "You knew about this?"

"Haha. Of course he does. I trained his father." Ganan slapped the table to refocus. "So I called them into work and set one group as a protection detail on a bit of information to which I'm privy, and set the rest toward an information gathering task against our newly arrived enemy. Just after that, our hostile invaders managed to knock out our communications with some sort of electromagnetic pulse.

"These guys sounded kinda amateurish,

but their tech — other than the piece of junk — was well made. But they had some military training. Seemed like their leader wasn't around. When they couldn't immediately catch me, they ransacked most of our deep caves looking for two things that I'm sure they would never find. Because we hid the one ages before my time, and we don't keep the other in stock. Hahaha." He slapped the table in time with his laughter.

"What were they seeking?" Briescha was on the edge of her seat.

"In a moment, my dear. So knowing what they wanted, I just let them look and kept my position concealed. But when they set charges, I signaled the rest of my team to retreat while I stayed a safe distance, or so I thought. But the blast radius was much larger than I thought, and I was caught up and got some mountain shrapnel in my face." His fingers brushed the pink scars. "Shredded one of my legs. I couldn't run away. Just about bled to death lying there. Hahaha."

"Ganan! That's nothing to laugh about!" Arcani slapped his arm, her eyes flashing her impotent worry and anger. She grabbed at his pants legs, trying to inspect him for the worst of his wounds. He caught her hands with a chuckle and kissed her fingers.

Arcani took a deep breath and sat down. Briescha knew that challenging look better than most. Ganan would hear from his wife for his indifference.

"Well, I'd just got the bleeding to stop with every trick I'd ever learned, and still managed to hold onto this old shell," he chuckled as only someone who escaped death could, "when they caught up to me. As it happens, I had a few contingency plans set up in the forest that prevented their quick progress, and only a few of those defectors lived to find me. And they thought they'd have a go at forcing me to retrieve one of those," he pointed to the corestone Briescha now wore, "and the schematics and excavation instructions for an extraordinarily important vehicle."

"But no amount of torture..."

"Torture, Ganan?" Arcani bristled at his flippant treatment of the serious situation. "When were you planning on providing that little detail?"

He smiled at her with such genuine love and deep-seated passion, then ruined it by saying, "I've just provided it." He even grinned at her challenging glare as she sat seething.

"They were dumb, though, the lot of them that came for what the Forge offered. They didn't see the tiny corestone shavings my young protégé had left in his workspace, luckily. Which I'd like to discuss with you, in a technical manner, when we have a moment, since I haven't had the honor of hacking away at the most precious stone in the known world, but you have." He leveled Jacan with a pained and mirthful expression.

"Oh, where was I?"

"Some nonsense about them being dumb," Arcani said, with measured impatience, "if you'll so kindly get to the part where you survived before we are all crispy with age."

"Ah, yes, my love." His eyes held that exclusive glance, just for his beloved. "Took them a week to realize that their buddies were long gone, having panicked and abandoned them when they realized the secret vessel was not within anyone's quick grasp, and was likely a fable." Ganan rubbed thoughtfully on his chin and gave a weathered, distant smile. "And it took another week for them to wear down their anger on me long enough for my Forgebound brothers to find us and dispatch all but the least dumb survivor, who lived long enough to spill every-thing he knew about this little excursion of theirs, with a little, ah, acute prompting."

"Prompting..." Briescha whispered the word. A wealth of new information about Daddy Ganan swam through her head.

"Yes." As he sought in her eyes an understanding, he lowered his voice. "In light, we act as we please, but in darkness, we act as we must. And always, we fail without skills appropriate to meet our challenges."

Briescha knew these words as para-phrased from the Master's oathbook. She found new meaning in them today. And she, in all her pain, accepted them as truth at long last.

"And as expected," Ganan continued at his conversational rate, "my dedicated brothers of the Forge informed me that I, in a fever, demanded a tablet and wrote out the full report on all my findings, as it was all still quite fresh in my mind, sealed it with all official titles and codes, instructed them to restore commun-ications if they could, told them to wake me soon so we could dig up a spaceship, and," this part he mumbled, "collapsed nigh unto death for over a week as they worked frantically to save my life."

Arcani stared at him in shock, rendered speechless by his flippancy.

"The conclusions are that digital communications will be down indefinitely due to the massive damage rendered to the entire system, at least Forge-side. The slimy stack of swaysnake spoor Deraddian is definitely involved, possibly leading the group. And as I overslept far beyond my expectations, I'm woefully behind on my priority excavation, at only ninety percent complete. And we had no intention of opening it before my girls got here. Except I was hoping that both of you would arrive, except the quakes gave me pause."

Briescha sat in silence, barely comprehending anything beyond Deraddian's involvement. She trembled in anger. Even her breath quaked with rage.

Daddy Ganan's sobering touch on her arm refocused her. "Are you ready to meet your spaceship?"

"Yes, I would love to leave as soon as I can."

Ganan's mouth pressed in a thin line that reminded her so much of Jacan's worried expression. Now she knew from whom he gained that face. "Then there is yet much to be done, my daughter, to ensure your safe passage. Shall we adjourn?"

She nodded.

"I trust that Dirco will remain with us until this business has run its course, his charge is delivered to her goal task before he delivers my report to Bridfar?"

"Yes, Sir, Forgemaster!"

Ganan delegated other tasks to those present, then waited until Briescha found her voice for a formal dismissal. Briescha allowed the group to file out ahead of her. She watched her fingers clench in determination on the smooth amethyst table. So much relief, albeit temporary. So much unknown future. And yet, she forged ahead on her path toward Silver.

"You really are just like your mother, and your foster mother." The voice belonged to Ganan. "That look of determination suits you all. Now come. I have much to show you."

Briescha sighed and straightened her shoulders, allowing Ganan to whisk her out of the room and along the way to the excavation site.

The group gathered before the gaping maw of Forge Mountain, looking out upon the vast plain below where a horde of workers hacked away at a specific point in the mountain on the other side. The mist of atmosphere blurred the object in her eyes. She reached out with her heart, knowing this miracle would maybe carry her beyond the stars into the arms of Silver.

"I can forgive anything, excuse anything but the loss of my sister."

"We all know this," answered Ganan. "We also know that Kyros has been implicated in the kidnapping. Although, the greatest mystery is this... I can't imagine why he'd go to such great lengths against those he appeared to love.

Briescha's heart arose to strangle her. She choked out, "Me neither. But I need to be prepared."

"We will do all we can." Ganan cast a glance at Jacan, an expression that was not lost on Briescha. "Anything and everything we can."

"Will you make a weapon for me?"

Jacan stepped forward to protest. Ganan placed a hand in front of his chest to stop him.

Arcani spun on her, instantly livid. "I won't have you getting killed, fighting gods-know-who with no experience! That's what your guards are for!"

"Your anger is justified," Ganan answered, seeing the fire in Briescha's eyes. "And none of us blame you. But Arcani presents a valid point. You've not trained a single day in combat."

"I can train until the day I leave." Briescha pressed his lips together. "Dirco will help?"

"So you can. And so he will." Ganan measured her with a long glance. "What will it be?"

"A sword, made with these." She held out the pouch for his inspection.

Ganan stared at her a long moment. "Then we shall make a weapon to outshine all others, to protect our dear Princess. Teardiamonds?"

"I gathered rubies from Silver, and teardiamonds from my own breakdown earlier. And you said you had shards of corestone? Could you incorporate all that into a sword?"

Ganan took the heavy pouch from her. The stones sifted through his fingers. "Red as Paz. Sparkling diamond. They're like night and day, and perfect to represent you both."

"But what will you do if it is him?" Jacan asked, the heat of anger and worry rising in him.

Briescha caught her breath. "I...don't know."

"Can you kill him?"

"I don't know." Briescha lifted her fist. "I must try. I must prepare."

Jacan snatched her shaking fist from the air with the gentlest grip. He pried her fingers apart. His scarred and handsome face leaned into the softness of her palm. "Then prepare we must. Please allow me to join you," he entreated. "I wish for nothing more."

"I cannot allow you." Briescha felt his pulse beating strong against her hand. "Someone needs to help Daddy Ganan and Arcani keep peace here, and who better than a man more kind and loving than any that ever graced Azela?"

Upon reaching the excavation site, Ganan disappeared among a throng of workers with questions and updates. Briescha heard their exclamations and caught a twinge of their excitement. The excavation went tremendously well. Almost the entire hull gleamed, despite centuries of dirt streaking its diamond surface. Her heart sank. *There is no time*, she thought. Not enough time to spend with my family, with Jacan. Not enough time to get to Silver. Time was against Briescha, and slipped through her fingers each moment. She felt Jacan's eyes on her and turned away from the ship to face him, masking her rising worry as best she could.

"What bothers you, my dear, sweet Jacan?" Briescha asked.

He looked up and blinked into the glare. "Just the brilliance, my Princess. Just the beauty. It seems so fragile," his voice cracked.

Then Ganan raised his voice for all to hear. "Continue, my friends! Your work is fruitful today. The task is important—do not so much as nick its surface, for its cargo is more precious than any!"

Briescha felt the brightness flood her cheeks. She ducked her head in embarrassment. When she raised her eyes again, Jacan met them with a pensive, yet somehow intense expression. "It is a beautiful creation, this Ship of the Stars our ancestors built," he said for Briescha's ears only. "I would have it stay here, and keep you safely with it, if the choice were mine. But as you love your sister, so do I. And to have her saves us all, in a way." He smiled a tragic little smile down at her. "However, my dearest Princess, your return will save my heart."

Azela protested the sweetness of the moment with a tumultuous jolt of her own. The ground shook several people from their feet; tools scattered across the ground; the newly revealed star ship threatened to career from the ledge it rested upon, where a mountain had earlier encased it. The remaining boulders that held the ship crumbled and rolled down the side of the plateau. All held their breath in suspense as the huge diamond vessel leaned this way and that with every quake.

Briescha's heart skipped in her chest. She leaped into the air and appeared beside the ship in an instant. She spread her palms across its side and sent a telekinetic jolt around the hull to steady it. Her lips flattened across her teeth in a desperate snarl as she pushed with all her might and mind. She rested her forehead on the huge monument to Azela's past attempt at star traversing. She fought the rocking with desperation and every ounce of power she had as others looked on helplessly, still knocked off their feet by the quaking of the ground. Several heartbeats later, the rocking slowed. The ground became still. The ship teetered to a stop. Briescha breathed a sigh of relief. Then she felt the effort drain her vision and consciousness. She stumbled from the narrow ledge. Arcani screamed in terror as her foster daughter plummeted from the sky.

Jacan scrambled to get below Briescha and dove forward to snatch her from the air. He cradled her in his arms, looking into her troubled face. Arcani rushed to their side, checking that Briescha was breathing and that her heart beat strongly.

"Now, you are to rest," she told her unconscious ward. "This way, Jacan."

She led him to the low-roofed Master's quarters and planning building. "Ganan said another day of work at least awaited them. Her journey requires her to be as rejuvenated as possible. Put her here." Arcani cleared some marked slates from the sleeping mat, fussing all the while how Ganan had been a slob in his solitude. "She is to remain here until she is fully rested."

Arcani arranged her on the sleeping mat with full authority. Briescha regained consciousness. Her head throbbed and her heart fluttered with an odd rhythm. Her protest was brief and half-hearted. When Arcani pulled a soft translucent blanket over her limp body, she couldn't keep her eyes open. Sleep came and wrested her into nightmare after nightmare of hopeless searching and danger, where her memory of Silver's scream tore through most often to jolt her almost awake. Then it would rise again to drown her in sorrow, into troubled sleep once again.

With Arcani at her bedside, Briescha settled into rest at last. She turned to Jacan. "What do you need to do right now?"

"I'll be ready when Father finds a moment." Jacan gestured to the pouch he set on the wide bench. "Briescha has requested a weapon, after all."

Arcani scoffed. "Even Silver, in all her meekness, spent more time learning combat than this dear child. But," and here, her eyes searched her son's, "with Fagan gone and Kyros a possible villain, can you blame her?"

"No, Mother." Jacan placed an arm across her thin shoulders. "I would do anything to take her place in this journey, if I could."

"As would I." Arcani leaned her head against his chest. "But we will serve as we can here, in her absence. And not allow all her hard work to unravel."

She kissed her son's scarred face. "Call me if she awakens, if she needs me." And with that, she left them alone.

Jacan sat at his father's workbench with a hearty sigh, in the center of the large, simple room with walls of soft jade and wide windows to let in the natural light. He sat with his slates of quartz, carefully designing the weapon his dear Princess requested, awaiting his father's input, carefully sorting the huge numbers of teardiamonds.

Deep in thought about his second love — his work — he felt the tingles of abrupt emotion course from each perfect stone as it passed from his fingers into sorted piles. So much pain had passed; so much pain to come. A tear of worry and sorrow and love slipped down his cheek and crystallized onto the table with a clinking noise that brought him out of his intense concentration. He looked at the perfect blue stone. Lapis lazuli, so rare, so deep. Then he heard her whimpering.

He lumbered quickly across the huge room to the low bed mat. She dreamed of something painful. Writhing in fear, she pushed at the menace that pulled her with it into darkness. Doing the only thing he could imagine, he took her reaching hands in his and kissed them as he knelt by her side.

Inexperienced though he was in manipulating emotion, Jacan concentrated hard on picturing her at peace with him, sitting in an open meadow of blue crystal with lesser Avians singing sweetly for them as he held her hands to his heart. Her shaking lessened and stopped.

Slowly her tired eyes opened on him. She smiled in apology and gratitude. He tried to release her hands so she could sleep easier, but she returned his grip and pulled him forward until her lips touched his cheek. The soft kiss sent tremors through his heart. He knelt motionless as she settled back onto the mat. He stared, wide-eyed, at the perfect creature gracing this bed with her supple body. He settled there, delighting in her every breath until she had been asleep for several minutes and her grip had lessened. He pulled the cover back over her and stood.

He tore himself away to his worktable to finish sorting and planning, every now and then stealing a glance at his secret love, wishing every moment that he had told her years ago of his feelings and wishing harder that she could stay with him forever.

*   *   *

Briescha awoke in the large jade living quarters built by the Master of the Forge, Daddy Ganan. She felt Jacan's presence some distance away, in a deep mine forge, hammering at something that glowed from the heat of a thousand fires.

Darkness had settled over the land; the only light in the room with her was a steady pulsing from the Heart of Azela around her neck. She clutched it and closed her eyes, speaking across space to her sister, who she hoped could hear. A slow panic that never went away leapt to Briescha's thoughts. What if Silver couldn't hear? What if she had been taken too far? But the core that Silver had claimed for Briescha still matched the Empress' heartbeat, for now.

She rushed to the door and out, glaring up at a glowing night sky. Several moons changed their light while she slept. The sleep had kept her all that night and into the following day and night. She felt furious with herself for sleeping so long, but the rest claimed her. She needed it, thanks to her impulsive, exhausting actions.

To her right, luminous in the moons' light, she saw the distant outline of the Ship of the Stars. *It is ready,* she read in the minds of those who slumbered around it, awaiting the morning and their Princess. All of Azela had been scurrying to accomplish their tasks in the time that she slumbered. She heard their whispers and thoughts drifting through the night.

The ship had been excavated and cleaned, but no one could find an entrance. Scribes sapped knowledge from her ancestor Darasha, the last Arkayn, pending any disaster at the attempt of transfer. All comforts to be sent had been boxed and packed into the encampment site around the ship. Gifts of cut gems overflowed from crates as barter for services rendered from those aliens who could not be convinced to volunteer. All was well and accounted for, so it seemed. Azela grumbled a retort that sent vague tremors across the plain, snapping some light sleepers awake and making others grumble in their dreams.

Briescha made her way a few strides farther from the low house where she had her last untroubled dreams. With the house and gaping maw of the mine behind her, she looked out on the plain that rested between her and the excavated ship that held her future. A deep slope led down to the broad expanse of land from where she stood amid large rock formations of crystal generated by the Mountain. Briescha walked out onto a wide, flat amethyst that jutted out over the sea of dense plants below. The grass twinkled blue-gray in the multicolored moons' light. A gentle breeze played across the field, making the whole of the grass swirl like the liquid crystal oceans in the South, with the surface dotted by tiny ruby flowers that looked like ships.

Briescha knelt on the faintly glowing stone and sat with her legs tucked partly beneath her while she supported herself on the other side with her hand and arm. She breathed in the familiar scent of life around her, felt the smooth, cool rock support her, and was more conscious than ever of the Azelan intricacies she took for granted her whole protection-focused life. She wondered how it happened that she had spent her entire life on this planet and not noticed the details around her.

The melodious humming of wild small creatures filled the night. Each plant was crystal perfection with facets that glimmered when the gentle breezed tossed them about. Color and beauty and form flooded her mind. She realized the possibility that she may never return from her noble journey — that despite her efforts, all may disappear in the blink of an eye because of her failure. Then a voice called to her, ever so faint with distance, for ever so fleeting an instant, but with such feeling and love that Briescha gasped at its power. Silver's mind-voice, always selfless, whispered into her soul.

Sister, I believe in you!

The Heart of Azela flared and fluttered quickly, brightly with Silver's presence, the power illuminating the entire amethyst boulder with its intensity. Then Silver was gone again, and the Heart resumed its calm beat. Yet Briescha sat in overwhelming emotion, so deeply moved in her spirit that her body was immobilized. Then came the tears, so pure with love they fell as blue diamonds. When the tears stopped, Briescha felt saturated with peace and confidence, knowing the love and resolve of Silver would get her beyond any obstacle she faced.

Time passed slowly, and she did not move from her place. The blue diamonds lay scattered across the stone and her lap, but she did not brush them away. They carried her love within them, a physical symbol of the faith her sister had in her. A stiff wind began to blow, lifting strands of her long onyx hair into beams of moonlight. She watched it all with the fascination of one at once condemned and empowered. Dreams and aspirations from thousands of Sentients drifted into her mind's vision.

Animals in the Sanctuary farther down the continent lifted lilting voices that she could feel in the stillness. The sparse flowers in crevices where she sat seemed to turn their petals to her, so she could see beauty. She drank all into her heart and soul. When at last the star Paz sent the first of its rays across the eastern horizon, Briescha had been steeped in life, drawing to herself everything she forgot to love about Azela. She knew what she fought for. She had known peace, and readied herself for the storm.

A presence pulled her eyes from the glory of the sunrise. Jacan stood politely out of sight, watching her. He seemed entranced by her every feature. She rose to her feet with such grace that the blue diamonds in her lap slid down the front of her longgown and barely scattered on the amethyst rock. He looked at her with the deep love and adoration that had always been there, just for her, and smiled a mournful smile.

All that I love about Azela.

The new day's light warmed his bare topaz face and chest. The scars shimmered on skin stretched tight over well-defined muscles and fine-boned hands. His hair had been tousled from his long hours of labor; red locks fell in front of sparkling ruby eyes — kinder eyes than any man she had ever known. All that she ever loved about Azela, she would soon leave, to find the only person she loved more.

"I saw that you were awake. I came as soon as we finished it. But you were just sitting there. I couldn't bring myself to disturb you. You just radiated peace and...and..." he whispered.

Briescha crossed the small distance between them in two long strides and leapt into his arms. She clung to him, cheek to cheek, with her arms wrapped tightly around his neck and shoulders. He was taken aback for a moment, unsure of what to do or how to soothe her. Then he realized she wasn't crying. He dropped the package he carried and slid his hands around her waist, then up her back. He held her like that for several moments, still confused at her display — she wasn't upset. She nuzzled his cheek. Then her smooth lips slid across his neck and around to his face. He caught his breath and hugged her more tightly. She stared into his face with half-lidded eyes, peaceful eyes that were the picture of enlightenment.

Pulling her head back, Briescha gazed into his perplexed eyes as her hands framed his face. Briescha gave him an encouraging smile. She closed her eyes and leaned toward his mouth as it opened to question her. Their lips met for the first time. Every shred of his suffering in his love for her, every denial of her love for him that she forced upon herself — these melted away in the sweetness of love's purest expression. Moments passed. Breathless, she collapsed trembling in his arms, which also trembled. Her cheek rested against his strong chest. Her hand found its way into his as he sank to the ground, eyes still wide with astonishment. His lips tingled with the kiss, his body still afire with the passion of long-suppressed desire. And she loved him! There was no doubt in her eyes, or her touch. No lie of tragedy deceived her. She decided to love him, in spite of it all.

"How long have you...?" he asked.

"Always."

He hugged her tighter, this precious gem he had adored all her life. Soon, she would leave him in body, but the knowledge of her love bound their very souls. Her love empowered him even more. And when, yes when, she returned, they could be together as one for all their lives! In the Great Peace during Silver's reign, all would prosper. All could love.

The red star's light shone fully upon the plain before they stood together, having neglected their duties long enough in watching the huge primary climb higher in the multihued sky. He leaned down and kissed her sweet lips once more, awkwardly but passionately. Then he knelt before her while reaching behind him for the package he had discarded in surprise. The long, narrow object was enshrouded with a shimmering translucent fabric that he unraveled layer after layer. Finally, he held the object up for her inspection. His shoulders slumped and he dropped his head. She felt the pain it caused him, knowing she might be in enough danger to use the item he and his father had crafted.

"Father ensured that his girl have a proper weapon fashioned to keep her safe during her travels," Jacan sighed, "since he is more experienced than I at warfare and weapons."

Briescha straightened her posture and looked down, steeling herself for what felt more and more like a final departure. Her first impression of the object was its flawless design. All the diamonds and rubies she had given him were unified in artful design and symmetry into a delicate looking short sword. An inner core of flawless ruby swirled down the length of the blade, having been joined into a single, nearly indestructible gem. Glowing in thin tendrils like flashes of lightning, the remaining shavings from her corestone wound around the ruby.

Encasing the ruby and corestone all around was an edged blade made entirely from unified diamonds, heated to melting then forced into shape by tools used by hands of unmatched skill, then honed to an edge so sharp only a diamond of unique hardness could hold it. The handle and hilt were all of diamond and ruby, with a deep red cloth wrapping the grip.

Embedded at the base of the blade and overlapping the hilt was a curious blue stone she had not given him to forge. It was rare lapis lazuli, and of exquisite quality. Her fingers grazed its surface, sending a flood of images through her senses: Jacan looked longingly at her while Silver gave her a ring he'd made; he bowed in his animated way to tease her and loved to see her smile and blush at the antic. She gasped. Every clue that ever existed to his love for her was reflected in the beauteous blue gem. Immediately, she knew the stone was his tear also, a gift of his long-standing love, to help protect her on her journey.

He watched her realize the gem's origin, saw the delight it sent coursing through her to know, and felt a sense of wonderful-beginnings-all-too-late. She caught his gaze, knew his thoughts, and joined him in kneeling on the ground. Briescha took the gorgeous weapon from him and set it aside. Her fingers pushed back the locks of ruby hair that fell in front of his eyes. She held him there, willed him to know her heart and mind and soul, and presented her pledge to him.

"As I promised my sister that I would cross the stars to find her, so I now extend my promise to you. You have my love. I will return, with my sister, and love you both so dearly with every breath that you will forgive me for neglecting your love for so long before." She smiled tenderly. "You may grow tired of such affections, but that is my vow."

"'Such affections,' my dear Princess, are more than I could have ever hoped of having in my life," he mused. "And, be careful what you promise to me, because I intend to collect on a vow that bounteous." His smile grew mischievous. He pulled her to him for a long, soul-shaking kiss that left both delighted, gasping for breath.

Across the plain, the campers awoke and finished their preparations, with Ganan's booming voice carrying above all. Everyone readied for the transfer of the last Arkayn in the Council and the awakening of the Ship of the Stars. Darasha consented to the long trip overland to reach the ship and arrived in grand style. The planet's few Sentients of Flight arranged an air carriage. They conveyed between them the precious cargo of Briescha's ancestor, the first Arkayn to leave the safety of the Hall after immobility in anyone's memory. Paz shone down on the open carriage, allowing Darasha to see the light of day once more, and all the glorious beauty of Azela.

Jacan picked up the sword and slipped it into the fine flexible sheath he had made for it; with his other hand he lifted the Princess to her feet, feeling the exquisite press of her body to his.

"It is time," Jacan whispered into her ear. "I don't want you to go, but I don't want you to deny Silver her return. I waited too long to tell you how I feel. Right when you are leaving me."

"I have a promise to keep. Don't forget that," she whispered back.

The words washed over him with new warmth. She smiled. She ran over to the amethyst boulder and scooped the blue diamonds of her revelation into a pile and gathered them into a fold of her longdress hem.

"Rule them in Silver's stead, along with Caslorius, Daddy Ganan and Arcani. And for each night I am gone from you, count one of these into a vase. On the last night of the last gem — that is when I plan to return to you!"

"But there are so many, easily a full cycle could pass. Or more!"

"But my love will not. Neither will my promise. It will be hope to you, and give you strength to govern Azela." She gestured to the Sentients gathering at the ship, clustering around Darasha's air carriage as the flight maneuvered to place it carefully beside the ship. "They will need your guidance. Calm the planet if you can, but keep the people united at all costs. It is their hope that will keep the planet alive until their Empress can restore order! Please, for them, and us... do all that you can."

He squeezed her to him once more and kissed her gently. Then he released her. He reached around her waist and fastened the sword belt in place, giving it a formal tug. Jacan, in customary stance, stepped back and folded his arm across his waist, then executed a perfect deep bow to his Princess. Briescha felt the white glimmer of a blush cross her cheeks as it had so many times in the past; now it seemed deepened by her full understanding of his teasing. She, in turn, curtsied with fluid grace before the man she loved, never letting her eyes leave his, even though his affectionate expression continually thrilled her heart into a faster beat.

He offered his arm to his Princess. She slipped her hand into the inner bend of his elbow. He covered her hand with the bronzed fingers of his other hand and led her toward the ship on the other side of the grassland. For once, she was content to walk, stealing a few precious moments with Jacan as the others finished their jobs and Silver inched farther away. The steady pulse of the Heart of Azela reassured Briescha that, thus far, Silver lived and awaited rescue. And in some small way, she guided Briescha every step of the way. The Princess straightened her shoulders and walked proudly with her love to the waiting Sentients gathered in support of the occasion.

Her arrival was heralded with respectful bows and hope-filled shouts of encouragement, while every eye that followed her held a glint of fear and worry. The events to come pressed each mind to anxious concern, spreading an atmosphere of suffocating heaviness throughout the ranks of Azelans that assembled. The Sentients of Flight settled their irreplaceable shipment on a flat area at the bottom of the incline leading to the ship. Briescha walked full of authority to the Arkayn, her beloved ancestor Darasha.

There was a delicacy to the crystal carving of Darasha's special carriage, all clear and smooth, allowing a full view all around of the landscape. Soft cushions lay under her on the bench and wide bands of cloth bound her arms and legs to the bench to prevent her from falling over on her trip. Darasha sat on her cushion, looking placid as always, her green eyes upturned and long black hair flowing all around her. Her face held its usual small, unshakeable smile.

The voice of her mind reached out to the emerald-eyed statue: *Wherein lies our method, now? All is in place, yet I've a worry. What if...?*

Let your heart, and hers, guide you. Not a single step you take will falter if you take it in confidence. Lack of confidence dictates failure. Now let your people know your intentions. Let their faith support you, the ancestor's mental voice rang through Briescha's head.

Briescha turned from Darasha, buoyed by the assurances of the Arkayn, to face the host of Azelans gathered to witness her success. Or shun her failure. The Sentients stood looking expectantly, hopefully. Lesser creatures of the wild had graced the air and ground with their jeweled feathers, pelts and scales; they mingled their melodic voices, blending them with the distant croon from the slanted crystal enclosures of the Sanctuary. All were her kin, to some degree. Most were her friends. All faced the same dangers.

Her hand went absently to stroke the hilt of her short sword, and then rested on the pommel. She closed her amethyst eyes and drank in their love and worry and support. The

Heart of Azela pulsed steadily against her own heart. When she opened her eyes, they at once met the ruby eyes of the Jacan, then of Daddy Ganan and Arcani. Every fear she'd held melted in the warmth and love she saw so deeply rooted within those people.

The deep breath she took was only slightly shaky; she drew in the fragrant atmosphere for one of the last times before she set off on her journey. All looked on, each with their different emotions. Briescha spread her hands in her placatory way.

The Princess of Azela, exuding confidence and power, began to speak.

"I have no eloquent words for these times, only an overwhelming urgency to do what must be done. Now, I hopefully leave my home and all I love to seek out the only thing I love more...my dear sister and the Empress of Azela." Briescha paused for the encouraging ripple through the crowd. "I also have no words that are strong enough to express my thanks to all who have helped me in life and in this endeavor. You have my fondest gratitude, you who have brought this possibility before me. For that, I must move ever forward to bring her back to us, and to bring Azela the peace it so desperately craves."

The crowd rang with an affirmative. Briescha glanced at each face she recognized and each face she didn't. The surreal feeling that no one had booed and hissed her decision in this group left her reminiscent about the rocky past that led her and her sister to the capitol.

A low thrumming began in her heart, reverberating in unison with the corestone against her chest. She felt a resonance to her right, where Darasha sat in statue form. The thrumming surrounded her and filled her. She couldn't speak any further.

It appears that all elements are near and in

place, dear child, Darasha cried, somehow breathless behind her frozen, placid face.

It appears you are right, Darasha!

Briescha managed a shaky flight up the incline to the ship. When she stood before it, the craft began resonating in time with the corestone. Briescha gestured to the Sentients of Flight, who brought Darasha up the incline and set her where Briescha indicated. Briescha touched the ship with one hand and felt it light up from within. Then she touched the side of Darasha's placid face with her other hand. Unifying all three entities with her touch, she felt electricity explode through her body, coursing in the direction of the vessel. The searing light flowed in intense waves for so long that she felt it would never end, that her body would be ripped apart in the effort.

After what seemed like an eternity, the light ebbed in her left hand and exited her right hand, and for a moment lingered warmly in her mind before it was gone. Briescha stood there, blinded outwardly by the ongoing pulses of light emanating from the ship, and shaken internally by the transfer she had attempted. Her knees trembled, so she slid down before the ship. Somewhere below, Jacan called out and she raised her hand to halt him.

"Darasha?" Briescha gasped. "Can you hear me?"

There was no answer from the emerald-eyed shell to her left. Panic rose in Briescha's chest. But the Heart of Azela pulsed steadily once more, and in time to the ship before her.

"Darasha?" No answer. A long moment passed.

I told you, dear child, that love is a master at miracles, did I not?

The light of the ship pulsed quickly with Darasha's lilting laughter.

"Oh my! It worked?" Briescha was in awe. "I have so many questions."

So do I, for the moment. She sighed. *It's a huge, cumbersome body, to be sure, so I'll need some time to learn how things work. Not much time, it seems. But a while.*

"Are you okay?"

I'm just fine, my dear. Just a bit stuffy. And it's odd having moving parts again, though they don't move the same as my former body. She laughed and sighed again. *But plenty of room for my expanded power. There are sensors and such. A door that forms from the wall to the outside. And, I'm afraid, there is a rather morbid cargo inside here, Briescha. Once these cameras work properly as eyes, I'll know more. But bring Ganan and Arcani. The ancestors buried this vessel for a reason.*

Briescha puzzled but a moment, then called Ganan, Arcani and Jacan. Jacan pulled her up beside him. "That was terrifying to watch!"

"Pretty scary to experience, too, if you ask me." She steadied herself against him and delivered Darasha's disturbing message.

Ganan rubbed his chin. "I had suspected as much, honestly. We'll all learn a great deal in the coming days. Looks like you'll be with us just a bit longer, my girl." He ran his hands across the smooth diamond hull, scrutinizing the handiwork of long-dead artisans.

Briescha drew a shaky breath. "You're right, Daddy Ganan." She sighed wearily and pushed herself from Jacan's shoulder. Her limbs tingled and her mind raced. The tingling dissipated after a moment. Given how much energy she just expended, she felt oddly rejuvenated.

"Darasha?"

Seems like we're linked in a different way

now, dear child. Can you feel the pulse of energy between us? Focus on the corestone.

Briescha did as she was told, and felt a remarkable oneness with the vessel that was now her Arkayn ancestor. And above that, the beat of Silver's heart resonated within the Heart of Azela more clearly than she remembered.

Also, I've discovered the mechanism to open the door, I do believe. And the cameras are working for me quite vividly now, with some ancient cargo before my eyes. Are you ready to enter your Ship of the Stars now?

"Yes, my dear Darasha. Please open the door."

16: SOULRIDER

Briescha steeled her nerves for the other side of a door that hadn't been explored since someone tampered with Arkayn memory. Arcani grabbed her hand and assured her it would be okay. She gave her foster mother a small smile, but her eyes betrayed her worry.

Stand back, Darasha lilted in their minds.

The smooth reflective surface rippled where Ganan touched it. He jerked his hand back. The hull flowed from an oval opening like molten glass, and then reformed into oblong risers that led into darkness. Briescha set her foot on the first riser and tested it to hold her weight. It didn't budge. Then another step and another. She touched the smooth oval doorway and bravely stepped into darkness.

"Lights, Darasha?" she whispered hopefully.

Working on it, Darasha said, her voice puzzling over technicalities. *This is quite the challenge, stretching my soul over so many working parts.*

Globes flickered to life overhead, followed by a flood of narrow bulbs around the perimeter of the room. The others followed her into a circular room with cushioned seats in the center. Access hallways radiated outward, shielded by translucent doors, each labeled above with the destination to which they led. CONTROL, STASIS, DINING, and several more. Darasha kindly illuminated the CONTROL label and opened the door as they approached.

"The concave surface makes it seem a lot larger," Ganan mumbled absently, reaching for the indention in the wall. "Organic and flowing lines, incredible artistry, in a machine, no less."

The hall glowed from both sides. The floor emanated a gentle warmth beneath Briescha's feet. Rooms angled off from the main path, but Darasha urged them forward, toward the main double-doored control room. Before the doors, Briescha paused and drew a deep breath.

I wish I could prepare you better, my dears.

Darasha opened the doors and globes flickered and glowed steadily. Ganan and Jacan stepped through ahead of Briescha with Arcani close behind them. Briescha stepped through and glanced around. The diamond hull thinned and appeared to dissolve almost a full circle around them, giving a full wall-height view of the sky and providing further illumination to the room.

"Oh no!" Arcani gasped and stumbled back. "Briescha, don't come forward."

Briescha disobeyed and stepped in front of her. "Who in the world?" Her hands flew to her mouth. Slumped forward in ergonomically carved seats, three bodies in archaic metal armor gripped three sets of controls.

"They died like this, at the controls?" Briescha clamped her mouth and leaned forward to inspect them. "And barely a day's decay? What in the world happened aboard this ship?"

I'm working on this information now. Darasha grew silent, then spoke again. *There are more eyes, ah, cameras in the room. Perhaps I can pull up any video files they may have. And the activity log immediately prior.*

"This place has been sealed since it was encased in the mountain?" Arcani asked. Darasha confirmed. Arcani continued, having regained her bearings with the mystery. "No air means no decay. But these bodies aren't gemflesh. I don't even think they're Azelan."

Ganan inspected all around the bodies. "We can move them now. The situation in which they died is pretty clear...stuck here, frozen for some reason. But why they died, we'll hopefully discover soon."

He called Jacan over to remove the bodies from their fixed position. In the natural atmosphere, they slumped easily to the floor with a metallic clink, two males and a female. "You're right, Arcani. They're not Azelan. At least, not that I can tell. I mean, the armor is Azelan. Archaic military. But they are not. See their rich skin and pale hair?" Ganan lifted a softened eyelid on the nearest male. "And pale eyes. Almost Delvan, except for the richly pigmented skin."

Arcani leaned down to inspect and confirm his observation. "I see what you mean by Delvan, my dear. But that hair lacks the gemstone pigmentation streaks that are common to Delvans. White hair, rich skin, pale eyes. Clad in Azelan armor, they may be, for whatever reason. However, the closest I can tell, these dead are Unatan."

"Unatan?" Briescha knelt beside the female, whose flaxen hair curled from beneath her helmet. "How in the world did they end up on Azela centuries ago, sealed in a buried vessel, with no record that Unatans had ever set foot on this planet?"

I hope to shed light on this mystery, Darasha began, *as it seems to be erased from*

Arkayn memory. Or prior to Arkayn collective consciousness.

"I wasn't aware that anything could be erased from Arkayn memory, Darasha." Ganan's voice held a note of warning. "And yet, this bit of evidence proves otherwise."

This hearkens back to a conversation I had with the girls about a great omission following the rule of The Nine. That's why I suggest that this incident either precedes the Arkayn collective, or belongs in that missing gap. She paused. *And the omission is still blurry.*

"Unless the right questions are asked to activate your locked knowledge?" Briescha's eyes lit up with the challenge.

Yes, my dear child. We will work at that bit of history soon, and it may take quite a while. As for now, I can display the video from the day these poor souls lay entombed in this vessel.

The front shield clouded and became solid once more. Then an intricate pattern of notches, triangles and circles spread across the surface. The symbols gave way to soundless moving images of the control room in which they stood.

Three young Unatans rushed about the room, settling into their positions. Other Unatans crowded around them, easily filling the space. Then, from somewhere off-screen, flashes of light blinded the primary camera. Unatans scattered and fell on the floor as militant Azelans burst from the hallway into the room, firing on them with unfamiliar weapons that shot out lasers. A group of the invaders dragged out the fallen Unatans.

The original three clung to the controls. The female reached for a central port in the helm and slid up the clear crystal covering it. The Azelans threw their hands up, alarmed at her seeming threat, and turned to retreat. They had barely cleared the door when the female Unatan buried her hand in the port, found the pressure plate or object she sought, then froze in triumph and...something far worse. Her eyes glowed in determination, then terror, then with the unnatural flood of energy that came from the ship. The light flooded the room. The retreating Azelans disintegrated into fine powder that blew away on the unseen gust. The light, as it receded back into the room and back through the female's hand, took with it the light in her companions' eyes, and the light in her eyes. She slumped there, her hand falling from the port it had occupied. The video ended.

And thereafter, the ship immediately sealed its doors and siphoned all atmosphere from the rooms therein, Darasha explained. *Not a soul in or out in all these years.*

Silence. Then Briescha remembered to breathe again. *I know what they did, why it killed them!* The Heart of Azela beat against her chest in time to Silver's heart, and now Darasha's. She pushed past Ganan and Arcani to the helm, staring at the port where the girl fed her soul to the ship. She slid the clear plate up along its track and peered inside.

"Wait!" Ganan snatched her wrist back as her fingers traced the edge of the port.

"It's okay, Daddy Ganan," Briescha said with a wan smile. "I know what happened, and I won't repeat it."

"You know?" He released her hand in shock.

She touched the Heart of Azela resting on her sternum and slid her hand inside the port. "They tried to use this vessel without an Arkayn soul inside to run it, and without an Azelan with Power Traits to pilot it. But they did acquire one thing they needed..." Briescha fished out a dull, glowing yellow husk of char. It's pulse felt weak and trembling. It was clearly at the end of its life, if such a thing lived on its own.

"A corestone to power it." Ganan took the dying husk from Briescha with trembling fingers. "I can barely feel its pulse. It has no effect anymore."

"The corestone burnt out the souls of everyone it could reach, even those Azelans who must've lacked Power Traits to resist its pull," Jacan whispered.

And lacking one of these elements, the vessel will not fly, Darasha chimed in.

"Does that mean it will be safe for Briescha to fly with you?" Arcani asked. "Since all elements will be in place?"

Darasha held her silence for a long moment.

"Darasha??" Arcani raised her voice in worry.

I had no intention of worrying you, dear Arcani. Her voice held true remorse. *I ran a diagnostic of this vessel. All systems, I do believe, are accounted for and online. I've stretched my legs, so to speak, and can reach into every crevice of this vessel. We have many systems and supplies for situational upgrades as the need arises. Far more advanced than any I have witnessed in my long tenure as an Arkayn who studies the cosmos. To answer simply, we should have no problems traveling, navigating, fighting if needed, and even thriving aboard.*

Arcani's lip stuck out, but she bit back the tears that threatened to fall. "That's all I could ever hope for my girls! Now, you two practice this thing and go get back my other daughter! And if you see them, my boys, as well!"

That somber note sobered Briescha's elation. She said, "I'll do everything and anything in my power to bring everyone back safely." And she meant it. She knew Kyros may be among the guilty, but she wanted him home.

She knew innocent, sweet Fagan was tied up in this mess, but she wanted him home. And most of all, she wanted her dear Silver back. At whatever cost.

"It appears we've work to accomplish, Darasha." Briescha whispered. "Let's get to it."

Before we begin, let us show respect to the dead. Please carry these poor souls to the stasis chambers I've prepared for them. Since we will pay a visit to our oldest neighbors on Unata, we will give them the opportunity to light pyres for them, and perhaps get help solving the mystery of their presence on Azela in the process.

"But what if they figure out you have their dead aboard," Jacan said in a panic, "and simply kill you instead of listen?"

Briescha gave a sharp, hoarse laugh as she reached for the ankles of the female Unatan. "Then suddenly this entire burden is someone else's to bear, though I wouldn't wish this on another."

"Briescha!" Arcani scolded her soundly, muttering under her breath as she lifted the dead woman's shoulders from the floor. "Dealing with the Unatans is no laughing matter!"

"They are the brutal and savage killers, the denizens of Fear Planet?" Briescha scoffed, and hefted the dead weight of the Unatan woman from the floor with a grunt of exertion. "I do not enter any leg of this journey without a healthy measure of fear." She paused for the door to slide open. "However, people are people. And the old Azelan hatred for Unatans is buried deep. I will solve that mystery as well. This may be the biggest and most tragic piece of the story. Or, like I said, it'll be someone else's mystery to solve."

Arcani groaned at her daughter's newfound sense of dark humor in the face of adventurous danger.

She laid the woman's feet in the blue gemstone case and helped Arcani lift her head and shoulders clear of the lip that surrounded the case. She arranged the woman's hands across her chest and straightened her helmet. She stared at her soft lips, devoid of light or blood. *They're not unlike us, just made from different stuff. Their queen must see my reason and innocence in this, or I really will be leaving my quest to another.*

A thin sheath of translucent crystal slid in place over the dead woman. The clear sides frosted with the sudden cold that would preserve her body in state. Brieschha stared, breathless from her efforts and considering her many future challenges.

*   *   *

Brieschha sat at the helm, staring around at all the technology that once seemed foreign to her. With Ganan and Jacan, and Darasha's direct help, she learned the function of every part of the ship by heart. The two men remained a constant presence, drawing diagrams and schematics of this Ship of the Stars, ominously "just in case". Though their diagrams were impersonal and cold, referencing the shell, Brieschha gave no effort to differentiating Darasha from the actual ship. Her light was the ship's light. Her voice, the ship's voice. It seemed wrong to Brieschha to address the vessel as anything but Darasha.

Darasha seemed content with this arrangement. She expressed exuberance about having regained some measure of mobility, albeit a foreign, expansive type of mobility, in her Arkayn years. She learned to fly, to zip through the crystal ocean as quickly as the sky of Azela.

The light of several Azelan moons changed

before Briescha and Darasha learned to work as a team piloting the vessel. Today, Briescha pulled the straps across her shoulders and pinned her body to the seat, which slid forward for easy access to the controls. The ship operated planet-side, and on minimal independent functions, without the corestone even leaving Briescha's neck. They'd tested the process and familiarized themselves with using the corestone as a power source. But today, Briescha readied herself to leave Azela's atmosphere for real, for the first time, and for a long time.

Today, her heart pounded as her family and her citizens gathered outside Darasha for the last time, to bid them farewell and to wish them both a safe return, whenever that may be. She remembered the crushing embrace of Daddy Ganan and the tearful, worried kisses of Arcani. She remembered Jacan's warmth all around her and the too-long kiss in front of the whole Forge community, and she remembered not caring that it was scandalous or that she was being judged. All that, only a moment ago. But it already seemed like a lifetime. *Yes*, she thought. *It is only proper that my final departure be from this place, where my heart resided for so long.*

She stared forward at her love, her Jacan. She stared the longest at him. Her fingers traced the edges of the ruby flower he made for her, a flower that pushed her hair back on that side. Then she pulled the Heart of Azela from her throat and slid open the clear cover on the corestone port.

Whenever you're ready, my dear, I'm ready. Darasha's voice pulsated with excitement mixed with revelatory gravity.

"Here we go, Darasha."

The port pulled the corestone from her hand and locked in place, the long silver chain draping down the front of the helm. Briescha steeled herself for the jolt of light that coursed through her body and through Darasha's shell. They were all one, at that instant — Darasha and her new body, Briescha and her body, and the corestone that beat in time with Silver's heart. Briescha knew and felt every movement of the ship as her own. The whim of Darasha melted with the will of Briescha. The vessel drifted upward at a speed that shocked the onlookers, without moving even a hair on their heads.

Preparing to leave the atmosphere, Darasha-Briescha said or knew as one. The hull of the vessel slipped through the resistance with only minimal shifting and not a degree of temperature change. *Atmospheric controls are constant,* they knew as one. *Gravity controls are switched off.* Darasha and Briescha reveled in the feeling of zero gravity a long moment. *Send the message back to Azela that we're on our way, and that we'll send word as we can.* Digital beeping sounded. *Sent.*

The navigational controls pulled up a three-dimensional map of the stars that rotated in holographic pulses all across the room. Darasha-Briescha twisted the ship with ease in the vacuum of space and locked in their course for Unata. Then, to those still watching below, the ship disappeared with hardly a trail, a rogue comet moving in daylight and gone in a flash.

17: SKYROAD

Starboard side, incoming! Prepare to evade.
Darasha sounded an alarm sequence.

"We're only showing halfway to Unata at this point!" Briescha spoke aloud. She felt drugged, unsure where Darasha ended and she began. The sudden pull from full-focus symbiosis left her feeling both sluggish and overstimulated, in the past. This full, functional dive left her mentally energized, if a little tired physically.

Briescha commanded, *Onscreen!* with her mind. The oblong object gleamed in the light from a distant star. *Scan!* Darasha's instant results confirmed that the object was not a weapon, but contained a single pulse of life. Briescha, returning to her single mind for a moment, contemplated her options. Possible contamination, for one. Possible enemy status. Possibilities are endless.

Whatever is in there, is in stasis, Darasha informed her. *I can detect no disease. In fact, the creature is in excellent health. Humanoid. Odd, though. This pod has no weaponry of any kind. Just set adrift in the great vacuum of space.*

Briescha, although permanently adhered to Darasha in some sense, knew she felt great sympathy for this unknown person. "Okay, but we can't do this for everyone we find adrift!"

Darasha's swell of excitement felt infectious, a state which Briescha earnestly hoped their newest tenant did not reflect. Infectiousness. Briescha often forgot that Darasha's singular specialty was cosmos-based. She literally survived to be in her precise element, through fate or luck or love. And she had every right to be excited about every bit of it. Darasha opened the outer hull into space and pulled the pod inside, sanitized the surface, then restored the atmosphere in the medical wing. Briescha entered the room cautiously.

You'll be glad to know that I confirmed his lack of disease. I don't quite know what he is yet, but I've begun the process of waking him.

"I'm not keen on your excitement in this situation, although I know we couldn't let someone possibly die." Briescha cocked her head to the side. "He?"

Yes, and he's been adrift for years and years. At least in space-time. He might be unconscious for a while, but if we can get him into one of our stasis modules, I can get him up to speed much faster if I calibrate the neural pathway transmitters for language.

The strange capsule sprang open with a hiss. Briescha shrieked, startled. The man, for Darasha had been correct, of course... The man's face was as angular and chiseled as his chest. Sight lenses, very old technology, lay across his nose. Briescha wondered at his pale, silken hair that spiked around his face, so pale it was almost translucent, taking on a violet hue from the surrounding lights. He drew a violent breath and gasped for more air, then his breathing came steadily.

"So to that module?" Briescha got confirmation from Darasha. "At least this one is alive when I move him! I sure wish Arcani was here to help. He's much larger than the last one!" If Darasha disapproved of Briescha's morbid commentary, she didn't reveal her thoughts. Briescha hauled the man to seated and slung his muscular arm across her shoulders, pulling him forward with all her might.

His limp body slumped against her and she stumbled but kept upright. Luckily, and to Briescha's immense relief, he shuffled his feet along for her when she got him upright, like a sleepy toddler who refused to be carried. She tucked him under translucent warming blankets in the stasis module, and a light began flickering over his head. Darasha would have his neural pathways lined out for language in no time! Still, she kept her distance, toying with the pommel of the diamond and ruby short sword at her side. Then he settled back into his deep breathing again.

He's not Unatan or Azelan. But he breathes this air with a little labor. Perhaps he doesn't receive much of his nourishment from the air as Azelans do? Darasha's tone was inquisitive. Infectious, still. *I'll be scanning and analyzing him for some time. All I can say is, his chemical makeup is definitely from Eranklaya, the water planet they refer to as Earth, from which you and Silver received your surname. But he's also not human. And not diseased, it seems.*

I appreciate your ongoing concern for my concerns, Darasha. Briescha laughed dotingly.

I'll stay the course for Unata on my own, but a bit slower without your help. Please keep our ward in sight for me.

Of course, my dear ancestor. Briescha rolled her eyes and laughed. Part of her was permanently ingrained in Darasha, and Darasha in her. Their thoughts could hardly be separated. Not the same as with Silver, but the feeling was one of contentment in the closeness. Briescha's impatience was tempered by Darasha's exuberance. And Briescha knew it to be a necessity.

Briescha stared at the man, studying his pale complexion, at his chest rising and falling for a long time. Then, despite her great affected indifference, she paid attention to other details. His finely sewn vest, a rich, deep blue like sapphire, was tucked in at the hips and open to the waist.

A little creamy white spiral hung from a heavy cord around his neck, halfway to his navel. *How had I not slapped myself with this before?* When her fingers, of their own accord, brushed the little spiral, she gasped at the wave of memories that flooded her. Such a small, four legged creature! White furred and cloven hooved, with a thin tail fringed in white hair, and a small spiral in the center of his forehead, he danced across a meadow with a clear spring, ringed by a vivid green forest.

"What did you see?" the man asked in her language, his voice full of gravel from sleep, but with a wonderful depth that surprised her. He peered at her through half-lidded, violet, white lashed eyes.

"I see the neural transmitter has done its job, for you to speak to me so soon." She felt so pleased with the technology that another possibility eluded her.

"Oh?" He chuckled, then cleared his throat. "No, dear. I see an Azelan before me, stunning and glorious as I expected. But of noble birth, by that opal skin you wear. So you see, it's only appropriate that I should show the courtesy of attempting to butcher your language!"

Briescha stared open-mouthed at his words. He laughed. The sound tickled the inside of her ears in a way that made her uncomfortable, in the most comfortable way. "You know my people and my language, and I imagine much more. Who are you, man from Eranklaya?"

"My rudeness is unsurpassed, dear noble lady." His Azelan dialect was older, slightly broken, exceedingly formal, but she understood him. He pushed his body up on shaking elbows and inclined his head in a bow. "My name is Sephandrum, of Earth, of the Carneya clan by the name of Alcourne, in this time, I do believe. A clan with whom I'd gratefully be returned, if possible, as something horrible has occurred there. I'm afraid I've been on a very long scholarly journey that has impaired even my manners, if you'll excuse me."

"Oh my!" Briescha cried out, flustered. She pushed him back to his lying down position with almost zero effort. "Do not bow! I get that enough. My name is Briescha and I'm on a journey to find my kidnapped twin sister. And it appears, good Sephandrum, that we will have plenty of time to discuss details once I've survived my next ordeal."

Darasha's lilting laugh drifted over the speakers. She wanted him to hear her. "Welcome to the Ship of the Stars. My name is Darasha, and I'm quite interested in knowing you, good Sephandrum."

"And I, you, Lady Darasha!"

Briescha smiled, excited for the moment when she realized Darasha was the ship herself. But that private joke, she held onto for a bit longer. But still, she smiled. "Why were you adrift in space?"

"You first. What did you see?" he repeated.

"A child, but an animal. Very small. Much like our Mietina animals on Azela, except without gemstone pelts. Did you hurt that child to gain his horn?"

Sephandrum chuckled, again a pleasant sound in Briescha's ears. He lifted the tiny spiral with a trembling hand, turning it in the light. "Your gifts are amazing. I assure you that no harm befell that child. It is a piece that is shed on occasion, and this first one is my treasure. He is a part of me, in many ways. But that is another story for another time." His hand settled on his chest, clasping the tiny horn.

He drifted into a deep sleep after that. She watched him rest, intrigued by the enigma he represented, and sure that he and she would see his fabled water planet at long last. She pressed a button that closed his medical wing module and left the room.

I like him, Darasha said.

You've never steered me wrong before. Briescha allowed the words in her mind to express the smile on her face. *I'm so glad you stopped to save him.*

They sat in fascinated silence for a long time, watching distant galaxies and stars zip past the screen shield, with the star Paz gleaming behind them. Then onscreen, in the distance, the planetary hologram popped alight, encircling Unata with a blue, glowing beacon. She recited everything she knew about Unata. Weak atmosphere resulting in oral consumption for survival, weak water for hydration only, harsh electrical fields and the most vicious reputation of any society in history. *Fear Planet.* She leaned forward in her seat, her throat dry.

Didn't you say that they're reasonable, just people, bound to understand you because you give them the chance? Darasha's playful questions irritated her, a loving irritation that she dismissed. *I've sent the peace beacon.*

"Thank you! Onscreen," Briescha rasped.

The planet Unata loomed on their screen. The hologram outlined landmasses and major cities that appeared as thick atmosphere in plain sight. Parisia, the landmass's capital city, spun into view.

"Scan." Briescha trembled in her seat. She reached for the sword at her side, capping her palm on the pommel for comfort.

Darasha's results took a moment. *There's life, of course. There is significant structural damage in the city-proper of Parisia. We've missed an important event, it seems. Hopefully, they'll welcome peaceful company.*

"I sincerely hope so." Briescha pressed her mouth into a thin line. "I'm no warrior. And their entire lives are war. They'll know I'm weak."

True, but only in body. Your spirit and heart will win theirs. You're the only one wh...

Briescha felt the alarm before it sounded. "What is that?" she cried.

Looks like they've locked onto our vessel with some type of tracking system. The weapons are lasers. Old tech. Not as sophisticated as ours, but big. Darasha finally sounded concerned.

"Well, *I* may be weak, but you are glorious, Darasha." Briescha choked on a nervous laugh. "Remember all that fancy flying we did together back on Azela? Think we can do it now? Dodge some lasers?"

Darasha's laugh drifted through her mind. *Of course, my dear.*

Briescha strapped on her belts and prepared to do a full dive with Darasha.

"They hate Azela. Time to find out why."

Oh, they've fired! So many times!

"It's *just* Fear Planet, right?" Briescha leaned into the controls. "Let's go make friends!"

###

Ready for more? The story continues in Solana, Book 3, A Novella of the Pathos Series, Available in Kindle Unlimited, Audible, and Paperback!

ABOUT THE AUTHOR

Tamara Henson lives in Kentucky with her precious little family, and all the people in her head. She's devoted to her son Elric and her man Will, and her kitty-brat Twitter-pater. She's a Sci-fi/Fantasy Author and Artist, Anime/Manga Fan, Legal Stabber of Tattoo and Piercing Clients, a Directionally-Challenged and Incompetent Gamer Gal, and a Workaholic Entrepreneur. Always improving, except in gaming, probably.

She is likely working on something creative, when she should be sleeping.

To access exclusive info and offers related to Tamara's PATHOS universe, go to her website:

www.tamarahenson.com

Discover other Pathos Series titles by Tamara Henson:

- Rowan Jun (Book 1)
- Solana (Pathos, Book 3, A Novella)
- Ariana (Pathos, Book 4, A Novella)
- Primorda (Book 5) *Fall, 2026*
- Incarnata (Book 6) *Spring, 2027*

Discover 3 NEW Romance Series by Tamara Henson (Series Titles TBA):

Cryptid (w/ a JACKALOPE SHIFTER!!), *Fall, 2026*
Dystopian and Dark Fae Romance Series
TITLES TO BE ANNOUNCED, COMING SOON!

<u>ABOUT THE PATHOS SERIES:</u>

Tamara Henson's ever-expanding Pathos universe spans space and dimensions beyond the waking world to bring fresh life to mythologies, folklore, and legends, spinning epic original locations and memorable, multi-dimensional characters in rich detail with her playful dialogue and direct writing style.

Join Rowan Jun in his path toward redemption from slave to warrior.

Walk the path of Briescha, a born diplomat so dedicated to her sister that she would shatter the cosmos to keep her safe.

Follow Solana into the wilderness as she escapes those who seek to harm her, and follows the voice of the mysterious Taiyo of the Flames.

Let Ariana guide you through her new life in the Mansion in the Mountain, where the mystery of her family is finally revealed, and her true trial begins.

Tread the path toward life and redemption, where suffering and pain hold the promise of a brighter, more joyful future. The Pathos Series!

Join the tamarahenson.com newsletter for updates on all Tamara's Upcoming Projects!